CW00505920

'Ruth Leigh's writing is sharp. [...] main character, Isabella Smugg[...] new heights but, right from the [...] hidden and perhaps tragic depths. Leigh's unique and cutting social commentary reminds me of Austen but with added Instagram, selfies and hashtags. Readers will keep turning the pages to see whether Isabella is capable of redemption.'
Fran Hill, author of Being Miss *and* Miss, What Does Incomprehensible Mean?

'Funny, smart, insightful. A *Bridget Jones's Diary* for the Age of Influencers. Recommended as a much-needed tonic, with a gin on the side.'
Paul Kerensa, stand-up comedian, speaker and writer

Dear Jane

Enjoy!

R

The diary of
Isabella M Smugge

ruth_leigh

instant
ap[]stle

First published in Great Britain in 2021

Instant Apostle
The Barn
1 Watford House Lane
Watford
Herts
WD17 1BJ

Copyright © Ruth Leigh 2021

The author has asserted her rights under Section 77 of the Copyright, Designs and Patents Act, 1988, to be identified as the author of the work.

All rights reserved. No portion of this book may be reproduced or transmitted in any form or by any means, electronic or mechanical, including photocopying and recording, or by any information storage and retrieval system, without permission in writing from the publisher.

Every effort has been made to seek permission to use copyright material reproduced in this book. The publisher apologises for those cases where permission might not have been sought and, if notified, will formally seek permission at the earliest opportunity.

The views and opinions expressed in this work are those of the author and do not necessarily reflect the views and opinions of the publisher.

This is a work of fiction. Names, characters, businesses, places, events and incidents are either the products of the author's imagination or used in a fictitious manner. Any resemblance to actual persons, living or dead, or actual events is purely coincidental.

Author's agent: The Tony Collins Literary Agency.

British Library Cataloguing-in-Publication Data

A catalogue record for this book is available from the British Library.

This book and all other Instant Apostle books are available from Instant Apostle:

Website: www.instantapostle.com

Email: info@instantapostle.com

ISBN 978-1-912726-40-0

Printed in Great Britain.

September

This morning, I woke up at 6 am, got up, did my stretches and forty lengths of the pool then said to myself, 'Isabella, you're a lucky girl. No cellulite to speak of, all your own teeth, a handsome husband, three beautiful children and a lovely house.'

I wouldn't want to give you the impression that all this (by which I mean our gorgeous Grade II listed Georgian house, grounds, indoor pool, gym and tennis court) has simply fallen into our laps. Johnnie works very hard for everything we've got, as do I. Since we first got together, we've gone after all our dreams. That's where so many people go wrong, in my opinion. Work out what you want and grab it with both hands!

I expect you know my name. My Insta account (issysmugge) has nearly two million followers. I post inspirational content on parenting, self-care, exercise, interior design and relationship enrichment. My book series, *Issy Smugge Says*, is a runaway success. I don't know where I find the time! Thank goodness for Sofija, my au pair. She's such a willing little thing, and the children love her.

One of the first things we did was to build my writing studio. I said to Johnnie, 'I can leave London, I can live without street lights and proper Laotian food, but I cannot keep improving the reach of my brand without a proper writing space.'

'No worries, sexy,' he said, slapping my bum. 'All tax deductible and when it's up, we'll christen it.' He laughed and winked at me. Even after nearly twenty years, my heart beats a little faster when he walks into the room. Piercing blue eyes, cheekbones you could slice an Iberico ham on and a great physique. He insisted on having the gym and pool installed before we moved in. I keep myself young with Pilates and regular swimming. I know he'd never stray, but it can't hurt to keep yourself trim. Mummy always told us, 'A man doesn't go out looking for burgers when he's got Wagyu beef at home.' Not that it worked out for her and Daddy, but that's another story.

I showered, dressed and ambled over to the house. It was the first day of term and I wanted to be there to make sure Sofija had everything she needed. She'd sewn in all the name tags, put the PE bags together and laid out the uniforms, but there are some things only a mother can do.

One of my favourite rooms is the kitchen. Originally, it was shocking. All pine cabinets, ugly tiled floors and no utility room, would you believe? We ripped the whole lot out and I found a wonderful local company who came in and designed the whole thing. I've got a huge central island, top-of-the range oven (ideal for entertaining), wine fridges and a dresser I picked up for a song. We went for hand-painted doors in a soft grey (so 'now') and I insisted on quartz engineered stone for the worktops. I flatter myself I've got a real eye for a kitchen.

Thank heavens for Brygita, my little Polish girl who comes and cleans for me three times a week. I work full-time, as well as keeping my marriage on track and parenting, and I simply don't have time for housework. It's so madly ageing, too – if you've got the money, we both think it's morally wrong not to contract out menial jobs. I mean, how would these girls manage if it wasn't for people like us?

I promised my followers a big reveal and gave them a teaser yesterday. The little Smugges' first day at their new school! My followers expect (and deserve) constant updates. I was all set up when the children came down the stairs. Finn is the oldest (nine), followed by Chloë (seven) and my baby, Elsie, who starts Reception today.

I'd already taken some shots of their breakfast (buttermilk pancakes with blueberries, strawberries and crème fraiche). Sofija's a great cook, but her presentation skills leave much to be desired. I reframed it all, posted some overhead angles, then posed them eating it. It took quite a while as they kept talking and looking the wrong way. Eventually I had what I needed and uploaded it all to my socials.

I'd told Sofija to get them all up half an hour early and have breakfast done by 8.15. Back in London, we drove to school and then on to Elsie's nursery, but here, everyone walks. I wanted to get some shots of them walking down the lane hand in hand to tweet later. **#firstdayofschool #mybabies #mumofthree**

We hit a bit of a snag when Elsie had a meltdown. 'Want my old school, Sofi!' she sobbed. 'Want my friends.' Say what I will about my au pair, she certainly knows how to cheer a child up. I was starting to worry that I wouldn't get the shots of family togetherness, which are vital for my brand, but after a couple of minutes, Elsie was walking along holding her brother and sister's hands just as I'd planned.

Johnnie leaves the children's education to me. Naturally, I'd thought about going private, which we can easily afford and gives the children such a good start in life, but as it turns out, the local village school is excellent. As my agent said, doing state school makes my brand that much more relatable. In Year Six, the girls will sit the exams for private school. Finn's been down for a place at Johnnie's old school since he was born, of course.

We walked on to the playground, which was surrounded by grass and trees. That's a bonus. I do like the children to get plenty of exercise and stay fit. They swim, of course, and they have tennis coaching every week and most years we ski in February half term and at Easter, but as I always say, you can't beat a bit of spontaneity! **#planningaheadforspontaneity**

I took Elsie's free hand and gave it a squeeze. 'All right, sweetie? What a lovely adventure you're going to have today! Lots of new friends!' She wriggled away from me and stuck her thumb into her mouth (I must talk to Sofija about that).

In London, I didn't particularly stand out, but here – well! Most of the women hadn't even bothered to put on make-up. There was a distressing preponderance of drooping leggings and tired leisure wear and everyone seemed to have at least four children. Nothing better to do, I suppose. The bell rang, I hugged Finn and Chloë, wished them good luck and trotted after Elsie and Sofija towards the Reception line.

It's a big moment when your youngest starts school. I was writing the content for my Facebook post in my head when a young woman with badly done highlights marched up to Sofija and said in a penetrating voice, 'You must be Mrs Smugge. I'm Miss Moss, the Reception teacher.'

'It's Smugge, not Smug,' I corrected her. 'As in Bruges. I'm Elsie's mother.'

Elsie was smiling at last, and consented to hold Miss Moss' hand as they walked in. I was surprised to see that quite a few of the mothers were crying. Some of the children were too. I remember being sent off to boarding school when I was seven. I admit, I cried at first, but I soon remembered Mummy's advice to be a brave girl. The worst bit was leaving Suze behind. Even now, I can see her face, contorted with tears as she broke free of Nanny and ran down the drive behind the car, calling my name. Funny, I haven't thought of that for years.

It was time to commence my social trajectory. I smiled graciously at the other parents in the line. Sofija was already chatting to a couple of women with pushchairs. She never dresses up much and today was no exception. Jeans, one of my old tops, trainers and her hair dragged off her face in a scrunchie. Shame, she's quite a pretty little thing if she'd only make the effort.

A plumpish woman was the first to break ranks. She had a little boy in a pushchair and was either pregnant or had shockingly lax abdominal muscles. She gave me a big smile.

'Hello! Are you a new mum? I'm Claire. I've got Becky in Reception and Hannah in Year Two. This is my youngest, Joel.'

I introduced myself. She had clearly never heard of me, so I tried to find another conversational topic.

'My daughter Chloë is in Year Two. My eldest, Finn, is in Year Five.' Tedious, but it had the desired effect. The woman's face was wreathed in smiles.

'Oh, how lovely! You must come over for a playdate. The children love having friends over. Whereabouts are you in the village?'

I explained that we had moved into the Old Rectory. The woman laughed. 'Well, we live at the new rectory. Not nearly so grand. My husband's the vicar at St Peter's and St Paul's. We've been here for five years. It's a very friendly village, lots going on, and of course the school is super. Hang on, let me get him over to say hello.'

She seemed wildly enthusiastic, but beggars can't be choosers, and I had factored in fifteen minutes for meet and greet in the playground. As the parents streamed out through the gate, a person dressed in what I believe is called a hoodie ambled over to us. Some kind of caretaker, I assumed. But no.

'This is my husband, Tom. Darling, this is Isabella who's just moved into the Old Rectory. Her girls are the same age as Hannah and Becky.'

I thought vicars were in their sixties, wore ill-fitting slacks and dog collars. This one looked as if he was off to the skate park and was quite startlingly good-looking. Not my type, but very nice just the same. Goodness knows how a woman like Claire managed to bag *him*!

He seemed perfectly friendly and chatted to Sofija and me as if we were old friends. He enquired after our spiritual leanings (subtly) and assured us that we would be welcome on Sunday mornings or any time there was a group, which seemed to be every day. Call me old-fashioned, but I thought the whole point of church was that you knew where you were. Carol service at Christmas, Harvest in September and so on. These people seemed gluttons for punishment.

'We do Messy Church on Wednesdays, Claire runs a mums' group on Friday mornings, we've got an Alpha starting next week…' I tuned out while smiling graciously. I had better things to do than hang around with a bunch of Bible bashers, although they seemed friendly enough.

At the gate, we divided, Sofija and I heading back up the hill to the house, the vicar, wife and pushchair trundling off towards the village centre. My phone was going crazy with notifications. I'm trending!

October

I flatter myself I can talk to anyone. Back at home, I used to say hello to the postman, the lollipop lady and even the dustmen. I pride myself on having the common touch. Johnnie thinks I'm a hoot.

'You're not exactly everywoman, are you, darling?' He poured us both another glass of fizz. It was Friday and we were unwinding after a crazy week. 'When's the last time you did the shopping, or worried about how you're going to pay the mortgage?'

It's true, I've never had to lose sleep over money, which has such a deleterious effect on a woman's looks. We lived with Mummy, Daddy and Nanny in our big house in Kent, handy for Daddy's work. Mummy used to laugh with that edge in her voice, like cut glass, and call herself the trophy wife. Suze and I didn't know what that meant, but we did know that all hell would break loose if Mummy had one too many G&Ts and spoke her mind when Daddy came home.

I don't want to give you the impression that we had a bad childhood. We had lots of toys, a treehouse, lovely parties and our ponies in the paddock. Nanny would whisk us off upstairs if Mummy and Daddy had one of their arguments, but often, when we were supposed to be asleep, Suze and I would creep out of bed and sit at the top of the stairs, listening to the voices shouting and the doors banging.

It hasn't affected me a bit, although Suze went through a bad time at boarding school which she always said was down to our home life. She's fine now. Absolutely fine. Not that we talk much.

We've all settled into country living. My followers love my posts about the simple life. The children seem to like school. Elsie has nearly kicked her thumb-sucking habit, which is a relief. She lost her first tooth the other day. Sofija sorted out all the fairy nonsense. I can't be expected to keep up with all the details of domestic life. That's what I pay her for.

I gave in to Claire's pleadings and scheduled an afternoon for coffee and chat. The new rectory is an ugly, modern house, softened slightly by a pretty garden at the front. Goodness knows what vicars earn, but it clearly isn't enough for a decent coffee machine and an ice-maker. I drank something calling itself 'instant' and accepted a cheap, sugary biscuit.

Claire chatted away about school, the children and the weather. How *do* people stay at home raising children and allowing their creativity to be stifled? I love my children as much as the next woman, but the thought of being in their company 24/7 fills me with horror. I need my space.

My hostess was pushing a luridly coloured flyer across the table. It was an invitation to something calling itself 'Messy Church' the next week. I had no intention of being sucked into religious activities but, out of politeness, I said I'd talk to the children and see. On the way home, to my amazement, Chloë started badgering me to take her along. She'd made great friends with Hannah, who is a mini version of her mother. Wednesday is our free night and with no Johnnie at home, I couldn't see any harm in it.

I'd say I believe in some sort of Supreme Being, and good and evil, but when I think about it at all (which isn't often), I suppose I think that all gods are roughly equal, if you do good things you should be OK and that there may be pie in the sky when you die, but probably not. Johnnie, on the other hand, is a full-on atheist.

'Look at all the trouble religion causes, Iss. Complete waste of time. They're all hypocrites.'

Of course, his father was a bishop, so I suppose it was inevitable.

Messy Church lived up to its name. When we walked in, Chloë rushed over to Hannah, Elsie and Becky hugged each other as if they'd been parted for years and various small, grimy children dashed about screaming. It was hell.

Claire and an older woman with grey hair and an unfortunate aversion to personal grooming seemed to be in charge. I was invited to take a seat, drink appalling coffee and eat something calling itself shortbread in the company of a gaggle of weary-looking mothers, some of whom I recognised from the Reception line.

I smiled graciously and tried to think of an opening gambit. It was easy back in London. You simply asked what their husband did and where they lived, and you were off. Here, the rules seemed different and I was surprised to feel like an outsider. It reminded me of my first term at boarding school. But I mustn't dwell on that.

I looked around for Claire, but she was wiping Joel's nose and talking to a young, skinny woman with purple streaks in her hair. 'Come on, Isabella,' I said to myself sternly. 'They won't bite.'

I smiled. 'Hi. I'm Isabella. We just moved here from London.'

There was a moment's silence, then they all seemed to come to life. 'All right?' 'Seen you in the playground.' 'You Elsie's mum?' That started us off and I treated them to my most charming manner, head on one side, lots of eager little nods and smiles. By the time Claire tapped the microphone and informed us all that it was story time, I knew that nearly all of them seemed to be called Lisa and that they had turbulent lives. Several of them left to go and smoke rolled-up cigarettes behind the gravestones with the girl with the purple hair.

Claire treated to us to a story about Noah and the ark. She got some of the children to play the animals. Believe me when I tell you that not much acting was required in some cases! My little Elsie was an elephant and did very well. I clapped and shouted, 'Go Elsie!' Some of the mums tittered. Apparently, it wasn't an immersive production.

After the story, the grey-haired woman seized the mic and led us in a stirring rendition of an action song. The children took to this with gusto, leaping up and down and bellowing the words with great enthusiasm. I took the opportunity to plug in my earphones and catch up on a podcast.

After that, there was another song which involved marching round the room shouting, 'Thank You, Jesus!' at top volume. I managed not to laugh, but only just. I never did find out what we were thanking Him for. I don't suppose it was the coffee. Claire took over and invited us to close our eyes and talk to Jesus. I closed mine and carried on listening to the podcast.

That marked the end of the religious portion of the afternoon. The children scattered to make an incredible mess with glitter, glue and Sellotape. I joined Elsie to help her make a badge. To my consternation, it read, 'Jesus Loves Me!' in huge letters. I'll put it in the recycling later. It wouldn't do for Johnnie to find it.

Busted! When Johnnie FaceTimed, Elsie spilled the beans.

'Daddy, we went to Messy Church, Mummy clapped and the other mummies said shhh!'

Johnnie raised his left eyebrow. When you've been together as long as we have, you know what every expression means, and the eyebrow is a bad sign. Thinking on my feet, I told him that Finn had been selected for the football team. That brought the smile back to his face and bought me some time.

The girls chattered away to him nineteen to the dozen. Finn played it cool, but I know he adores Johnnie. They chatted about football while I loaded the dishwasher. I felt so connected, pottering about in my beautiful kitchen, wiping surfaces and rearranging the flowers. Let no one accuse Issy Smugge of not being relatable!

After a while, Johnnie said, 'OK, kids, off you go and play. Mummy and Daddy time.'

'What's all this, darling?' he asked. 'Surely you're not playing the little housewife? Although you do look very hot in that apron. Where's Sofija got to?'

I explained that I'd given her some time off. She was missing her friends in London and the social whirl, and when you find good staff, you need to make sure you treat them right. She was staying with my friend Nicki's au pair. They were great friends back in London and Nicki very sweetly lets her stay over on her days off. Johnnie shrugged. He leaves all the HR to me.

We talked about work. Part of keeping a relationship alive and vibrant is pretending to be interested when your husband talks about what he does. Johnnie started out on the trading floor at one of the big investment banks, then jumped ship to another one when we were twenty-seven, netting a fantastic pay deal in the process. Three years later, he was off to Credit Suisse. His mother is from Interlaken and he's fluent in German, so that was a no-brainer. These days, he's a hedge fund manager, raking it in and highly respected in the industry.

People say we're lucky, but they forget all those years of hard work, tough decisions and risks. We shed a few friends along the way, but that's life.

'You know I don't want you and the kids getting involved in religion, Iss.' He was frowning.

I kept it light. That's always best when Johnnie is in a mood. Turns out Tom the skater-boy vicar went to Cambridge. Johnnie likes to know the right sort of people and his face lightened when I told him.

'There's no harm in the kids playing together, and I suppose if you're hanging out with the wife, I can get to know the rev a bit. What's his background?' Johnnie's always keeping an eye open for potential networking and deals.

I only knew that he came from quite a good family and had given up a career in the law to become a vicar. Johnnie snorted. 'Idiot! He could have been earning decent money by now if he'd stuck at it. Get them over for drinks one weekend, sweetie, and I'll play the gracious host.'

Weirdly, although Claire could drop a couple of stone, do something about her hair and really benefit from a course of chemical peels, she seems to be one of the playground kingpins. She talks to everyone, even the clutch of scowling mums with tattoos from the council estate. I have to admit, she's growing on me. It seems that the key to village life is to know a few of the right people, but I'm finding it relatively tough.

Some of the other parents say hi when they see me, but most of them stare at me as though I were some rare bird of paradise. In my line of work, you have to keep up your appearance. I get my hair done monthly, nails every week, regular massages and of course a good diet and exercise regime. I don't have to bother going clothes shopping much as my favourite designers send me a selection every season. That's the joy of being an inspirational lifestyle blogger. Sofija must be the best-dressed au pair in the county, what with all my cast-offs. **#aupairupcycling**

I had Claire and the children over to ours after school. Part of my success is my ability to stay humble and relatable, but I get quite a thrill when I see visitors' jaws drop as they walk in.

I fired up the coffee machine which I'd imported from the States. Fiendishly expensive, but worth every penny. I made Claire the best cappuccino she'd ever had, then we went and sat in the family room while Joel pulled himself up on the sofa and plumped himself down again. He seemed easily amused.

'How are you finding village life, Isabella?' asked Claire, savouring her coffee, as well she might. 'It must be a huge change after London.'

I was missing the hustle and bustle, all my friends and, now I came to think about it, Johnnie. Back home, we'd have weekly date nights, take off for little weekend getaways, leaving his mother or Sofija in charge or sneak off to the bolt-hole for a bit of R&R. I was seeing less of him than ever before, but spending much more time around the children. I felt a tiny little ice-cold finger prod speculatively at my gut. I'd taken my eye off the ball.

I wasn't going to tell Claire any of that. 'Fine, fine,' I trilled. 'I miss my friends and the social life, but it's a sacrifice worth making. The children seem happy and Sofija loves it, which is the main thing. Happy au pair, happy Issy!'

'Have you connected with any of the other mums?' Claire asked, hauling Joel on to her lap and wiping his nose. He is the most remarkably snotty child, although quite sweet if you like toddlers. I never did, much.

'Not really. I say hello when I see them and they talked to me at your craft afternoon thing, but I don't seem to be making much headway.'

She put her cup down and leaned forward. I felt a moment coming on.

'Can I be honest, Isabella?'

I braced myself. Is it my fault that men find me attractive? I'd seen the looks in the playground. Some of the women could have been quite presentable with the right clothes and a makeover, but if you will let yourself go, what can you expect?

'I think they find you just a little intimidating. They're afraid that you might look down on them a bit, so they're not reaching out as they normally would.' She looked anxious. 'I hope I haven't hurt your feelings.'

I'm known for my problem-solving abilities. To me, a problem is simply an opportunity to grow.

'How about if I have them all over for coffee over half term?' I suggested. 'They can bring their children and get to know me.'

'I think you might be biting off a bit more than you can chew.' Claire was looking worried. 'Maybe just have two or three over at a time?'

Sofija would have done all the donkey work, of course, while I did the meet and greet, but I bowed to Claire's superior wisdom. We walked down to school to pick up the children and I worked the playground, giving out my mobile number to the women indicated by Claire as potential social acquaintances.

I was worn out by the time I got back home, and never have I been so glad to see Sofija. The children all hugged her as if she'd been away for years. Elsie was holding her hand and talking non-stop about being an elephant, Chloë was holding the other hand and chatting away about her sleepover with Hannah while even Finn was smiling and laughing. He's been such a grump lately. I've had to work so hard to get him to pose for my 'Easy Family Meals' series.

Sofija had finally taken my advice and got her hair done properly. A closer inspection revealed that she'd had her eyebrows done and, if I wasn't very much mistaken, had bagged herself a full set of lashes. Now she wasn't sporting her old Shaggy Peasant look, she really did appear quite presentable.

We chatted as she cooked tea and I checked my notifications. She'd had a great time in town, gone out with her friend and blown her birthday money on the hair, lashes and eyebrows. And why not? Living with one of the UK's most successful inspirational lifestyle bloggers was clearly rubbing off. I asked if I could feature her in my next 'From Tramp to Vamp' series. She looked a bit uncomfortable, but eventually agreed.

Johnnie's home tomorrow night! I've booked a table at the trendy new oyster bar on the coast and got some new underwear that'll knock his socks off! Really, I am the luckiest girl in the world, although as Mummy always says, 'You make your own luck, Isabella.' Maybe you do. **#luckygirl #keepingitreal**

November

November in the country is dull as ditchwater! There are endless school and church-based activities for the socially constipated, but I'm being careful not to get too involved. I've hardly seen Claire. I texted her to ask her over for coffee, but she replied that this is one of her busiest times of the year and she's rushed off her feet. Who knows what she's doing? How hard can it be to organise a carol service?

The only thing keeping me going is Chloë's eighth birthday party. We're having the whole class round for a pool party and pizza afterwards. What with designing the invites, making up the party bags, ordering in the cake from town and organising the collage of the birthday girl from birth to now, my socials have gone crazy! Numbers are up and my daily posts about my baby girl's party are getting my followers very excited. No one does a party like me.

Sofija makes the most heavenly pizzas, so she's in charge of the catering. I'll be doing the mocktails and dressing the pool room, and we'll both do the party bags.

We're having the party on Friday night, straight after school. I've told Johnnie to make sure he's back. He missed her last two and it's not the same without him.

I was as good as my word. I had a batch of mums over every day of half term and I gave them the full Issy Smugge experience. Would you believe, most of them have never even heard of me and don't follow anyone of any importance. I made sure to point them in the right direction.

The girl with the purple hair (Lauren) and I have hit it off. She was flatteringly impressed with my interior design. Her three little girls were very well-mannered, I thought, although of course Finn rushed upstairs as soon as he saw them on the drive and didn't appear again until they'd all gone. He's in that awkward stage where he hates girls. I must get him and Johnnie to go away on a little male bonding weekend. Sofija says he just needs a bit of one-to-one time. I see him twice as much as I ever did back home in London, maybe even more. How much one-to-one does he want?

Chloë's party was a triumph! Sofija surpassed herself. The mums all seemed to like her and were bombarding her with questions about Lithuania. Or Latvia. Wherever it is she comes from. I always get those two confused. I'd ordered in loads of inflatables and they all splashed around and had a great time. I got some fabulous posts out of it and so many retweets it was untrue! **#issysmuggesays**

The only downer was that Mummy came to stay. Goodness only knows why she's suddenly showing an interest in my children, but she rang a couple of weeks before the big day and invited herself. Johnnie groaned when I broke the news.

'Oh no, not your mother! She'll stink out the place with her fags and put you down over supper. And you know she hates me, Iss. Can't you think of an excuse?'

The thought of forbidding Mummy from visiting was delightful, but hardly practical. I suggested that we ask his mother up to balance out the Mummy effect, but when I texted, she said she was away with some of the girls for a spa weekend. I love Silvia. She's got to be the best mother-in-law a girl ever had. Her social life is nearly as good as mine.

Mummy doesn't drive any more (as Johnnie says, losing your licence once may be regarded as a misfortune, to lose it twice looks like carelessness). She told me to be at the station ten minutes before her train came in as she doesn't like standing around being stared at. I sent Sofija.

'Don't forget the red carpet!' Johnnie called after her. 'Her Majesty will be expecting the Changing of the Guard at the very least.'

The poor girl looked baffled. I wish Johnnie wouldn't tease her like that.

I suppose you have to accept people as they are. Suze and I weren't deprived of love and affection as little girls. I wouldn't want you to think that. Mummy loves us both, and at some level she's proud of us, not that she'd ever say it. I suppose it's her generation and, dare I say it, her class. I get all the love and affirmation I need from Johnnie, my followers, Silvia and the children. I'm thirty-eight years old (not that I'd admit to it), although you wouldn't think it from the way Mummy speaks to me.

She was hardly in the door before she started.

'The house is smaller than I thought. Good heavens, darling, what on earth are you wearing? Aren't you a bit old for that shade of pink? Where are my grandchildren?'

Mummy looked the children over then offered her cheek to be kissed. Out of the corner of my eye, I saw Johnnie making a low curtsey and waving his hand regally. Our eyes met and I tried desperately hard not to laugh. She began the ritual interrogation.

'Finn, are you keeping up with your swimming? I hope you're working hard at school. Chloë, your hair looks much better like that. Do stand up straight, child. Elsie, if you keep on sucking your thumb, no one will ever marry you when you're a grown-up lady.'

Her grandmotherly duties done, she sat down at the island and lit a cigarette. She does it deliberately to needle Johnnie, I know. He coughed ostentatiously, which was my cue.

'Mummy, you know you're not allowed to smoke in the house. Go out into the garden.'

She snorted. 'In this weather? I'll catch my death.'

Behind her back, Johnnie put his hands together as though in prayer and cast his eyes heavenward. He always makes me laugh. Such an attractive quality in a man.

We compromised. She grudgingly agreed to lurk in the boot room with the door open. I'll warn the gardener to look out for fag ends in the agapanthus.

The week unfolded as expected. Mummy slept in and assumed that she could treat Sofija like a slave. I put my foot down. I won't have her taken advantage of.

'Mummy, Sofija is like a member of the family. And she works for us, not you. If you want breakfast in bed, you'll have to come down, make it yourself and carry it back upstairs.'

She gave me a sly, sideways look. 'She's *not* a member of the family, though, is she, darling? She's staff. You know my policy on the help. Don't get too familiar. It always leads to trouble.'

'For heaven's sake, Mummy,' I hissed through clenched teeth. 'It's not the 1950s! Sofija's been with me since Chloë was born. I won't have her treated like a second-class citizen!'

That shut her up, but I didn't like the way she looked at me. She makes me feel like an awkward teenager instead of a successful, happily married woman and renowned blogger.

Mummy lasted ten minutes at the pool party before exiting stage left. I rolled my eyes across the pool at Sofija, who grinned back at me and shook her head. I don't know what I'd do without her. I must get her a little something to let her know how much I appreciate her. Sofija's worth her weight in gold and I would do anything to keep her from leaving. Not that she will. She couldn't ask for a better employer than me. **#soblessed**

You could cut the tension in this house with a knife. Mummy loathes Johnnie and treats Sofija like a scullery maid. She puts me down and makes the children nervous. Johnnie hates having her in the house and drinks too much at dinner to compensate. The fag ends are building up in the shrubbery.

In town, I was always out in the evenings, but here we spend more family time together. We've got into the habit of sitting down in the family room after tea and watching television. Only things I can tweet about, obvs! No reality or anything like that. *So* not my brand.

Mummy was particularly obnoxious at teatime and we were all feeling rather fragile. I needed some time away from her, so I pretended to be unsure about how to redecorate the south wing. I've already decided to go with a fresh new take on British Farmhouse with lots of classic prints while playing around with whimsy. My colour palette will be muted primary tones and botanicals. Mummy doesn't know that, however. I gave her a stack of interiors magazines, a notebook and a pen and begged her to help me. It was a vermilion rag to a bull! Off she charged, leaving Sofija, Finn, Chloë and me alone together.

I never sat down and watched television with the children in London, but in the country things are different. I did a little teaser on Insta last week and my followers absolutely loved it! A gorgeous little shot of the three of them lying on their fronts in their pyjamas watching something educational.

Sofija has got us all into *Miranda*, which I am surprised to find that I enjoy. Even Finn likes it. We were watching the one where Miranda and her mother were at the funeral when Mummy came barging in. Miranda had just fallen into the grave. I was laughing so much I forgot to tweet! **#preciousfamilytime**

'Good heavens, isn't that Diana Hart Dyke's oldest girl? What on earth is she wearing? What's Patricia Hodge doing? Now I do like her. Wonderful cheekbones and, of course, she enunciates so well.'

I sighed and tried to explain, but she was wasn't paying attention. I decided to employ humour, not something I bother with normally.

'Such fun!' I bellowed. The children and Sofija fell about laughing. It was lost on Mummy, of course, but it did have the effect of sending her off to the boot room to fill her lungs with tar.

I don't think I've ever made my children laugh before.

On Wednesday morning, I was in the kitchen when the post arrived. The children were at school, Sofija was upstairs and Mummy was in the boot room, puffing away and searching for something to criticise. I sorted out the bills, statements, a few handwritten ones (early Christmas cards) and a parcel covered in colourful Hong Kong stamps. Suze never forgets a birthday or anniversary.

Mummy walked back in and helped herself to a coffee. She skewered me with a look.

'Is that from your sister?'

I sighed. 'Who else do we know in Hong Kong?'

'There's no need for that tone, Isabella. Have you spoken to Suzanne recently?'

'I've been rushed off my feet, Mummy, what with the move and settling in up here.'

'*We* speak every week.' Mummy took a sip of her coffee. 'Lily is doing so well at school. Top of her class, Suzanne says. Such a beautiful child. Of course, Orientals often are.'

Mummy is such a racist without realising it. She got out her phone and her reading glasses.

'Look at these photographs! Lily at the water park with Suzanne and Jeremy (such a keen swimmer); there they all are on her birthday having dinner. Oh, and here she is in her school uniform (a proper blazer and pleated skirt, not like those common little pullovers your children wear) — what on earth you're thinking sending them to some back-of-beyond little village school when there's a perfectly good prep up the road...'

I tried to tune out but there was no stopping her. There seemed to be no end to Lily's accomplishments. Of course, Mummy always preferred Suze to me. She would have done much better with sons. As she droned on about Jeremy and his wonderful job, I had a flashback of her shouting at me.

'If only I'd had a boy! Your father would never have left.'

I'm pretty sure he would. Mummy's best friend Arabella Pryke-Darby had been having a raging affair with Daddy for five years before it all came out. We were away at boarding school when Mummy threw him out. But I mustn't think about that.

Only twenty-three more hours until Mummy leaves. Only twenty-six more shopping days until Christmas. **#yuletidejoy #jinglebells**

December

For an award-winning blogger like me (Best Lifestyle Blogger for three years running, Most Inspiring Mum Blogger twice, Influencer of the Year more times than I can remember and no stranger to *The Sunday Times* Bestsellers List), December is the month where all my Christmases come at once. Metaphorically. And, of course, literally.

People think that what I do is easy. I can assure you it's not! I work very hard and put in a great deal of preparation, which is why everything looks so effortless. I've got the best agent in the business, of course, which really helps. Mimi talented-spotted me when I first started blogging. I shudder to think of the amateur content I used to put out. Finn was a few months old; we were living in Highgate and I knew virtually nothing about monetising. I can't believe I was ever that young!

Between us, we're an unbeatable team. We've got Christmas all planned and have had for months! **#bloggingwins #planningahead**

Mimi and I Skype every Monday morning. I checked my make-up and clicked on her icon (Mimi Stanhope Creatives). Her rasping voice and narrowed eyes leapt on to the screen.

'Sweetheart! How's my favourite client? Great stats – what a buzz about Clarissa's party. We need to do a tie-in.'

'Chloë,' I reminded her. I might be her favourite client, but she's got a terrible memory for names.

Mimi took a huge drag on her cigarette and waved her hand. 'Chloë. Yeah. Sorry. And how's that handsome husband of yours?'

Johnnie can't stand Mimi, and she knows it, but they keep up the pretence. As I pointed out halfway through his last character assassination, she's the best agent in the business and is 100 per cent behind Issy Smugge's brand. OK, she's left a trail of disgruntled clients in her wake, is on her fourth husband, smokes like a chimney and is rumoured to sleep in a banana-leaf coffin, but she's the best you can get.

'Darling, she's a two-faced old moo. I swear she's got no reflection. Did I ever tell you about the time I saw her at Shucks opening an oyster with her teeth?'

I put Johnnie's voice out of my head and pitched my latest, 'From Tramp to Vamp'. Ever since we came up with the idea, it's been incredibly popular, even featuring on quiz shows. 'Which well-known lifestyle blogger invites members of the public to smarten themselves up and then posts the results on her Instagram page?' **#trinnyandsusannahwho? #moveoverauntiegok**

'OK, sweetheart, who have you got for me?'

'Sofija! She's just had her hair properly done, plus a full set of lashes and brows. She looks amazing!'

Mimi frowned. 'What, the Russian girl? Your cleaner? I'm not sure about her. There are limits, darling!'

I put her straight. 'Not Brygita. Sofija. My au pair. She's Lithuanian. Or is it Latvian? I never can remember.'

'It might have legs. How old is she? How rough did she look before?'

The conversation was interrupted by Sofija herself walking into the kitchen with a full laundry basket. I hoped she hadn't overheard.

I reminded her of our conversation. She's seen plenty of my 'From Tramp to Vamp' makeovers in the past and, to be honest, Sofija didn't have nearly as far to go as some of my previous examples!

'I am not model, Isabella. I am au pair.' Sofija tends to drop her definite articles when she's stressed.

'You're perfect! We'll go through my clothes and style you. It'll be fun!'

'I must do washing now, Isabella.' Off she went to the utility room.

Mimi was smiling. 'Dig out some unflattering pics and we'll put something together. Let me know when you're ready to style her.'

'From Tramp to Vamp' sorted, we moved briskly through the overview for the next three months.

'Spring, darling!' Clouds of smoke were pouring from Mimi's lavishly lipsticked mouth. 'I'm seeing fresh air, nature, the great outdoors. I'm seeing the whole Smugge family doing – well, whatever it is people do outside the M25.'

Sofija marched past again with a pile of ironing. With six of us in the house, the washing never stops!

'Now, sweetheart, one more thing before we finish.' Mimi coughed and lit yet another cigarette. 'Lots of your competition are doing charity now (it's the new big thing) and we need to get you associated with some social action. Nothing too heavy – just a bit of doing good in the community.'

I was baffled. Do my followers really want to see Isabelle M Smugge opening garden fêtes and endowing hospital wings? It's all a bit Duchess of Gloucester, if you ask me.

'I've checked the feel-good power list. Since you've been relatable and sent your children to a state school, you can show how generous and community-minded you are by giving them a chunk of cash. We need to make sure it's image-driven, so I'm thinking swings, slides, a tree with flowers on it, something like that. You can write most of it off against tax.'

Mimi carried on.

'You wouldn't catch *me* venturing outside the M25' (here she laughed in a gravelly baritone), 'but since you've taken the leap, you can probably spread your nets a bit. Churches are very in this season. Ancient stonework, stained glass, gravestones, that kind of thing. Is there one near you?'

I pointed out that the Old Rectory was, naturally, bang smack next door to the church. It was lost on Mimi, who doesn't do sarcasm.

'Excellent! Is it falling down? Any bits looking like they might drop off? Let's schedule the school for spring and the church for autumn. Before and after pics, grateful vicar shaking your hand, soft-focus children frolicking in the background, some local history. It adds depth to your brand. Makes you look caring.'

I hadn't noticed anything falling apart, but Claire would know. I texted her.

'Hi Claire. Is anything broken at the church? Let me know xx'

Mimi was still going strong.

'I don't suppose you could have another baby, could you, sweetheart? Lots of your competition are. Newborns really sell, and they're the gift that keeps on giving to the lifestyle blogger.'

There I had to put my foot down. 'Absolutely not, Mimi. Three elective C-sections is quite enough, thank you very much!'

With a final hacking cough from the depths of her much-abused bronchioles, Mimi was off.

'Fabulous sweetheart, love you, miss you, mwah, mwah!'

I put on my organic faux fur gilet and walked briskly down to my writing studio. **#awomansworkisneverdone #keepingaheadofthegame**

Last week, my publisher sent me crates of the reissued *Issy Smugge Says* series of books to sign. I expect you've seen my Christmas campaign, 'Fill your Stockings with Issy Smugge this Christmas!' and, 'Issy Smugge Says: Find Me at the Bottom of Your Bed'. Orders have gone through the roof, which is making Mimi very happy.

My florist sent up our Christmas trees at the end of November. I've gone for an icy palette of silver and blue, fairy lights and sprayed pine cones, wreaths and table decorations. Sofija and I spent the day dressing the house and I took hundreds of shots for editing. Christmas is such fun!

This year, it's a family affair. We've got Silvia, Mummy and Johnnie's brother Toby and his horsey wife, Davina. It will be a full house, which I love. Sofija is flying home for a fortnight the day after school breaks up. **#perfectfamilychristmas #issysmuggesays**

An hour or so after I texted Claire, she replied. *'Soz, what? I don't understand LOL. RU on school run? xx'* I was, as Sofija was up to her eyes sorting out the children's clothes and clearing out the play room.

Claire was walking up to the school gates as I came down the lane. We were a few minutes early, so we went and sat down on one of the benches in the playground. No one around here seems to understand how monetising, endorsement and earning revenue from blogging works, so I gave Claire a brief overview of my reach, how followers respond and why, and charitable community donations.

'Is there anything at the church that needs an injection of cash? Maybe some new chairs, or a window, or something like that. I'll mention it on my socials, tag the church, put up a series of images and find a good hashtag. It might even put a few more bums on seats.' I was aware that I'd been talking for quite a while and that Claire was looking confused.

'A fourteenth-century church always needs money. We can apply for certain grants, fundraise, do appeals, but there's never enough. Are you saying that you would appeal for money via your blog? I'm not sure what the bishop would think about that.'

'No, I'd *give* you the money as a charitable donation.' I hadn't expected to make such heavy weather of the conversation. 'As a relatable blogger, it's important that I tick all the boxes, and since I'm part of this community, I wanted to talk to you about making a donation.'

Claire took a sharp intake of breath. '*Give* us the money? Oh, my goodness, Isabella, you're an answer to prayer!'

To my amazement, she started crying and hugging me. The bell rang, the doors opened and the children came pouring out. 'Come back to mine for coffee and we can chat properly – I can't wait to tell Tom!' she called over her shoulder.

My offer had clearly made her day.

Back at the vicarage, the girls rushed off to play while Finn sulked on the sofa. I had to be quite sharp with him while Claire was making coffee (you have to believe me when I tell you she was using an actual kettle, rather than a boiling water tap – are we in the Dark Ages?). Claire came back in with the coffee and offered him a glass of squash and some biscuits. That cheered him up slightly. You would not believe how many biscuits a nine-year-old boy can eat. We get through bags and bags of organic oats and cocoa nibs at home (Sofija makes the most heavenly flapjacks).

Claire hugged me again and started talking about something called the PCC and how pleased it would be. I smiled and nodded graciously, as we must always do when we find ourselves in a baffling situation, but she may as well have been speaking Serbo-Croat.

'Tom will be so happy – honestly, you really are the most incredible answer to prayer!'

Vicars' wives presumably have some kind of hotline to the man upstairs. I indicated that I had no problem with the good news being shared and sipped my coffee. Frightful. No depth of flavour.

A couple of minutes later, Tom joined us. He too was looking emotional.

'Claire's told me about your incredibly generous offer, Isabella. Thank you so much!'

He started telling me about the roof. Normally if I were addressed by a vicar, I'd smile charmingly and tune out, but I actually wanted to hear what he had to say. The trouble was, I couldn't understand above half of it. The PCC (them again) had held an emergency meeting the night before with the churchwardens (were these like holy traffic wardens, I wondered) and were on the point of launching a brand-new appeal and Gift Day. He carried on in this vein for some time until I felt my eyes beginning to glaze over.

Now, I wouldn't want to give you the impression that I'm a complete heathen. I know all about God and suchlike from daily chapel at St Dymphna's. Even now, I can belt out quite a few hymns from memory, thanks to our music mistress, Miss Napier. 'Sing up, girls!' she would bellow in her hoarse contralto, bashing away at the Bechstein. 'Let's make those windows rattle!' I always enjoyed chapel. It was a peaceful interlude away from the hurly-burly of prep, lessons, games and the dorm. Since I left, I haven't really had much to do with the CofE. I asked Tom to translate.

'I'm sorry, Isabella, I'm talking Christian jargon.' He smiled, and ran his hand through his thick, corn-coloured hair. His teeth are incredibly white and even. He really is delightful to look at. But I digress.

It would appear that the Archbishop of Canterbury is the CEO (God presumably being the founder), overseeing the branch offices run by bishops. All the vicars report to their local bishop and are in charge of their own micro-businesses, but ultimately responsible to the CEO (I think that's right). The PCC, apparently, is an executive committee which runs each micro-business (or church). The churchwardens *are* a bit like traffic wardens, since they are meant to set a good example to the flock (no parking on double yellows or breaking the Ten Commandments) and keep an eye on the fixtures and fittings.

The long and the short of it was that there wasn't enough money to fix the roof, pigeons were nesting in it and water was starting to trickle down the east wall. You can't just call in the local builder. Because the church is so old, it can only be worked on by accredited workmen and this costs twice as much.

'We held our meeting last night to find some way to raise enough funds. All the rain has exacerbated the problem and it's only going to get worse. The sooner we can authorise the work, the better. We prayed for a miracle and it seems that God has answered that prayer!'

There was a short silence as we gazed at each other, broken only by the sound of my son munching his way through a plateful of custard creams. Suddenly, the penny dropped.

'Oh, I see! You mean me. I'm sure it was a coincidence, but I'm so happy to be able to help. Reaching out into our community is very important to me. I truly feel that giving back is part of my social responsibility. I've worked hard for my success and I want to enrich the neighbourhood in which I find myself.'

Without realising it, I'd lapsed into socially aware blogger speak. It was my turn to talk in jargon, which was going right over Tom and Claire's heads. I translated.

'I'm pleased to help. I've been so fortunate myself and I believe in giving something back.'

We agreed on a figure and, with hugs all round, I gathered up the children and splashed back to our house, where Sofija had something delicious bubbling away on the stove. #hunkyvicar #reachingout #socialresponsibility

December in the country is a mad whirl! If it wasn't a Christmas fair or a Christmas shopping evening with wine and nibbles (very poor quality, not a blini in sight, and I suspect that the

wine was blended), then it was a class assembly, or a morning of making the most frightful mess with glitter and cardboard. I managed to dodge the latter (Sofija went), but did my maternal duty for all the others.

At pick-up, Lauren invited us over for a playdate the following week. She seems genuinely friendly. Most of the other mothers ignore me, or give me the briefest of nods, but Lauren is one of the social kingpins.

In the time it took us to walk over to the veranda, she'd given me a rundown on the six main village families, who's married to whom, who's divorced from whom, who isn't speaking to whom and what to expect at the Nursery and Reception Nativity. (Chaos, apparently. If you don't arrive at least forty-five minutes before the curtain goes up, you're relegated to the back row – utterly shaming and complete social suicide.)

As we stood in the playground together, she gave me a running commentary, *sotto voce*.

'Lisa J was a Rozier, but she married a Jarmin. They're all big drinkers. Debs Plummer's mother was a Ling, but she married Bob Plummer, then they split up and she married Barry Clarke and had three more children with him, including Lisa C. So, Debs and Lisa are half-sisters, but they don't speak. You must never slag off a Spalding, a Kersey or a Bloomfield because they're all inter-married with the Roziers, the Plummers and the Lings.'

I got the feeling she would have told me more, but at that point the bell rang.

'See you, babes,' she called to me as she disappeared in a welter of short people. She seems to be the pied piper of the playground as she rarely goes home with fewer than six children. Her house is playdate central. I must have her over.

By mid-December, I was in need of a break. Mimi was delighted with my figures; my socials were going crazy and my *Issy Smugge*

36

Says series was selling like hot cakes. I was feeling tired and lacklustre. There was only one place that could give me back my irresistible sparkle, and that was London! I messaged the girls and we booked a night of cocktails, nibbles and fun!

I tried to kiss Finn goodbye at school on Monday morning. He scowled at me and muttered, 'You are *so* embarrassing!' before stomping off to his classroom. Sofija drove me to the station. Johnnie very sweetly changed his work days around so that I could have the flat to myself.

Sitting back in my seat and watching the countryside whizz by, I found myself reminiscing, something I rarely do. I gazed out of the window and drank in the flat, leafless Suffolk countryside which reminded me of the view from the train on my way back to school. After that terrible first term, I made some friends, got into the rhythm of boarding school and taught myself to stop missing home. It was then that I began to build the foundations of the blogging phenomenon that is Isabella M Smugge.

Back then, I was Isabella Mary Neville; every item I owned was labelled with my name. Nanny spent hours sewing my name tags into the school uniform while Suze and I took it in turns riding on our rocking horse, Mr Fazakerley.

Up in the nursery, I felt completely safe. Mummy and Daddy only came up at Nanny's express invitation and there were never any raised voices or icy silences in her domain. Suze and I could play to our hearts' content, read, draw, or whatever took our fancy. Nanny was always there, a smiling, warm, encouraging presence entirely on our side.

Not that I want to give you the impression that there were sides. Mummy and Daddy were quite often happy and smiling. I can remember the parties they used to throw and how we would be dressed in our best frocks and brought downstairs to be shown off. Mummy looked so beautiful in her sparkly dress and Daddy was tall, jovial and handsome. If only it had always been like that.

I was so absorbed in my thoughts that we were at Liverpool Street before I knew where I was. Party time! **#friendsreunited #christmasshopping #cocktailswiththegirls**

Johnnie had left me a bottle of fizz in the fridge and a flirty note on the table. Tonight, I was going to have a night off from being Isabella the wife, the mother, the worker. I was going to get myself dressed up to the nines, put on my heels and have fun. The girls and I had arranged to meet at Freudian Sip, our favourite cocktail bar. I was so happy and excited.

I'm not a crier, but for two pins I could have burst into tears and sobbed all the way home. It's painful to recall what happened. I had been so looking forward to it.

I was the first at the bar, then the girls surged in in a cloud of expensive perfume, did the usual kissing and hugging and complimenting of outfits and talked solidly about themselves. No one asked me how I was. There were a few snidey remarks about being buried in the countryside, and Meredith had the infernal cheek to ask me if I was growing my lowlights out. I missed one hair appointment. One!

It was no better at the restaurant. It felt just like that first terrible night at St Dymphna's. I was surrounded by people, but totally alone. They clearly weren't interested in my new life. I pretended not to care and drank as much wine as I could to numb the pain. I kept on smiling and laughing until the minute I got into my cab, and then I stopped.

Issy Smugge doesn't dwell on painful things, so there we will leave it.

Back home, the children seemed to have missed me – even Finn, who gave me a reluctant smile and the briefest of hugs. Sofija had cooked my favourite dinner. I felt safe. It was a bit like being back in the nursery with Nanny and Suze.

In bed with Johnnie, he said, 'What happened, Iss?'

I told him the whole sorry story and burst into tears. I feel so safe in his arms. Nothing can hurt me when he's there.

In the blink of an eye, there were only nine sleeps to Christmas, as Elsie put it. My cards had been written and sent, my presents wrapped and the Christmas food ordered. I'd been especially well organised, as I had so much photography to do. Great images don't take themselves. Johnnie snapped at me as I tried to get a picture of everyone in the dining room.

'Honestly, Iss, do you have to take photos of everything? I'm off to the loo – why don't you join me and let your followers share yet another intimate moment?'

Then Sofija asked if she could change her days. She wants Mondays and Tuesdays off from now on, which is perfectly OK with me. I checked with Johnnie who said if I was happy, so was he. Which is fine. **#flexiblefriend**

Claire invited us to Carols by Candlelight the Sunday before Christmas Day. Johnnie may be anti-religion but he likes to go to church at Christmas. I always tease him and say he's paying his insurance, just in case there is a God.

We walked through the garden gate into the churchyard. It was a cold, still night and the stars were blazing overhead. I closed my eyes and took a deep breath of crisp air into my lungs.

Turning round to look back at our house, I felt a surge of pride. The floodlights bathed the walls in a warm, pinkish glow and the Christmas trees and lights twinkled at the windows. It looked beautiful. We definitely did the right thing uprooting ourselves and moving here. I took Johnnie's hand and squeezed it. #christmasjoy #carolsbycandlelight

I felt so proud of my family as we stood singing words of joy and hope. I don't delve into the past too much (so draining), but the carols and the candles bathing the church in a golden glow took me back to our childhood Christmases. Johnnie sang all the carols, prompting surprised looks from the children. With a father having made his career in the church, he is well versed in all the facts, but can't believe all that far-fetched stuff about resurrection and forgiveness and so on.

It's a shame about his father. I always liked him. The media can be so cruel. Johnnie always says the shock contributed to that final stroke. I wish the children had known him. I can't believe there are only three days till Christmas! #perfectfamily #issysmuggesaysmerrychristmas

January

What a great Christmas! We had a houseful, but we've got the room. I had fresh flowers in all the bedrooms, scented candles from a marvellous little woman I've discovered just up the road and a selection of books and magazines to keep all my guests happy.

Mummy and Silvia are like French chalk and artisan Swiss cheese. Mummy was her usual brittle, critical self, but when MIL is around, I don't mind so much. Toby and Davina are nice enough. He's a crashing bore and she looks remarkably like a horse.

I don't mean that rudely. Davina has got a long face, slightly prominent teeth and a shaggy mane of hair. I almost expect her to snort and paw the ground with her hoof when she enters a room. The two of them are fine in small doses and it's nice for the children to see them. They haven't bred, yet, and are unlikely to now, I should think. He's engrossed in his work and she's with her hunters in the stable block round the clock. I was tempted to lay in a stock of hoof oil for her over Christmas, but resisted. #whateverworks #takesallsorts

Johnnie didn't have to go back to work until the beginning of January. We chilled out, playing board games, watching awful television and eating leftovers. I suspect that this is what ordinary people do. My followers certainly expressed surprise that Isabella Smugge is a dab hand with cold turkey and ham and a demon at Scrabble. #notjustaprettyface

Everyone was a lot more relaxed on the first day of term than we had been back in September. I took some lovely breakfast images. Homemade porridge with bananas and cinnamon and mugs of hot chocolate (made with oat milk as we're all doing Veganuary). Finn was his usual awkward self and refused to pose until Sofija took him to one side and had a quiet word. Honestly! What's got into him?

In the playground, some of the mums smiled at me and asked how my Christmas had been. I detected a slight thaw. It was my turn to host a playdate, so we agreed that Lauren and her girls would come to play on Friday. I'm going to Claire's on Thursday. The social whirl!

January can be a rather dull time of year, but Mimi and I had agreed to focus on nature. In London, post-Christmas it's pretty frightful, with everyone sneezing and coughing, grey skies, Tube strikes and a general feeling of malaise. Up here, I can focus on the Great Outdoors, a gift to the creative blogger.

You may be surprised to learn that I'm a bit of a whizz when it comes to horticulture. Mummy always had green fingers – her planting charts and seasonal bedding plans were legendary in our part of Kent. Issy Smugge knows her hostas from her heliotropes and her camellias from her ceanothus.

I spent a couple of days building up a portfolio of shots to scatter throughout my posts. Holly berries gleaming on a dark-green background, leafless trees, pretty houses, the village pond with ice on it and, of course, that old standby: my own delightful interiors.

The big news in January is Finn's birthday. Ten years old! It seems like yesterday that I was telling Johnnie the news. I can remember the emotion welling up in me as I silently promised my unborn child that I would never put him through what Suze and I had experienced with Mummy and Daddy.

I started the birthday build-up with some new hashtags and a different photo collage every day. From the minute he was born, I made sure I had plenty of beautiful shots. Pretty soon, **#tenyearsold** and **#mybabyisten** were trending.

At teatime, I asked Finn what he'd like to do for his birthday. He banged down his knife and fork and said he wasn't doing anything babyish this year. He and Jake wanted to go go-karting and then have pizza at some kind of café. I pride myself on being an indulgent and flexible mother.

'If that's what you want, darling, that's what you shall have. I can do some lovely shots of you whizzing round the track. Is it indoors or outdoors? I'll have to think about the lighting.'

'No! You're so embarrassing! I want to hang out with Jake and have pizza. You can drop us off and sit in the car.'

We had a row, which ended with him storming upstairs. Could it be hormones? He's a bit young for that, surely. I made a mental note to start work on *Issy Smugge Says: We've Got a Teenager on Our Hands*.

'He is growing up so quickly, Isabella.' Sofija was pouring oil on troubled waters. 'He is getting such a big boy and he wants to do what all his friends do. We can have little party for him here, just family. It will be OK.'

She laid her hand briefly on my shoulder as she loaded the dishwasher. She's a treasure.

On Thursday, we walked up to the vicarage after school. The girls rushed off to play and Claire and I were left to relax on her sofa (unfashionable colour and not very well sprung but surprisingly comfortable) while Joel played at our feet.

We caught up on Christmas. I never did get to Midnight Mass. I felt it was politic to keep Johnnie happy as he'd been quite uncharacteristically snappy about my need to take photos throughout the holiday period. I asked Claire if they'd had any family staying.

'No, Tom's parents were spending Christmas with one of his brothers in Hampshire. We'll probably see them at half term.'

I was surprised. Claire and Tom strike me as the cosy family type.

'What about your family? I can't imagine Christmas with just Johnnie and the children. Hosting lots of guests is part of the fun for me.'

Claire put down her mug and shifted in her seat. I could sense that I'd struck a nerve. Just then, Joel fell over, banging his head and sent up the most frightful wailing. Claire scooped him up, mopped him down and cuddled him. After a few minutes, he calmed down, snuffling and sucking his thumb. Young children make such a mess. If it isn't smelly nappies it's runny noses, vomit or other revolting smearing. Thank heavens I always had such good help with mine.

'Forget I asked. I was being nosey.' I was all ready to move on to talking about Finn's party when Claire interrupted me.

'I don't mind talking about personal things. That's how friendship develops, isn't it?'

I smiled and nodded, although this had not been my experience to date. Friendships for me had been based on having children in the same class, shared interests and being seen with the right people. With a jolt, I realised that Claire and Lauren didn't seem to care about any of those things.

Joel had fallen asleep with his mouth open, his little hand clamped to Claire's jumper like a starfish. I can't say I miss the early years, but just for a second, I had a brief flash of memory.

I was sitting in our flat in Highgate. My baby was fast asleep in my arms, his tiny hand gripping my finger as he slept. His perfect little face and delicious newborn smell flooded me with love. How had that adorable creature become such an angry, withdrawn little boy? I felt tears prick my eyes, but Issy Smugge doesn't allow herself to give in to emotion, so I blinked them back. Natch.

We chatted about our families for a little while. I'd love her to meet Suze. I think they'd get on. Mummy, on the other hand, looks down on everyone. Thinking about it, when she starts ranting on, maybe I should employ one of Finn's stock phrases. 'You are *so* embarrassing.' I can't imagine what she'd say!

I was curious to know a bit more about Claire's background. I imagined her cosy family life – mum at home cooking and singing hymns while she made jam, dad out at work, providing for them all.

'How about your family?' I enquired. 'Do you see much of them?'

She shook her head. 'I haven't seen my parents since I was eight years old.'

Well, you could have knocked me down with a Hungarian goose-down feather. I genuinely did not know what to say.

Claire looked steadily at me. 'Isabella, we can leave it there, or I can tell you more. I don't want to burden you or embarrass you. I haven't had the easiest of lives.'

I was intrigued and shocked all at the same time. I was also feeling a ridiculous sense of flattery that Claire would confide in me. Back in London, my gang all promised to keep each other's secrets, but of course we didn't.

'No, please do go on if you'd like to.' An old and long-repressed emotion was welling up in me. The thought of my friend being hurt upset me. This was how I had felt about Suze until I learned to crush those feelings and lock them away where no one could find them.

'My dad drank heavily and could be violent. My mum had severe clinical depression and became addicted to painkillers and that made it hard for them to look after us. I was the oldest and looked after my brother and sister.'

'But who took care of you?' I was shocked.

'No one. The rest of the family stayed away because of my dad. Things came to a head one Christmas…' Here she swallowed and looked down. 'Dad came back from the pub extremely drunk and lost his temper with Mum because the Christmas tree wasn't up. They had a huge fight. Dad threw a chair at her and smashed the place up. He didn't mean to hurt us, but I got in the way and ended up with broken glass in my arm.'

She pulled up her sleeve to reveal a long, jagged scar. My head was spinning. The cosy picture of a happy family in suburbia was fast receding and in its place was an image of terrified children cowering in the corner while their home was destroyed before their eyes.

'I couldn't stop the bleeding. My little brother ran out on to the street. The neighbours found me and called an ambulance. Social services got involved. We were all fostered, but separately. It broke my heart.

'No one wanted to adopt me. I was angry, and lashed out in ways that made it very hard for anyone to have me living with them. My last foster parents took me on when I was thirteen. They were amazing people, but I was so angry by then that I couldn't accept the love they gave me.'

She stopped speaking and looked down at Joel, gently stroking his head. I couldn't think of a single thing to say.

'I started bunking off school and got in with the wrong crowd. I was desperate for love and attention, but I was looking for it in all the wrong places. I felt unlovable. I'd failed to protect my brother and sister. I felt that it was all my fault.'

There was a long silence. I hate silences. I literally could not think of anything to say that wasn't patronising, disrespectful or downright nosey. After a little while, Claire carried on.

'I started smoking weed and I hardly ever went to school. My foster parents never lost patience with me, though. I ran away several times, and when I was seventeen, I left for good. I got on a bus and went up to London, which was the worst possible place for me. I can't remember a lot about those years. I was usually drunk or out of my head on something.'

I felt I had to speak.

'Claire – thank you for confiding in me. I'm not used to it. My friends never went this deep. I assumed that you'd had the sort of life that everyone does.'

She smiled. 'I don't think I have.'

We sat in silence again, but I didn't feel awkward. I felt –
well, something else. I couldn't tell you exactly what it was, but
it wasn't uncomfortable. I don't think anyone has confided in
me so openly or generously since Suze, that last time. Again, I
felt tears in my eyes. Letting them spill out on to my cheeks and
fall on to my jeans was the bravest thing I've done in a long
time. Claire reached out her free hand and took mine and we
just sat there, neither of us speaking, for a long time.

My conversation with Claire was the last thing I thought about
as I went to sleep that night, and the first thing that popped into
my head when I woke up in the morning. I felt anxious walking
down to school and couldn't work out why. As Chloë and Elsie
chattered away and Finn stalked off ahead of us, I tried to
process my feelings of fear and anxiety.

I hung back a little in the Reception line. I felt strangely shy
and planned to leave the minute Elsie got into school. My
brilliant plan was scuppered by Lauren, who came up behind
me and started chatting about our playdate.

By the time the children were in, it was too late to escape.
Claire was walking over with a big smile on her face. The three
of us wandered over towards the gate, me homeward-bound for
yet more photography editing, the two of them off to the
vicarage for Claire's group. I listened as they chatted, but I felt
as though something heavy was sitting on my chest. To my
horror, I began to feel light-headed and sweaty. I took deep
breaths, but my head was swimming and my heart was beating
so fast I could hardly draw breath.

It's been years since I had a panic attack. I've worked hard
on putting painful memories behind me. The thought of Claire
and Lauren seeing me in such a state filled me with horror, but
as we approached the gate, I felt so faint that all I could do was
lean on it and try to breathe.

'Isabella! What's the matter?'

I couldn't reply. After a few minutes, I began to feel the horror receding. I breathed in deeply a few times and stood up straight. Perhaps I could brazen it out.

'I'm fine. I didn't have any breakfast...' (That was a lie. I did.) 'I think I must be a bit dehydrated.' (Another lie. Issy Smugge drinks water like it's going out of fashion.) 'This coat is very heavy – I should have worn my lighter one.'

'You don't look fine. You look like death warmed up.' Lauren was her usual forthright self. 'Why don't you come down to Claire's for the group? You can chill out a bit.'

Well, I wasn't going to do that!

'I'm absolutely fine, honestly. I'll go home and have a little rest, some tea and a nice breakfast. I feel so silly!' I attempted a light laugh, which came out more like a whinny. I've been spending too much time with Davina.

'Lauren, grab my keys out of the buggy. Can you take Joel, get the kettle on and lay out the biscuits? I'm going to walk Isabella home.' I tried to insist that I was fine, but Lauren was already pushing Joel down towards the vicarage and Claire had taken my arm. How much worse could the day get?

I conserved my energy on the walk up the lane to the house, feeling ridiculously weak. I gave myself a good talking to as we walked up the drive towards the front door.

'For goodness' sake, Isabella, pull yourself together! What on earth's the matter with you?'

Claire brought me a glass of water. She seemed reluctant to leave, in spite of my assurances that I would be fine.

'Honestly, Claire, I was in a rush this morning so I skipped breakfast and I got a bit overheated. That's all.'

At that very minute, Sofija appeared. Claire looked relieved.

'I'm so glad to see you. Isabella had a bit of a turn in the playground. She'll need some breakfast and plenty of water. She's feeling a bit light-headed.'

I willed Sofija to keep her mouth shut about the vegan pancakes with fresh fruit compote I'd eaten for breakfast, but she seemed not to see my pleading eyes.

'Isabella had breakfast today. She says it's the most important meal of the day.'

Claire stood up. 'I'd better run. Lovely to see you, Sofija. Isabella, text me if you need anything.'

There was an awkward silence. No one knows about my panic attacks and I want to keep it that way. Sofija seemed jumpy. She kept playing with her hair, which is a sure sign there's something on her mind. To avoid yet another embarrassing situation, I explained I'd taken the wrong coat off the peg and overheated. I took another gulp of water and stood up.

'Well, this won't get any work done. Lauren and the girls are coming back after school for a playdate, so I'll do pick-up.'

With a final dazzling smile, I headed off down to my studio. **#awks**

After a solid day's work, I felt ready for the challenge of the playground. Issy Smugge prides herself on openness and authenticity, but I seemed to be in a strange place with my au pair. I hadn't worked out the origin of my episode in the playground and until I did, I wasn't ready to explain myself to Sofija. Not that I needed to explain myself. I wouldn't want you to think that there isn't complete confidence between us. I will confess that I felt a little peculiar about being caught out in a lie. I can still remember being walloped with a hairbrush by Mummy for fibbing about borrowing her perfume. I never did that again. **#smellsjustassweet #naughtyissy**

In the playground, Claire was chatting to Lauren and a group of the scary mums. With Mummy's words ringing in my ears ('Stop being such a baby, Isabella!'), I walked over to join them with a bright social smile on my face.

There's something about Claire. I can't put my finger on it, but I find myself saying things to her that I never would to anyone else. I sat down and blurted out the truth. She seemed fine with it and told me that she had suffered not only from panic attacks but also from rampant post-natal depression and crippling anxiety for years. I found it difficult to reconcile the mumsy woman before me with the anxious, damaged person she described.

'How did you get through it all?'

'Meeting Tom had a huge impact on me. He loved me for who I was, the real Claire. I couldn't believe that anyone that sorted could like me and want to be with me, but he did. And my faith has carried me through. I don't know where I would be without that.'

There was a silence while I processed this. I was struggling to see how the angry, lost teenager could have met up with a trainee vicar. I was more interested in Claire's story than I had been in anything for quite a while.

'When did you meet him?' I asked.

Claire smiled. 'I was nineteen. I was dependent on alcohol, I smoked weed every day and I was in a terrible state. One night, I was sitting on some steps, drinking. I was cold and lonely, feeling really bad about my brother and sister and genuinely thinking about ending it all. Who would miss me? I decided to get drunk and stoned the next night and throw myself into the Thames.'

I couldn't believe what I was hearing. This wasn't the kind of backstory I expected to hear from a rural vicar's wife.

'I was sitting there crying when a voice asked if I was all right. I won't repeat what I said to him, but it wasn't terribly polite. In spite of my suggestion that he push off immediately and never return, he sat down next to me and said he was happy to listen if I wanted to talk. I gave him another mouthful then looked up.'

She giggled. 'When I first saw Tom, my heart started beating in double time. I went from being a rough sleeper with a drink problem to a moonstruck teenage girl. I'd never seen anyone so handsome in all my life. He explained that he volunteered with the church group and that he was training to be a lawyer. Even that didn't put me off. We agreed to meet the next night and he wrote down his number and gave it to me. I couldn't ring him, because I didn't have any money or a card for a phone box, but that scrap of paper was a ray of hope. I've still got it in my bedside cabinet.'

I was desperate to hear what happened next, but Lauren and the girls came over and it was time to go home.

'I'll text you,' I called over my shoulder as we started to walk up the lane.

You can't replicate a conversation about a suicidal homeless alcoholic meeting a trainee lawyer via text. I know, because I tried. I haven't felt this desperate to know what happened next since Sherlock threw himself off the top of Bart's. **#cliffhanger #whathappensnext**

On Monday morning, I virtually drop-kicked the children into school.

Breathless with anticipation, I rang the vicarage doorbell, was admitted, sank into Claire's shabby sofa and waited for the next instalment.

'I went to a homeless shelter, got myself washed and dressed in clean clothes and borrowed some make-up from another inhabitant. I wanted to look nice for Tom, even though I knew that someone that normal couldn't possibly want anything to do with someone like me. I was still young enough to have hope. Another few years and it would have been too late. I couldn't pretend that my experiences with men until then had been anything to do with romance.'

I nearly choked on my soya latte.

'So you fell in love, became religious and lived happily ever after.'

She laughed. 'It took a bit longer than that. Tom and I met regularly, and soon I realised that I was coming to rely on him more than I ever had on drink and drugs. I joined an AA meeting. I even started going to the church most weeks, although I had no idea what they were on about.'

Words failed me, and that's not something you'll hear Issy Smugge say very often.

'For me, it was a huge leap of faith going to regular meetings and confronting the pain and fear that had led me to contemplate suicide. No one judged me. They were all so incredibly supportive.'

'So, hang on, how did Tom become a vicar? And what about his family?'

'Tom's parents had their hearts set on him qualifying as a lawyer. He finished his degree but then decided that he had a calling to the ministry and went to theological college. When he introduced me to them, they almost passed out. I wasn't the kind of person they'd envisaged as their daughter-in-law.'

'Well!' I sank back into my seat, amazed. 'How do you get on with them now?'

Claire sighed. 'They've accepted me as best they can, but they don't really approve. They think that if Tom hadn't met me, he'd be a successful lawyer with the right sort of wife. I used to feel so guilty, but he says that being a lawyer would have turned him to drink if I hadn't come along.'

I assured Claire that her secret was safe with me.

'It's not a secret, Isabella.' Claire looked surprised. 'It's part of who I am. When Tom applied for the job, we were honest about my past. The diocese was amazing about it, but some of the congregation felt that they couldn't continue coming to a church with a vicar's wife like me. That really knocked me back. I'd had terrible post-natal depression with Hannah in our last parish, and everyone had been so supportive. Becky was only a baby when we came here and I was tired and anxious, struggling to be a good mum and wife. Tom tried to shield me from the worst of it, but it all came to a head with a special church meeting. I'll never forget his face when he came home that night.'

To my horror, two big tears trickled down her cheeks. I found myself putting my arms round her and holding her while she sobbed. Issy Smugge doesn't do emotional outbursts or public displays of affection, but this was different. I couldn't think of anything to say to make it better, but a wave of indignation swept over me.

Claire gently disengaged herself and blew her nose. 'Sorry. I'm still working through my feelings on that one.'

I'd assumed that once you became religious, everything got sorted out. I thought that you made your commitment, received the free gift (pie in the sky when you die), went to church, stopped swearing, didn't covet your neighbour's ox and that was that.

I felt very cross. 'That's the trouble with the elderly. They get stuck in their ways.'

'Oh no, it was the young families who had a problem with me. We lost four of them, which pretty much wiped out the children's work. It was a small congregation to begin with, and once they left, we had to start again.'

Walking back up the lane with the girls, I was lost in thought. Maybe my panic attack had been triggered by the sad thoughts I'd worked so hard to bury. Could it be that chatting to Claire and hearing her story was having an effect on me? I'd have to be careful that I didn't go soft. Isabella M Smugge has worked too hard on herself to let that happen. #eyesontheprize #stayingstrong

When I got home, I made dairy-free milkshakes for everyone and reminded them that we were talking to Suze the next morning, so it was early bed for everyone. I was so worn out that I wasn't far behind them. I didn't even check my notifications before I dropped off. I had unsettling dreams about running down corridors trying to find someone who was just out of reach. I woke up twice and had to refresh my lavender and Roman chamomile sleep mask to drift off again.

The children get so excited when we talk to Suze. They all love her, and even Finn softens and forgets that he's too cool for school when they chat. I dialled her up and after the usual clicking and buffering (the internet in the countryside is shocking), her face appeared. I felt a stab of pain when I saw her familiar features. We were so close when we were little, allies against Mummy and Daddy, protectors of each other at school. And now this. I know it's all my fault, but I can't seem to find a way through.

'Auntie Suzie! Look, I lost a toof!' Elsie always had trouble with the 'th' sound, and the massive gap in her mouth wasn't helping.

I waved. 'Hi, Suze.'

'Hi, Bella. How are you?'

We exchanged pleasantries. I made myself a soya latte and sat back while the children bombarded her with questions. Finn thanked her in advance for her present and told her all about his go-karting trip. Suze is loving and warm and knows exactly what to say. Their faces light up whenever they see her. I wish they would when I come home. But I must not, simply must not, go down that road.

'Auntie Suzie, when you are coming to see us? Our house is very big and there are lots of rooms for you and Uncle Jeremy and Lily to sleep in. Please, please come and see us. We miss you!' Chloë is particularly close to Suze and I know she's dying to meet her cousin.

'Well, that's up to your mummy and daddy, darling.'

'You're welcome any time, Suze. You know that.' And I meant it. While part of me dreaded seeing her again, another part of me simply wanted to hug her tight and tell her how sorry I was. Because I was.

At that point, Lily appeared. The girls squealed with excitement and that was it on the adult conversation.

We chatted till 8.15, then, reluctantly, I said goodbye. Outside, the skies were leaden and the rain was lashing against the windows. **#sadface #longingforspring**

February

Thank heavens January's over! I quite enjoyed being a vegan for a month, but it didn't go down too well with the children and Johnnie. There was a painful incident with some toasted cheese which I'll draw a veil over. Suffice it to say, we all fell on bacon sandwiches on 1st February with great relief. My **#veganuary** posts were popular, but I don't know if I've got the strength to do it again next year.

I was expecting Sofija back on Tuesday evening as usual, but at lunchtime, she rang up from Nicki's to say she was ill. With Johnnie at work, that left me high and dry. She sounded awful. February is high season for illness. I stay healthy with a cocktail of vitamins. When I told Johnnie, he flew into a rage.

'Iss, she's taking advantage of you! I know you're attached to her and she's good with the kids, but if this keeps happening, I think you should let her go.'

I was shocked. I couldn't possibly manage without Sofija. I made Johnnie promise not to say anything and texted Sofija a get-well message with lots of emojis.

This weekend, Johnnie suddenly said, 'Shall we have the vicar and his wife over soon, sweetie?' I texted Claire and we fixed on the following Friday at 7.00 for 7.30.

Johnnie got back home on Thursday night. I packed the children off to bed and planned a romantic supper. We need to spend some quality time as things aren't working out as I expected. The plan was that he'd be in town three days a week and spend the rest of the time with the family. More often than not, he leaves first thing on Monday morning and we don't see him again until Friday teatime.

We've always talked about retiring at fifty – our hard work brought us financial security. No mortgage on the house (which is in my name), trust funds for all the children, the London flat, the chalet in Verbier and a string of buy-to-lets across east London. It's a good little portfolio.

Johnnie went upstairs to shower and came down looking and smelling delicious. I'd dimmed the lights, lit the candles and had half a dozen oysters reclining seductively on a bed of crushed ice. **#foodoflove #romanticdinner**

Ironically, Mummy used to give Suze and me the benefits of her marital wisdom. 'Remember, girls, when a man comes home from work, he isn't interested in what you've been doing all day. Make sure you've got a drink ready for him, dinner in the oven and that you look nice.'

Trouble was, Mummy may have looked nice when Daddy came home (and she did keep herself up, to be fair), but she'd usually cracked open the gin a good hour before he walked through the door. I certainly wasn't going to fall into that trap.

I poured us both a glass of wine and asked him how his week had been. He talked for fifteen minutes by the clock while I looked interested. I wasn't, particularly, but Mummy did occasionally stumble upon some half-decent advice and I have to confess she was right on this one.

The oysters slipped down nicely. I leaned over Johnnie as I took his plate, grazing the top of his head with a sultry kiss. I didn't want a heavy meal, for obvious reasons, so I served him a beautifully cooked lemon sole with crushed minted potatoes, petit pois and a simple butter and lemon sauce. I was sending pretty clear signals across the rose quartz granite. Oysters, perfume, crisp white wine and not even one photo of our repast. If that doesn't tell a man what the next course is, I don't know what does! **#cometobedeyes #cheeky**

Johnnie's definitely working too hard. 'Perfunctory' would be the word I'd use to describe our post-supper activities. He fell asleep straight away and made noises that in a lesser man could be called snoring. I was left lying awake, staring at the ceiling and wondering if I should have gone all out and got a dozen oysters. Oh, well. Issy Smugge takes everything in her stride and will be planning ahead for more spontaneous dinner dates.

We haven't done much entertaining since we moved, and it's a shame, as the house lends itself beautifully to social occasions. On Friday, I placed fresh flowers around the house, laid the table with our best china and silver and lit the candles. Sofija was in charge of keeping the children at bay (they can smell a dinner party at ten paces) and I did the cooking. Issy Smugge is no slouch when it comes to sauces and soufflés. I just can't bear the daily grind of meal production for people who don't know or don't care that I've slaved over a hot stove for hours, and children are very much included in that bracket.

I prepared some cheeky little *amuse-gueules* to go with the welcome drinks. Tiny chilled glasses of strawberry and beet consommé, thinly sliced rare beef wrapped round asparagus (wickedly expensive, but worth it) and miniature salmon tartare. They took ages to make, but it was worth it to engage with my followers. Mimi gets terribly excited when I throw a dinner party. 'All those lovely trending tweets, sweetheart!' **#dinnerisserved #issysmuggesaysbonappetit**

My menu was perfect. Beefsteak tomatoes, avocado and buffalo mozzarella dressed with extra virgin olive oil and crispy basil leaves; roast venison with a blackberry jus, fondant potato, braised cavolo nero and honeyed carrots, followed by a local cheeseboard with quince jelly. I planned to finish with a flourish, serving my justly famed raspberry soufflé. Thank goodness it's February. Mushrooms and tahini are all very well, but nothing beats organic free-range meat and three veg.

Johnnie always sorts the wine out when we have friends over. I mentioned that Claire and Tom don't drink. He looked appalled.

'What am I supposed to offer them? Water?' The poor man was visibly shocked.

I pointed out that I'd stocked up on elderflower pressé, pink lemonade and bitters and urged him to imagine we were doing **#dryjanuary**, but he merely shuddered and gazed longingly at the wine cellar door.

Just after seven, the front doorbell rang. I relieved Claire of a rather lovely bunch of sea holly, forsythia and euphorbia and we walked through to the kitchen. Johnnie had the charm turned up to eleven and was transfixing our guests with his hypnotic social patter.

I passed round the *amuse-gueules* which met with a rapturous reception. Johnnie poured two flutes of champagne and offered them to our guests.

'Not for me, Johnnie, thank you. Do you have anything soft, Isabella?'

I ran through my extensive menu of fruity fizz and sorted Claire out with a strawberry lemonade with a cheeky little polished steel straw. **#livinglight #issysmuggesaysgogreen**

'Come on, it's not a school night! Are you more of a beer man? I've got a lovely local brew here.' Johnnie was determinedly playing host. Like Claire, Tom politely declined and I supplied him with an elderflower pressé with a dash of lime.

At 7.45, I ushered them through to the dining room. It looked beautiful, warm candlelight reflecting from the glasses and the chandelier twinkling in the firelight.

Tom and Claire doggedly quaffed their strawberry lemonade and elderflower pressé while Johnnie sipped a particularly good white Buzet our wine merchant sent last month. I showed solidarity with our guests and washed my tomatoes down with sparkling water infused with organic Italian lemons.

When I served the venison, Johnnie took the opportunity to switch to a rather kicky little Shiraz. To my consternation, there was a definite air of tension hanging over the table. I racked my brains for a suitable topic of conversation, but try as I might, nothing came to mind.

Johnnie broke the short but awkward silence as we all munched our venison. 'Do you ski, Tom?' he enquired, taking another mouthful of Shiraz.

'I used to. My family are all very keen skiers. A vicar's salary doesn't run to that kind of thing, unfortunately.'

'I bet!' Johnnie raised his left eyebrow and slurred his words just the tiniest touch. To an onlooker, he would have seemed perfectly in control, but to me, red flags were flying.

'And where have you skied? I don't know if Iss has told you, but we've got a little place in Verbier. My mother's Swiss, otherwise we'd never have got it.'

Tom put down his knife and fork. 'We went to Grindelwald one year, I seem to remember, but mostly France.'

The conversation carried on in this vein through the main course. I cleared away and brought in the cheese. Johnnie rose to his feet and went off to the cellar. He returned with a dusty bottle and my heart sank. Our guests had made it abundantly clear that they didn't drink. Why wouldn't he let it go?

'This is a very special port,' he announced. 'My father gave me a case of '85 when Iss and I got married. I'd love you to join me in a toast to our lovely hostess here.' He gave me a wolfish grin. 'I think we can all agree that she is more than just a pretty face.'

I didn't like the way this was going at all. Johnnie was putting Claire and Tom in an incredibly awkward situation. I pushed my chair back.

'Darling, will you come and help with the cheese, please?'

In the kitchen and safely out of earshot, I pushed him up against the fridge and hissed, 'What do you think you're doing? You're being a complete idiot. I told you they don't drink!'

'Have I touched a nerve, darling?' he drawled. 'Surely a little port won't hurt the neighbourinos.'

'No! Stop forcing drink on them!'

'Okeley dokeley,' he replied, irritatingly, and we walked back up the passageway to the dining room.

'Sorry about that.' I launched into a grand tour around my cheeseboard. East Anglia is not quite the culinary desert I'd imagined. With a few pistachios, some organic oatcakes and quince jelly, I'd produced something I wouldn't have been ashamed of back in London.

Johnnie hadn't finished. I thought that the swift kick to the ankle I'd given him by the oven would have driven my point home, but apparently not.

'My wife tells me I'm being an utter cad by insisting that you join me in drinking some of the contents of my cellar. May I take this opportunity to apologise wholeheartedly and remove any temptation from the table?' With that, he stood up and removed the port.

I could feel my cheeks reddening. What was the matter with him? In desperation, I fell back on Mummy's advice, and that's not something you'll hear Issy Smugge say very often! She used to tell Suze and me to remember that people absolutely love talking about themselves. Whether it was their family background, county of origin or the school they went to, a few well-placed questions and a look of utter fascination should be enough to fix any sticky social situation.

'So, Tom,' I said, in what I hoped was a soothing voice, 'Claire tells me your family come from Hampshire. Whereabouts, exactly?'

'Near Whitchurch, at the foot of the North Wessex Downs. It's a pretty little place.'

I managed to keep the conversation going for another five minutes or so, chatting about the New Forest, wild ponies and ferry sailings from Portsmouth. Johnnie was leaning back in his chair and putting away the Shiraz at an alarming rate.

I was just starting to think about the soufflé when Johnnie rejoined the conversation.

'I know Hampshire quite well. All four of us went to school there. Did you board?'

'Yes. I think our parents felt that we'd get more out of the boarding experience if we were a bit further from home, so we were up in Surrey.'

'Iss was at St Dymphna's. Lots of jolly hockey sticks and pashes on the French mistress, eh, darling?' He chuckled. 'And where were you educated, Claire?'

My mouth was dry.

'State school all the way, Johnnie.' Claire had put down her knife and was looking my husband straight in the eye. 'The local primary followed by a comprehensive, which I didn't bother gracing with my presence too much. I didn't go to university and I haven't got any GCSEs or A levels. Delicious cheese, Isabella. Is this a Cambridge Blue?'

That shut him up. I rose to commence the soufflé. I felt it would be politic to take Claire with me. Four soufflés are a bit of a challenge at the best of times, and I didn't want the highly charged atmosphere to cause my *pièce de résistance* to sink. #lightasafeather #raspberrysoufflé

I put the soufflés in the oven and apologised to my friend. 'I don't know what's got into Johnnie tonight. He's not normally like this.' I grabbed my timer and set it to ten minutes.

Claire joined me at the oven door as we stared at the mixture.

'Can I be honest, Isabella? I think he's feeling a bit threatened.'

I was rather taken aback. Johnnie is never thrown by anything or anyone.

'What do you mean?'

'Well, you're the one who's settled into this new life, braved the playground, made friends and managed to balance work and parenting. He's only here at the weekends and suddenly he's meeting two people he doesn't know from Adam.'

Eyes fixed on the slowly rising soufflés, I considered this.

'I suppose it could be something to do with the religion thing. He isn't a fan, and his father being a bishop did have an effect on him. That's no excuse, though. I just feel so bad that he went on about alcohol. I didn't tell him about how you and Tom met because I didn't think it was any of his business.'

'You can tell him if you want.'

Pale pink and feathery light, the soufflés were ascending heavenward in my second-best ramekins.

'I think he's a bit thrown by Tom being – well, more like him than he expects a vicar should be. You know, the public school education, going to Cambridge and all that.'

That made sense. I love Johnnie devotedly, but in his own way, he can be a bit of a snob. He gets that from his father.

The timer went off. Claire stood next to me like a theatre nurse assisting a surgeon. I opened the oven door and lifted out the precious cargo. A triumph! With silent respect, we put them on the plates and walked back to the dining room holding them aloft.

Once dessert had gone down the hatch, we had coffee in the snug. It turned out that that Johnnie's brother Rafe had been at Cambridge with Tom. As always in these cases, they found that they knew lots of the same people from school and university. The atmosphere was slightly more relaxed, thank heavens.

Food-wise, the evening had been a triumph. Socially, I wasn't so sure. At ten, we called it a night. Claire and Tom had to get back for the babysitter. It makes me realise how fortunate I am to have Sofija. I never have to worry about childcare and that gives me huge freedom. I suppose there must be so many women out there who can't go and do what they like when they like because they have to think of their children.

As we waved our guests off, I felt my anger rising. I love my husband, but he had behaved like a complete idiot and needed to be told. He was making come-to-bed eyes at me, but I wasn't going to leave the dining room and kitchen in a mess for Sofija to clear up the next morning. I made him load the dishwasher before we went upstairs.

I marched into our en suite, turned the shower on full and let rip. I didn't want the children or Sofija to overhear. We were yelling at each other for a good twenty minutes and I certainly wasn't going to let him off the hook. I may come across as a sweet-natured woman, but inside Isabella M Smugge there is a sleeping tiger who will not let anyone hurt those she loves.

By eleven, we were in bed. It's vulgar to grade such things, but if I were a different kind of woman, I might say nine out of ten. #makeupsex #healthydebate

We had a wonderful weekend. Johnnie brought me breakfast in bed with the papers while Sofija took the children out on a bike ride. It was a bright, almost spring-like day, so we took full advantage of it.

On Sunday morning, I lay in bed listening to the church bells ringing and wondering what it must be like to go every week. Rather a bore, I think. Still, the steeple looks pretty against the icy blue sky and the sound of the bells reminds me of our childhood when Suze and I used to lie in our beds listening to the bell ringers' practice before we drifted off to sleep.

My followers and Mimi were delighted with my weekend images, as I knew they would be. I came up with a great new hashtag – **#curatedperfection** Says it all about my brand. I was feeling pretty perky when my phone rang. It was Mrs Jenkins, Finn's teacher, asking if I could pop in for a chat about Finn. What a joy for her to have someone like him in her class. Perfect manners, well-spoken and, of course, very bright. I may be biased, but he does seem to have inherited the very best from Johnnie and me.

I haven't had much to do with Mrs Jenkins, but as she ushered me into the conference room, I felt that I was in the presence of an expert. She also knows how to dress for success. Beautifully cut black trousers, nice little top and very on-trend chunky silver accessories. I was pleasantly surprised.

I don't know what I was expecting her opening gambit to be, but it certainly wasn't this.

'Mrs Smugge, I've called you in for a chat as we've had some issues between Finn and some of his classmates. I've talked to the boys involved and we've chatted about interpersonal relationships in PSHE, but it hasn't got any better.'

Naturally, I was horrified to think that my boy was being badly treated, and said so.

'It's slightly more complex than that. Since he joined us, he hasn't been focusing on his work and he's been behaving in an unacceptable way to a couple of the other boys in his class. Our ethos here is that we show respect to each other and that we work through any issues rather than letting them fester.'

It seemed that Finn had been taunting some of the boys about having divorced parents. I could hardly believe my ears. He and Jake had been told off for fighting a couple of times and things had turned nasty when one of the boys fought back.

Mrs Jenkins was very much in charge.

'Boys of this age can start to jostle for position and become a little more aggressive. I'm meeting with the other parents and

I have spoken to Finn about it. I would be grateful if you and your husband could address the issue at home. We don't want this getting out of hand, and of course we've got secondary school to think about next year.'

Here, I put her straight. 'Finn's been down for public school since before he was born.'

After a few more awkward exchanges, I was ushered out. I stood in the rain for a few minutes, my mind racing. I thought about texting Johnnie, but what would I say? *'Our son has been taunting other boys. Come home at once.'* I did the next best thing and texted Claire.

A few minutes later, I was installed on Claire's sofa and had a cup of instant coffee in my hand. Like persistent toothache or fallen arches, after a while you get used to it. I poured out the whole sorry story to her and she was marvellous. After a chat, I felt much better and ready to talk to Finn when he came home from school.

I apologised again for Johnnie's boorish behaviour on Friday evening. My menfolk weren't exactly covering themselves with glory. I thought Claire looked pale and tired. I must get her a little something to thank her for being such a good friend to me.

On Monday night I had a chat with Finn. He flew into a rage and told me he hated me, then stomped upstairs to his room. I could have cried. I didn't, obviously. Crying solves nothing and ruins your lashes.

I was worn out. I put Elsie to bed, then half an hour later kissed Chloë goodnight and shouted kindly salutations through Finn's bedroom door. I was in bed by ten. What have I become? #earlytobedearlytorise

It's cold and I'm barefoot. I've lost Suze. I can hear her calling, 'Bella! Where are you?' I'm running as fast as I can, but my feet are like lead. I run towards Suze's dorm. The door is locked and it doesn't matter how hard I bang on it and shout her name. I'll never find her again. Mummy will be so cross with me. I sink down on to the floor and burst into tears, calling her name over and over again.

I've found her! Her curly blonde hair has worked its way out of its ponytail and she's wearing a pair of little pink pyjamas. She's cuddling me and wiping away my tears.

'Oh, Suze, I thought I'd lost you,' I sob, holding her close. 'I'm so sorry. I promise I'll look after you.' I can hardly speak for tears.

'Mummy, don't be sad.' The little girl lying next to me, stroking my face, isn't Suze. It's my own sweet Elsie. 'I had a bad dream so I came in to find you. Why were you calling me Auntie Suzie?'

Mothers are supposed to cuddle their children and comfort them and wipe away their tears. Not that mine ever did. I sit up and rub my eyes and try to compose myself.

'Mummy was having a nasty dream, darling. Let's lie down and see if we can go back to sleep.'

Elsie snuggles down beside me, pops her thumb into her mouth and goes straight to sleep. I lie gazing at her for what seems like hours before I finally fall into a restless slumber. I can't remember the last time I've been this close to one of my children. Elsie looks so much like Suze. The same hair, the same mouth, the same peaches-and-cream complexion. She's so beautiful. Just like Suze.

In the morning, I woke up feeling terrible. There was no way I could do the school run, so I reached over for my phone to text

Sofija before I remembered she was in London. Short of telling a bare-faced lie to the school and claiming that all three children had been laid low by some terrible disease, it looked as though I would have to get up, have a long hot shower and apply some very expensive concealer. It didn't work. No matter how much I caked on, I still looked about a hundred years old. I couldn't even wear sunglasses because who does in February? I didn't think that even I could rock that look in a cold, wet Suffolk playground.

In the Reception line, people said hi and then did a double take. I wanted to attribute this flattering attention to my statement red lipstick and oversized designer bag, but Issy Smugge is a realist. It was the eye bags.

'You look rough, babes!' It was Lauren. 'Were you out on the lash last night?'

As if! Claire came over and expressed concern at my huge eye bags. I shall certainly be looking elsewhere for my cosmetics from now on.

I should have gone home and got going on *Issy Smugge Says: Spring's Here!* but I didn't have it in me. I invited Claire and Lauren back for coffee. Lauren was busy, but said she'd try to look in later. We splashed up the lane, Joel's howls competing with the noise of the rain drumming on the road.

Claire asked for decaf. She must be on a post-Christmas health kick. After my hideous night, I was on full strength and going easy on the steamed milk. I dug out a tin of Christmas shortbread. Issy Smugge doesn't generally do comfort eating, but my eyes were burning, my head ached and my stomach was in knots. I felt like a sad little girl, and on days like that (not that I have many of them), shortbread made by people employed by the future king is the only thing that hits the spot. #yummyscrummy #thankyouprincecharles

The biscuits didn't even touch the sides; we took a huge gulp of coffee and let out a loud sigh. There are many things in this life that I treasure. The crisp champagne snow on a red run in Verbier early in the morning, the new season's collections, a tiny pot of caviar with a flute of champagne. On this rainy February morning, however, a really good coffee and shortbread in the company of my friend were certainly hitting the spot.

It felt good to sit in my beautiful kitchen with my friend, like a normal woman. The trouble with being an internationally renowned blogger of my calibre is that it's work, work, work and one rarely gets to relax and enjoy the fruits of one's labours. If you'd told me a year ago that I would find comfort and happiness in the company of a mumsy vicar's wife in the wilds of Suffolk while stuffing my face with organic shortbread, I'd have laughed in your face.

We ambled through to the playroom and sank down on to the sofa. A little voice in my head was shouting, 'Get on with your work! What do you think you're doing, lazing around?' but I ignored it. It sounded remarkably like Mummy.

Claire broke the silence. 'Did you have a bad night, Isabella? You do look tired.'

I explained that I'd had a terrible dream and woken up to find Elsie in bed with me. Claire laughed.

'Tom and I are lucky if we spend two nights out of seven alone. It's either Joel waking up and needing a cuddle, or one of the girls having a nightmare or wanting to be taken to the loo. I quite like waking up and finding a little person in bed with me. They're so cuddly.'

'Johnnie's not a fan of co-sleeping. I had a horrible nightmare about being back at boarding school, looking for my sister. I took ages to get back to sleep. Hence the bags!'

'Your sister's in Hong Kong, is that right?'

I ran through the basics. Suze is two years younger than me and married to Jeremy. They adopted Lily last year. She works at the British Consulate, part-time since Lily came along. Jeremy is a merchant banker, but in spite of that is a lovely man.

'I'd love to meet her.' Claire was looking wistful. 'I'd give anything to see more of my brother and sister. Are you close?'

How could I tell her that we used to be as close as two petit pois in a pod, but now found ourselves unable to bridge the chasm between us? Sweat prickled around my hairline. Could I really tell Claire the truth? I took a deep breath.

'We were incredibly close when we were young. Life at home wasn't easy. When I went to St Dymphna's at seven, we were heartbroken. Suze came to school two years later. She got bullied but I soon sorted that out.'

I smiled as I remembered the metallic 'snip' of the scissors and the hair falling to the ground.

'Daddy went off with Mummy's best friend, Arabella. She and Mummy ran a business called Carobella together. I expect you've heard of it. Interior designs. Mummy sold it a few years ago but the new owner kept the name. A year after Mummy and Daddy split up, Daddy and Arabella were on holiday in Italy and came off the road on a hairpin bend. When we came home for Easter, Mummy had sold our ponies. That wasn't the greatest of years, but it did bring Suze and me even closer together.'

Claire was staring at me as though I was wearing Neo-Gothic two seasons after it went out.

'Oh, Isabella, that's awful! Losing your father twice over and being away at school when he died. That must have been so traumatic.'

I shrugged. 'I suppose. You cope, don't you?'

There was a silence, broken by the sound of Joel contentedly filling his pants. Claire went off to the cloakroom to change him, leaving me with an acrid tang in the air and a feeling of vulnerability. Why was I telling Claire such personal things? What had happened to the old Issy Smugge who kept her cards so close to her chest?

Once I escaped from the cloisters of St Dymphna's, I had to go up against Mummy. Would you believe that she expected me to attend some terrible finishing school in Switzerland? Her own sojourn at an exclusive establishment had left her with perfect posture, the ability to whip up a *tarte tatin* at a minute's notice and the belief that the best thing a girl could aspire to was a good marriage. I had no intention of spending two years in some reactionary canton learning how to make ganache and mend china.

At school, I excelled in art. Above all other subjects, this was the one I wanted to pursue. Daddy would have backed me up, but he was dead and buried, so I had to do it for myself.

I won a place at art college to study drawing, art and photography. That was one in the eye for Mummy.

Claire was engrossed. 'And how did you meet Johnnie? Was he there too?'

Anything less likely I couldn't imagine!

'We met through a mutual friend. It was love at first sight for both of us.'

Claire sighed. 'How romantic! I bet your sister was delighted for you.'

If this was a TV miniseries, we'd have a heart-warming scene where the older sister tells the younger that she's found love and everything goes into soft focus. This being my actual life, however, things hadn't quite worked out that way. If Claire hated me after I told her the truth, at least I'd been honest.

'Suze got a place at Durham and rang me just before Christmas to tell me she'd met someone. I can still hear her saying that she thought he might be the One. She fell hard for him and he seemed to feel the same way. That Easter, she invited him home. She was bubbling over with excitement, so in love and so happy that she was going to introduce the man she loved to her family.'

I stopped for a minute to gather my thoughts.

'They were due in on the late train, so I drove to the station to meet them. I'll never forget the first moment I saw him. It was love at first sight. He told me later that he felt the same. There was an electrical charge between us, the most incredible magnetic pull. Suze introduced us, holding his hand and gazing up at him with such love in her eyes. I remember gripping the steering wheel so hard on the way home that my knuckles went white.'

I broke off. I'd had a flashback of Suze, face white, eyes full of tears, whispering, 'But I trusted you, Bella. How could you do this to me?'

I gazed at my lap, reliving the shame and the guilt. I'd tried to justify our actions a thousand times over the years, but when it came down to it, Suze had fallen in love for the first time and then been dumped by her boyfriend for her own sister. By the time we got married, there was a shaky connection between us again, but nothing was ever the same.

Claire reached over and took my hand. For the second time in twenty-four hours, I found myself with tears pouring down my cheeks. At this rate, the eye bags would become a permanent feature.

Thank heavens for Verbier. March was nearly upon us, with the promise of spring, and soon I would have a huge stock of gorgeous photos of snow, schussing and Smugges. #smuggesinthesnow #climbeverymountain

March

Issy Smugge is revitalised after a week in the Swiss Alps. We had a marvellous time! Finn perked up no end and spent lots of time with Johnnie, which had a mollifying effect on his behaviour. Say what you will, it's far easier to chat to a child dangling hundreds of feet over an alp than it is over *spaghetti alle vongole* in the kitchen at home.

Johnnie thinks we made a mistake sending the children to state school. I can't agree. We had a lively discussion about that one evening over fondue. His view is that Finn will naturally struggle in a state setting and that the sooner he goes off to private school, the better.

Once upon a time, I would have agreed. Now, I remember the stiff fabric of my school skirt rubbing against my seven-year-old legs and smell the institutional aroma of St Dymphna's. It brings all the terror flooding back. I have to be logical. If I really feel that it's not the right thing for Finn, I'll talk Johnnie round. Somehow.

It's Johnnie's birthday this month. I'm doing presents, cards, cake and a celebratory meal, but we've been apart so much of late that I feel a really special treat is called for. Johnnie and I are rock solid, of course, but all couples need to make sure they keep the sparkle in their relationship. In *Issy Smugge Says: Turn the Lights Down Low*, my bestselling relationship book, I share my Top Ten Tips for a long-lasting and mutually fulfilling partnership.

At breakfast on Monday morning, I gave Finn a stern talking-to about his behaviour. I made a point of walking up to the Year Five line to smile graciously at Mrs Jenkins, who was wearing another very well-put-together outfit. I don't know many of the parents in Finn's year, apart from Jake's mum, Charlene, of course. And I don't really know her. Year Five seems to have a disproportionately high number of scowling mothers from the council estate. Several of them turned to look at me as I stood in the line.

'Go away!' Finn hissed at me. 'What are you doing? I'm not a baby. You are *so* lame!'

I ignored him and tried to catch the eyes of some of the mums. One woman did more than catch my eye. She bored into it with what I believe is termed a death stare. She was clad in a pair of skin-tight jeans, high-heeled boots and a leather jacket. She had spiky blonde hair and heavy eye make-up. She looked absolutely terrifying. I stopped smiling and scuttled back to the Reception line where nearly everyone seems to like me.

It was a relief to see them all as I returned to my rightful place in the playground. I consulted the oracle.

'Who's that skinny woman with the blonde hair over there?'

Lauren peered into the distance.

'That's Liane Bloomfield. Zach Bloomfield's mum. Apart from Zach, she's got a couple of kids at high school, the little girl in Year Three and the baby. She's a real hard nut.'

I explained that she'd been giving me evils. I believe that's the term.

'You don't want to get on the wrong side of her! She's all right, but if you upset her you'll know all about it. Plus, she's a Bloomfield so she's related to half the village.'

The name was ringing a vague bell. Now I came to think about it, Zach Bloomfield was the name of the boy who had hit Jake and started the whole business with Mrs Jenkins. Issy Smugge doesn't believe in cheapening her utterances with coarse language, but if ever there was a time for a naughty word, this was it.

At pick-up time, I smelled trouble. Mrs Jenkins was eyeballing me across the playground. I was tempted to put my head down and scurry home, but she could probably teleport if she put her mind to it. I bowed to the inevitable and trudged over to her.

'Hello, Mrs Smugge. Nice half term? I'm afraid we've had an incident. Finn and Zach Bloomfield had a fight on the field at lunchtime and we've taken away their playground privileges for this week. There seems to be some tension between them. We're working on it in school, but if you could speak to him, please, I'd appreciate it.'

I could have wept. Zach Bloomfield! Son of the terrifying blonde Amazon. I smiled and promised that I'd try to get to the bottom of it.

I shared the news with Lauren and Claire. Lauren shook her head and looked concerned and even Claire appeared to be rattled. My son had chosen the very worst person with whom to tangle. I could only hope that Mrs Jenkins' superpowers and my excellent parenting could combine to sort this out.

Back home, I locked myself in the downstairs cloakroom. I wondered what Claire would say in the same situation and suddenly realised that I might have hit on the solution. By acting like the vicar's wife, a former addict and alcoholic, I, one of the UK's best-known bloggers, could perhaps reach out to my own child. I found my eyes filling with tears as I realised that Finn's behaviour might have something to do with me. I thought I'd given him everything to make him happy, but I appeared to have forgotten something vital.

Dinner was organic quiche with quinoa and beetroot, but as I came out of the loo, wiping my eyes, a new idea came to me. My voice was a bit wobbly.

'Who fancies fish and chips?'

Well, you'd have thought I'd said that they never had to have a bath or clean their teeth ever again.

'Come on, then. Coats on. Let's go and get it.'

I found myself in the unusual situation of sourcing nourishment for the family myself, and from a takeaway establishment at that. I'd noticed the fish and chip shop in the village but, of course, I'd never been there. The windows were steamed up, and as we pushed the door open, a wonderful smell hit us. It reminded me of going down to Whitstable with Daddy when we were children. He'd always buy us fish and chips, which we'd eat on the beach. Why hadn't I thought of this before?

I directed the children to the large handwritten menu. We shook salt and vinegar onto our chips and I bought a pot of mushy peas to show willing. We walked back up the lane to our house with the delicious smell of fish and chips in our nostrils.

The old me would insist on proper dining round the table, or at least at the island, with knives and forks. This new me walked into the family room with cutlery and invited the children to choose something funny to watch while we ate off our laps. Finn was looking at me as though I had been transformed into someone else. And I suppose I had. I was enjoying myself so much I completely forgot to take any photos.

After we'd finished, I took Elsie up to bed, leaving Chloë and Finn to tidy up downstairs. As I tucked her in, I kissed her and told her I loved her. She threw her arms round my neck.

'I love you too, Mummy. I like it when you put me to bed.'

She gave me a huge, gappy smile. For a moment, it could have been Suze lying there in her bed, waiting for me to arrange all her teddies for her and check under the bed for monsters. Once again, my eyes filled with tears. What on earth was happening to me? I kissed Elsie again, turned out the light and said goodnight.

The diary of Isabella M Smugge

Ruth Leigh

"For an award-winning blogger like me (Influencer of the Year more times than I can remember and no stranger to The Sunday Times Bestsellers List), December is the month where all my Christmases come at once. Metaphorically. And of course, literally."

...loë were tidying up and loading ...ssed. Sofija has taught them well. I ...e bedtime warning and checked my ...'d texted Johnnie earlier, but he hadn't

...the loaded dishwasher and sent it to Sofija to ... good job the children had done. She didn't come ... either. I expect she was out with her friends and couldn... ...r her phone.

I chased Chloë upstairs and into the bathroom to clean her teeth. No wonder Sofija's so skinny. It's exhausting looking after children! I kissed her goodnight and left her reading her book. I know she'll be sensible and turn her light off when she's tired.

As I walked downstairs, I wondered what Claire would do. I was pretty sure she wouldn't shout or judge. She'd listen intently to whatever Finn had to say and take her time before replying. I decided that this was the way forward.

I settled myself onto the sofa and thought about what to say. As I was pondering, Finn started things off.

'Mum, no offence, but there's been some stuff going on at school and it's about you.'

He looked at me sideways as if to gauge my response. I stayed calm, nodded and said, 'None taken. I'm listening.'

He looked down at his lap and twisted his hands together. Whatever it was, it had clearly had an effect on him. I managed to keep my mouth shut and let the silence unfold.

'When we were in London, all the mums looked like you and I didn't stand out. Since we moved up here, everyone stares at you in the playground and some of the people in my class say horrible things. I tried to ignore it, but Jake told me to punch Zach Bloomfield, so I did.'

He broke off and looked down again. I took a minute to marshal my thoughts.

'So, you were standing up for me. Is that what you mean?'

Ruth Leigh

Obsessive book-lover,
word-queen, author,
blogger, speaker.

socials:

'S'pose.' He scratched his ear, always a sign of concern. 'I don't want to upset you, but Zach and some of the others said you're really stuck-up. They found you on Instagram and kept whispering stuff in lessons. I told Sofija and she said not to worry you because you're so busy and just to ignore them. So I did, but then it got too much and I had the fight with Zach.'

I was surprised to hear that a ten-year-old boy had access to Instagram. They're not my usual demographic.

'I told Mrs Jenkins. She told him off for using bad language and not being respectful, but she said I shouldn't have hit him and I needed to think carefully about my choices. Thing is, he says I'm a stuck-up posh boy who doesn't belong here. I wish we were back at home. I liked it there.'

This wasn't turning out at all as I'd envisaged. My phone beeped. It was a text from Sofija. There were lots of emojis. I showed it to Finn, who smiled weakly.

Johnnie and I had spent ages deliberating over the move. We wanted to invest in a property outside London. We were looking ahead to our retirement and, of course, with three children, you've got to think about schooling, health and future weddings. The garden here will make the perfect venue for their receptions and the church is just next door. I'll be the best mother of the bride and mother of the groom ever. #countrywedding #perfectday

With a stab of pain, I realised that I was doing to Finn exactly what Mummy had done to me all those years ago. I always spoke to Nanny about everything that really mattered to me, and she would instruct me not to bother my mother with my troubles because she was so busy. The difference was that she was merely playing bridge with her cronies and fiddling about with the campanulas, whereas I am engaged in building an empire, but the fact remains that I haven't been the best mother I could be to Finn. That picture of my tiny sleeping newborn flashed back into my mind again, and I swallowed hard.

'I'm so glad we're having this conversation, darling.' I reached across and touched his arm and, for the first time in months, he didn't flinch and pull away. 'What can I do to help?'

'Nothing really. Jake said the best thing is to keep my head down and if Zach winds me up again, punch him behind the games shed.'

'Maybe ease up on the punching,' I suggested. 'They don't like that kind of thing at school. They never did at mine.'

Finn looked surprised. 'But Dad says it was all playing hockey and singing hymns at your school.'

I laughed. 'There was a lot of that, but some punching did go on from time to time. You can't have hundreds of girls locked up in a school without the odd row.'

Finn looked unsure. Was it time to reveal the awful truth about his mother? Issy Smugge is pro-diplomacy and abhors violence, but Isabella Neville was a different kettle of fish. To my surprise, I found myself letting out what could only be described as a belly laugh. I usually express amusement melodiously and appropriately, but recalling the scene behind the lacrosse pavilion and feeling my fist connecting with Lavvie Harcourt's eye was extremely satisfying, even so many years on.

Since I seemed to be getting through to Finn at last, I was loath to stop.

'I don't know if I should be telling you this, but I punched someone at school once.'

Finn's mouth fell open. 'No way!'

'Yes way!' I riposted, feeling ludicrously young and giggly.

By the time I'd been at St Dymphna's a while, I'd bedded myself in and made some friends. Suze struggled from the start. Things got even worse in her third year, when a new girl arrived. I disliked her the minute I clapped eyes on her. She was very pretty with long blonde hair which she wore in two plaits. Her eyes were a deep blue, she spoke with a soft and demure voice and I knew immediately that she was a wolf in sheep's clothing. And so she proved to be.

In the Christmas hols, Suze was very quiet and subdued. Mummy didn't notice, of course. That was the last Christmas Mummy and Daddy would be together, although we didn't know it at the time. Nanny had gone (Mummy had told us to say goodbye the week before Suze joined me at St Dymphna's. I still feel such rage whenever I think about that) and it was just the four of us in the house.

We lay in our beds on Christmas Eve, sleepless from excitement and anticipation while Suze poured her heart out to me.

'Lavvie Harcourt is so horrible to me, Bella. She got me in trouble with Mademoiselle in French, she put a dead mouse in my bed and everyone laughed when I screamed. The teachers think she's a nice girl, but she isn't. I hate school. Can't we run away together and live somewhere until we can leave home?'

Poor Suze. She was only nine and was finding out how vile people can be. I got out of my bed, put my arms around her and told her I would make sure Lavvie Harcourt never upset her again. We fell asleep cuddled up together, and when we woke, our stockings were full and it was Christmas morning, with the bells ringing and snow on the ground.

Back at school, I hatched my plan. Lavinia was extremely proud of her hair. Suze told me that she brushed it 200 times each night. It was beautiful hair, I must admit, the colour of spun gold in a fairy tale. Anything less like a princess than Lavvie Harcourt, however, you couldn't imagine. She had a gaggle of girls who looked up to her and who would do her dirty work, the mouse being a prime example. I decided to hit her where it hurt.

I fixed on suet pudding night, gambling on the fact that the overload of heavy carbohydrates would ensure sound sleep. I left most of mine. I didn't want to nod off and miss my chance.

I sneaked a pair of dressmaking scissors into my pocket and hid them under my pillow. When everyone was asleep, I crept out and down the stairs towards the Third Year wing. As the school clock struck eleven, I arrived in Suze's dorm. The sound of deep breathing was proof of the pudding.

I took the scissors from my dressing gown pocket and gently teased one of Lavinia's long, golden plaits out from under the blankets. This was the crucial moment. If she woke up, I couldn't possibly explain why I was out of my bed standing over a helpless Third Year with a huge pair of dressmaking shears!

I took the scissors out of my pocket and cut off a plait. There was a loose floorboard in the corridor outside the dorm which squeaked whenever you walked on it. I prised it up, coiled up the shining plait and stowed it there. It's probably still there to this day.

I glanced at the clock. It was late and a school night. I decided to carry on. It's not every day that you get to confess what you got up to at school! **#sneakyschoolgirls** My son agog, I continued the story.

Suze's dorm was awoken by a piercing scream from Lavinia Harcourt.

'My hair! My plait's gone!'

Uproar ensued. Lavvie Harcourt was sitting bolt upright in bed, screaming at the top of her voice. Suze had to work hard not to burst out laughing.

The St Dymphna's investigative squad swung into action. Everyone was ordered to take their mattresses off their beds and open up their tuck boxes. It was assumed that someone in the Third Year had committed the crime and this belief persisted well into the afternoon. The headmistress addressed us all in a grave and solemn manner at chapel. Lavinia was not one of our number. She had been taken to the sickbay to lie down and be fussed over by Matron.

'I am horrified to think that a St Dymphna's girl could play such a barbarous prank on a fellow pupil. I simply cannot believe that any young lady in this school could possibly commit such an act!'

Miss Trent continued in this vein for some time, fixing us all with a steely glare which reduced several of the younger girls to tears. After twenty minutes or so, we were reminded of the school motto: 'Duty, Obedience, Kindness'. There was a respectful silence as we all gazed up at the stained-glass window upon which these words were emblazoned. Miss Napier struck up 'Onward Christian Soldiers' on the Bechstein and we marched out two by two.

'What happened?' Finn enquired. 'Did they find out it was you?'

'Oh no. They never noticed the squeaky floorboard. The next day, Miss Trent gave it to us with both barrels, assuring us that if the culprit owned up, justice would be done but mercy would be shown. Obviously, I wasn't going to say anything. Lavinia came back from the sickbay later that week with the other plait cut off too. She looked ridiculous. Matron had tried to keep her hair even, but it was ragged and messy, and even with a nice hairband in it looked silly.'

I grinned as I recalled the chastened Lavinia skulking around the corridors until her hair started to grow again. She and her gang were ominously quiet. Suze overheard them in the showers one day after lacrosse and reported back.

'Lavvie was saying she'd find out who cut her plait off if it was the last thing she did and she'd get revenge! What if she finds out it was you, Bella?'

I assured her that she would never discover the truth. I should have known that Miss Lavinia had something up her sleeve.

It felt good to be back in our bedroom at February half term with Mr Fazakerley and all our familiar books and toys. We chatted non-stop about Lavinia and her clique and her missing plait.

Our two best friends, Penny and Minty Pryke-Darby, were the same ages as us but attended the local private school. Their mother, Arabella, was my godmother and Mummy was Pen's. We loved Arabella. Her house was big, like ours, but had a completely different feeling. It was always a bit messy, but whenever you turned up, Arabella would greet you with a big hug and the offer of cake. To this day, I can't work out what it was that drew Mummy and Arabella to each other, let alone made them start up a successful business together.

Arabella was the complete opposite of Mummy. Like her, she loved gardening, but she also adored horses and was a member of the local hunt. She'd helped Daddy to choose our ponies. She was warm, loving and lots of fun, with a loud, dirty laugh and hair pinned up any old how. The Pryke-Darbys' house was a second home to us. We'd play for hours in the big, rambling garden, climbing the trees, swinging on their low branches and engaging in never-ending games of hide-and-seek. Those times are some of the happiest memories of my life.

One day, Daddy took us down to Whitstable, to give Mummy a rest, as he put it. A rest from what, I couldn't tell you. I know now that things between them were bad, and that he and Arabella were close to being discovered. Suze and I had one last perfect day with our father. We walked on the beach, ate ice creams with Flakes and sauce and sprinkles, collected shells and pebbles and had a huge fish and chip lunch. We walked along holding one hand each and chatting away to him about school.

Suze let it out. I thought Daddy would be furious, but he threw his head back and laughed. He put his arms around me, picked me up in the air and whirled me around. Sometimes, just before I fall asleep, or when I'm half-awake in the morning, I have a vivid memory of the rough feeling of his coat, the smell of his aftershave and cigarettes, and his laughter pealing out over the cold grey sea.

Back at school, Lavinia was unnaturally quiet. One cold March day, I was summoned to Miss McDonald's office. My heart was beating fast and my palms were sweaty. To my surprise, the door opened again and in walked Suze. I was convinced the game was up. However, my Head of Year was smiling kindly at us.

'Girls, I've called you in because your mother rang up this morning. Now, don't worry. No one is ill or hurt.'

She paused and smiled at us again. Suze reached over to take my hand. I squeezed it.

'Your mother told me that she and your father have decided to separate. That means that when you go home for Easter, he'll be living in a different house. You can still see him whenever you want, but things will be a little different. I want you both to know that you can come and talk to me any time you would like to. Have you got any questions?'

I couldn't think of a single thing to say. After an awkward silence, we were dismissed. As we walked down the corridor together, Suze said, 'Does that mean Mummy and Daddy don't love each other any more, Bella? Do you think we did something wrong?' She started chewing at her fingernails.

I didn't like the idea of Daddy living somewhere else. I instructed Suze not to tell anyone. There were lots of girls at St Dymphna's with divorced parents, but I had no wish to broadcast Mummy and Daddy's marital troubles.

I don't know how Lavinia found out that our parents had split up. She started taunting Suze. The next time we saw each other, my little sister's fingernails were chewed to the quick and she'd started ripping off the skin around her nails. I made her tell me what had been said, and when I heard the cruel words, Lavinia's fate was sealed.

I bided my time. I was the lacrosse monitor, my job being to make sure that everything was tided away in the pavilion and that the door was securely shut. Since maths was after lacrosse,

I was dawdling around, wasting time. I hated maths. Suddenly, I saw a figure walking across the pitch. It was none other than Lavinia Harcourt, on her way back from her violin lesson in the music block.

I waited until she was almost upon me, then stepped out of the pavilion. Her eyes narrowed.

'You leave my sister alone, Lavinia Harcourt. If I hear that you've said a single word about our family, or anything else, I'll... I'll...' I paused briefly, thinking of what I would do.

'You'll... you'll... What?' she mocked. 'Cut off my plait? I know it was you, Isabella Neville. I'll make you sorry. No wonder your father left your mother, if she's anything like you and your idiot of a sister.'

It isn't particularly becoming in a young lady, but I was overcome with the urge to punch Lavinia Harcourt. So I did. It was incredibly satisfying. My fist connected with her eye and she staggered backwards. I would have left it there, but she came back at me with lightning speed, grabbed my hair and started pulling it. It really hurt so I punched her again. Then she scratched my face and kicked me in the shins. I'd just knocked her over when Miss Napier appeared.

We got a severe reprimand from Miss Trent; our parents were written to and we lost all our privileges that term. I didn't care. I'd have done it all again to protect Suze. Lavinia was left with horrible short hair and a massive black eye. My bruises and scratches were a small price to pay.

Finn was gazing at me in what I can only describe as awe.

'You punched that girl and cut her hair off? Why didn't you tell me all this stuff before?'

How do you introduce such a thing into everyday conversation? 'More spinach, darling? Oh, and by the way, did I ever tell you about the time I punched Lavvie Harcourt's lights out?'

I looked up at the clock. It had gone ten. I arose.

'Bed, young man! We'll be fit for nothing tomorrow morning.'

I walked up the stairs behind him, stood respectfully outside the bathroom as he cleaned his teeth and, for the first time in many months, was permitted to enter his bedroom to say goodnight.

As I climbed into my own bed, I felt happier than I had for months. If I were religious, which I'm not, I would probably have thanked God for breaking down the barrier between Finn and me. I drifted off to sleep between my crisp, 500 thread count percale sheets, a smile on my face, thinking how much I'd have to tell Claire the next time we met.

I jumped out of bed the next morning and ran down to the kitchen, to find Finn making himself a hot chocolate. I don't swim on Sofija's days off as I need to be downstairs sorting out breakfast, uniform and teeth cleaning. It seems to take me twice as long to get everything done when she's not here. When she asks the children to do something, they do it immediately. It takes a bit longer when I'm in charge. I'm not sure why.

'Good morning, darling.' I walked over to the coffee machine and fired it up. 'How are you today?'

Finn grinned. 'Can I tell Jake what you did, Mum? I still can't believe it.'

We giggled and I took the risk of giving him a hug. He didn't pull away. Result!

Coffee made, I sat myself down at the island and ran through the bill of fare. Fresh fruit and yoghurt, sourdough toast with avocado, pancakes with blueberries, granola. We both went for granola, which was nice and easy. It felt pretty good sitting at the island in my dressing gown with my boy, eating breakfast in a companionable silence.

I still wanted to do something to help Finn at school. He wouldn't let me talk to anyone (too embarrassing), but I really wanted to be the right sort of mother.

'Can you try to look like everyone else, Mum?' he asked. 'Don't do your hair up all fancy and put on make-up. None of the other mums do.'

Never in many a moon has Isabella M Smugge left the house without a full face of make-up and perfect hair. Suze inherited Daddy's thick blond curls, whereas I got Mummy's thin red-gold hair which needs to be washed every day to avoid the dreaded lank look. We compromised. I would apply foundation and mascara, but leave it at that, and put my hair up in a ponytail. I also agreed to wear jeans, no heels and leave my handbag at home. This, it seems, is the standard mum look which will not cause Finn any grief.

We agreed that he would try his very hardest to ignore Zach Bloomfield's taunts, stay with Jake at all times (except in the loo) and report back to me and Mrs Jenkins on a regular basis. At this point, the girls came down, half dressed and rubbing their eyes. Finn jumped up and poured them both a bowl of granola. Things feel pretty good in Issy Smugge's world this morning! #happyfamily #bondingwithmyboy

My new look went relatively unnoticed in the playground. I made sure to stay well away from the Year Five line but noticed Liane Bloomfield staring at me as she walked out of the gate. It took me right back to Lavinia Harcourt giving me the evil eye halfway through 'Dear Lord and Father of Mankind' in chapel all those years ago.

Tom was on the school run. I wandered over to say hi once I'd waved Finn, Chloë and Elsie off. He smiled his dazzling smile at me. He always makes me feel that there's no one he'd rather see. Claire is one lucky lady!

'How are things, Isabella?' he asked. 'What are you up to today?'

I had a busy day planned, editing, writing and posting, but I wanted to have coffee with Claire if I could fit it in.

'She's not feeling very well, unfortunately. Hence I've got Joel.' He indicated the pushchair, which contained a sleepy-looking Joel clutching a small teddy bear and a tatty cloth. My face must have fallen, as he added hastily, 'I'm sure she'd love to see you, though. Maybe text her around eleven and see how she's doing. I'd better run – see you!'

He trotted off in the direction of the village hall, trailing behind a long line of other parents with prams and pushchairs. I was left to walk out on my own.

I got back home, loaded the dishwasher, put on a wash and cleaned around the kitchen surfaces. I made myself a cappuccino and walked over to my studio to start work. At eleven, I gave myself a break and texted Claire.

'Hi, how ru? Fancy a visit xx?'

A couple of minutes later, she replied.

'Feeling terrible. Been sick as a dog. Soz, can we take a rain check? Maybe tomorrow xx'

Oh, well. It could wait. I replied.

'Poor you! Do you want me to take the girls after school? Xx'

Back came her reply.

'You angel! That would help so much. T has got funeral at 2.30 so if I don't have to do school run, could stay crashed out on sofa! xx'

I worked hard until pick-up time and braced myself for my extra call with Mimi the next day. We had lots to talk about. She wasn't very happy that I'd sealed the deal with Tom before sorting out the school, and worse, had agreed to contribute to the roof repairs rather than something more visible.

'How are you going to get up there to take inspiring photos? I'll have to work pretty hard to make lead replacement sexy.'

I put Mimi's contorted features out of my mind and walked down to school. I stopped myself from putting lipstick on and washing my hair. I looked shocking, but a promise is a promise!

Issy Smugge is the queen of playdates! Everyone occupied themselves while I pottered about in the kitchen making creamy tagliatelle with portobello mushrooms and bacon. Just as I was clearing up, Sofija walked in.

Chloe and Elsie rushed up to her and hugged her, talking non-stop. Finn looked up and waved. I was very pleased to see her, but thinking back on it, I hadn't been counting the minutes until she pulled up on the drive as I would once have done. I'm a hands-on mother!

She looked very well. Her trips to London suit her. I gave her a big hug and asked her if she'd had fun. She gave me a full rundown. Drinks and dinner with her friends, a film and some shopping. I am such a good employer! **#familydynamic #playdatequeen**

Mimi loved the idea of a romantic birthday surprise for Johnnie, as I knew she would. I fixed on the following Monday. I planned everything with my legendary eye for detail. I'd drive up to town, park at the flat, dress it with candles and rose petals on the bed and have oysters and champagne chilling in the fridge. I'd then get a cab to the airport to pick up the birthday boy. Johnnie was going to be in Frankfurt from Saturday first thing to Monday teatime. Before we had the children, I'd often go with him on his European trips, but that's a thing of the past.

I'm so excited! I've packed a little case with the bare essentials. Perfume, make-up and not much else! We all need to keep investing in our relationships, as I say in my blogs. It's all too easy to take a long-term partner for granted. Johnnie will be thrilled.

On Friday night we were in bed by ten as Johnnie had to be up and out by five the next morning. I kissed him goodbye, bursting with my surprise. The next time we met would be at the airport. I felt deliciously young and romantic.

I'd just nodded off when my mobile rang. It was an unfamiliar number, so I ignored it. On the third time of ringing, I took the risk and, to my surprise, heard Johnnie's voice.

'Iss, I must have dropped my phone in the cab. I've told them to search for it and deliver it back to the flat if they find it, so don't worry if you don't hear from me straight away. I'll call you from Andreas' place [Andreas being the business associate he was visiting in Frankfurt]. Got to dash, love you!'

Saturday was dry, so we went on a bike ride then spent the afternoon in the pool. I invited Lauren and Claire and their families over, but Claire was feeling ill again, so we ended up with just Lauren and her girls. Rather than sulking and retreating to his room, Finn fell on his own sword and entertained them for half an hour before privately asking if he could be excused. He seems so much happier.

On Sunday, I broke the news to Sofija that I needed to change her days off. She looked shocked.

'I have plans, Isabella. I have booked tickets and cannot get refund.'

'I'll make it worth your while, I promise. I know this is incredibly short notice, but I didn't realise you had plans. Let me know how much the tickets cost and I'll refund you all the money and pull some strings to get you in on another performance.'

I was hoping that bribery would work, but Sofija was unsure.

'I cannot let my friends down. We have been looking forward to this for months.'

She started fiddling with her hair and gazing at the floor. I felt bad, but I am the boss, after all.

'Sofija, I know I should have given you more notice. But it's Johnnie's birthday. You wouldn't want him to miss out, would you? Honestly, I'll do anything you want to make it up to you.'

She kept saying she was sorry, but she couldn't change her plans. Eventually, I wore her down and we agreed on a full refund for the tickets and an extra week off in April so she could go home to see her family.

I felt guilty about spoiling her night out, so I did the girls' baths and gave her the rest of the night off. It was utterly exhausting. I don't know how people without au pairs do it.

The next morning, I told Sofija to have a lie-in, but when I got back from school, she was bustling around in the kitchen. I felt strangely awkward. I couldn't put my finger on it, but something felt a bit off. I ran upstairs, grabbed my suitcase, gave her a big hug and thanked her again.

'You really are such a treasure. I truly don't know what I'd do without you.'

As I drove down the M11, I saw the clustered towers of London on the skyline and felt my heart beat a little faster. Driving in Suffolk is nothing like driving in London. By the time I came off on to the A13, I'd been beeped twice, cut up three times and had a lorry nearly crash into the back of me. It felt like home.

I pulled into the underground car park and felt my heart flutter with excitement. I'd got candles and bags of rose petals packed, the food and drink were being delivered and all I had to do was set it all up. As I opened our front door, I closed my eyes for a second to savour the moment.

You know when you see something and you can't quite process it? On the table in the front room was an enormous vase full of flowers. There was a note attached. I read it and blushed. My husband is so cheeky! In the fridge, I discovered champagne chilling, plus the makings of a delicious meal. My mouth watered. We'd just have to have my food for breakfast the next morning!

I felt incredibly touched. Johnnie had obviously had the same thought as me and, unwittingly, I'd chosen the same day to do my surprise. No wonder Sofija had been so reluctant to change her day off. She must have been in on it!

I scattered the rose petals on the bed, placed the candles and touched up my make-up. I was about to text Sofija when the doorbell rang. It was the food delivery service. I stowed the champagne, oysters and turbot in the fridge and ordered my cab.

I had five minutes so I took lots of shots of the flat, arty images of the oysters and close-ups of the flowers. Mimi would be delighted! **#soromantic #keepingitfresh #naughtyboy**

At the airport, I felt unaccountably nervous. Johnnie and I hadn't been spending much time together of late. What if he didn't like my surprise? I had to give myself a good talking to. What man wouldn't be over the moon to be met by the woman he loves and whisked off to a romantic rendezvous?

The plane was late. I was getting quite jittery when suddenly I saw him. I feasted my eyes for a minute or two. He was head and shoulders above any other man I'd ever met. Even just off a plane from a business trip, he was so handsome and well put together. I stood behind a pillar, watching him and savouring the moment. He stopped and started looking around. He must have ordered his own car. I stepped out from behind the pillar, crept up behind him, put my arms around him and whispered, 'Surprise!'

The look on his face was all I'd hoped it would be. In fact, to be honest, it was a great deal more. He genuinely looked as though he had seen a ghost! A very well-dressed, well-coiffed one, naturally! He gazed at me as if he'd never seen me before.

'What... what on earth are you doing here, Iss?' he asked.

'Happy birthday, darling! I thought I'd surprise you.'

I stood on tiptoe to kiss him. I nestled into his chest and stood there, holding him, as passengers streamed past us. I could feel his heart beating fast, and no wonder! It would be beating a lot quicker by the time I'd finished with him!

'Who's looking after the kids? Isn't today Sofija's day off? I never can remember since she switched them.'

I explained that I had crossed Sofija's palm with a refund and an extra week's holiday to get her to change her days off.

'You and I are off for a romantic evening, birthday boy! Come on, our car's waiting.'

Johnnie seemed absolutely stunned. I was expecting a big reaction, but not quite as big as this. I reached across and took his hand as we climbed into the cab.

'I know all about it. No need to keep your secret any more. You and Sofija must have been planning it for ages.'

Johnnie looked even more shocked.

'What do you mean, Iss?'

'I mean *your* surprise, silly! I've already been to the flat. Flowers, food in the fridge – I can't believe you were planning a romantic evening for me and I chose the same day for you! We're so in sync.'

I leaned against him and closed my eyes. What bliss to be speeding towards our love nest with the man of my dreams.

'I had it all planned. You were going to be picked up after the school run and brought down to the flat. Sofija was going to pretend to go off, then come back just in time to look after the kids. It was all organised! I've even got a lovely dinner in the fridge for you.'

There were tears in my eyes. I felt so special and loved. #romance #truelove

The next morning, I lay in bed waiting for my husband to bring me coffee and breakfast. I'd have to have a shower before I

headed home, as the rose petals had proved strangely adhesive. We'd had the perfect night, made even better by a ring at the door just before we sat down for dinner. Johnnie was reunited with his phone, which made him very happy. I'd already texted Sofija.

'I can't believe you managed to fool me! I believed every word you said. Now in the flat with Johnnie having a lovely romantic evening. See you tomorrow x'

Issy Smugge is one lucky lady!! **#happybirthday #romanticsurprise #cheekychappie**

April

The Smugges are flying off to Verbier for two blissful weeks of snow, sun and Sancerre. Mimi adored the shots I took in the flat and she'll go crazy for Easter Egg Hunts in the snow, champagne in the hot tub and gorgeous shots of pine trees and blue Alpine skies.

I don't know what I'd do without my twice-yearly ski trips. I find the clear air so revitalising and it's good to have special family time. Sofija is flying out with us for the first week, then carrying on over to her family in Latvia, as agreed. I'd come up with a little *aide memoire* so that I could remember her country of origin. It was easy really. 'Sofija from Latvia.' I don't know why I didn't think of it before. Three syllables ending in a. **#sillyissy**

I'm still on a high from our romantic getaway at the flat. The only cloud in my sky is Sofija. She seems jumpy, on edge and not herself at all. Whenever I ask her what's up, she claims everything is fine. Issy Smugge is empathy personified. I'll get her to open up to me over a glass of wine.

I'm going to give Messy Church a go again. Lauren says they're doing an Easter Egg Hunt and a bring-and-share tea. I imagine it will be a smörgåsbord of poorly constructed sandwiches, mass-produced fried snacks and shop-bought sausage rolls. They don't call me the Party Queen for nothing. I shall whip up Romano peppers stuffed with cream cheese and walnuts and an organic quiche. As it's on a Wednesday, I can take the girls and Sofija can keep an eye on Finn at home. I feel that village society needs a taste of my justly famed finger food.

Exciting news! Claire is pregnant. Which explains the peakiness and puking. I can't believe I didn't put two and two together. The baby is due mid-September. She's really suffering. Terrible morning sickness, feeling faint, hardly eating and worn out all the time. Lauren and I have agreed to offer help and support wherever it's needed. I am genuinely excited about the prospect. Thank heavens my baby-making days are over!

When I returned from the school drop—off, Sofija was bending over the dishwasher. In response to my cheerful greeting, she let out a muffled scream and dropped a plate, which shattered into a million pieces on the floor. She fell to her knees and burst into tears.

I am surrounded by a swirling soup of hormones! If it isn't poor Claire and her fourth little bundle of joy, it's my au pair and what I can only assume is a rampant case of PMT. I joined her on the floor (my joints are remarkably supple; I put it down to all the swimming and my fish oil supplements) and attempted to comfort her. She was inconsolable, sobbing that she was so sorry, over and over again.

After a few minutes of shoulder patting, I rose gracefully to my feet and fired up the coffee machine. Sometimes, only an espresso will do. After a few sips of the good stuff, Sofija calmed down a bit. I assured her that the plate didn't matter a bit and enquired delicately after her feminine health. When my offer of sourdough with mashed avocado and beet compote fell on deaf ears, I suggested she went and had a lie down, leaving me to sweep the floor and finish loading the dishwasher. Latte in hand, I walked over to my studio to commence the day's work. #lookingafterthestaff #hormones

By Friday, Sofija seemed herself again. I laid in a stock of gingko, ginger and evening primrose oil to be on the safe side, although I don't know why primroses picked in the evening are any better than the ordinary sort.

We've got into a nice cosy weekend routine. Johnnie comes home for supper on Friday, the children stay up a bit later, we watch a film. The rest of the weekend is devoted to exercise and leisure, with a bit of homework thrown in. Sometimes I miss those old carefree days when we could go out and find a little Peruvian bar or check out the latest Tasmanian tapas craze. Up here, the most exciting thing you can do is hang around the bus shelter or vandalise the public toilets.

Sofija is doing the school runs for me this week. I'm very busy, what with setting up the shoot for the church, writing new content for all my socials and checking the proofs of my latest bestseller: *Issy Smugge Says: Let's Move to the Country.*

I was deep in concentration when my phone rang. I hate being interrupted in the middle of something creative. The professionally cheerful tones of the school secretary, Mrs Hill, tinkled in my ear like a ring of little silver bells. I'm sure they teach them to talk like that whenever important news is to be imparted. Overdue library books, uncontrollable nits in Year One, a nosebleed, copious sickness in assembly or, as in this case, a punch-up.

'Mrs Jenkins would appreciate it if you could just pop in, Mrs Smugge. Anytime between twelve and one today. Bye!'

My heart sank but there was nothing to be done. I logged off and went to tell Sofija where I was going.

The village primary is absolutely nothing like St Dymphna's. It's a pretty little place, well kept, but there are no stained-glass windows, no Latin mottos up on the walls, no oil paintings of former heads. Instead, there is the ever-jolly Mrs Hill with her friendly smile, directing me to take a seat on the threadbare chair in reception. After five minutes, Mrs Jenkins shimmered up the corridor and ushered me down to the meeting room.

The Isabella M Smugge who faced her son's teacher today was not the same woman who was summoned to her lair back in February. Whatever has gone on, I was in full possession of the facts and would fight for my son if required.

'I'm sorry to say that things have deteriorated again between Finn and Zach. Today, there was a serious fight between them at break time. Some school property was damaged and both boys sustained minor injuries. Nothing that a wet paper towel couldn't put right...' (Here, she smiled, glacially.) 'But you must understand, Mrs Smugge, that there will be serious consequences.'

I sat bolt upright and fixed Mrs Jenkins with a look. I'd give her serious consequences!

'Finn has been completely honest with me about the reason for the friction between him and the Bloomfield boy. It seems that Zach has been using extremely inappropriate language – ' (I treated Mrs Jenkins to a selection of it) ' – insulting me and constantly goading my son in front of the other boys. I wonder how you would react if you were told daily that your mother was a stuck-up old moo?'

I sat ramrod straight in the chair (St Dymphna's training. 'Don't slouch, girls!') and held Mrs Jenkins' gaze. I was using my special voice, rarely brought out and guaranteed to stop a charging rhino at ten paces.

My trained eye detected a slight ripple of surprise play over the teacher's professional face. Whatever she'd expected me to say, it wasn't this. She gave me another burst of catchphrases. Poor choices, consequences, golden rules, self-control, etc. **#blahblahblah**

I cranked the special voice up a notch and adopted the special look. The combination generally makes grown men weep and promise never to do it again, but Mrs Jenkins was made of sterner stuff.

'I appreciate that Zach's language and sentiments are completely inappropriate. No child in this school should be saying anything of the sort. However, that said, the boys need to learn to control themselves. We cannot have fisticuffs in the corridors.'

I leaned forward in my seat.

'What do you suggest? I don't know if you've noticed, but I have taken significant steps to reduce my "stuck-up old moo" look. Limited make-up, no handbag, off-the-peg clothes.'

Mrs Jenkins sighed.

'Mrs Smugge, I've been a teacher for long enough to know that children of this age can be cruel. There are – issues – at home for Zach, and his acting-out is a reflection of that. I fully appreciate that Finn is struggling with the taunting and it does him credit that he wants to stand up for you. Let me say that he is a pleasure to teach. The weak spot is his tendency to lash out.'

I switched off the special look. Now we were getting somewhere. We chatted, woman to woman, for a quarter of an hour and agreed that a summit between both boys, myself and Liane Bloomfield, refereed by Mrs Jenkins, would be the sensible way forward. Inwardly, I quailed, but Issy Smugge never allows the opposition to smell her fear. **#facingfacts #feelingthefearanddoingitanyway**

On Messy Church day, Lauren and I walked up the hill to the church. I was relieved that Sofija had changed her days. Rather than dragging a reluctant ten-year-old along, I could relax and enjoy myself.

Inside, it looked like a jumble sale. We came in through the big glass porch, hung up the girls' coats and book bags and headed over to where Claire and her sidekick were laying out tubes of glitter and piles of coloured paper. Tom, with a howling Joel in his arms, was fiddling about with a pile of rubbish in the corner. Someone seemed to have left all their recycling in the church, which I thought was terribly disrespectful. On closer inspection, however, it turned out to be something calling itself junk modelling. It's called junk for a reason, people!

After a few more minutes of chaos, Claire seized the mic and addressed us. Various craft stations were set up, there would be an Easter Egg Hunt in half an hour, we would be singing a couple of action songs and then enjoying a meal together. I availed myself of a glass of water and ambled over to the food table.

I was confronted with a sea of beige and unacceptably high levels of packaging. Don't these people cook? There were packets of nasty-looking sausages, shop-bought dip with limp vegetables and a mountain of crisps. Someone had made a platter of jam sandwiches and there appeared to be a preponderance of soggy pastry-based items. I sighed and shook my head as I pushed a particularly revolting pile of sausage rolls out of the way to place my quiche. I heard Lauren come up behind me.

'Who thinks it's acceptable to bring this sort of trash to a bring and share?' I enquired, *sotto voce*. 'How hard could it be to buy some sausage meat, make your own rough puff and knock up a batch?'

My eye fell upon a depressed-looking dish of grapes. Believe me when I tell you that there were no grape scissors in sight! I ask you. I pointed this out to Lauren as well, my *voce* perhaps not quite so *sotto*. To my amazement, she poked me in the back, hard, and shouted a very rude suggestion in my ear. I turned around, only to be confronted by an angry Liane Bloomfield. Great.

I stared at her for a moment, wondering what to do. A grovelling apology for insulting her sausage rolls probably wouldn't cut it, nor would turning tail and fleeing to the toilets. The only remaining option was to look her in the eye and take whatever she threw at me. Which turned out to be a torrent of abuse.

Halfway through the observations on my looks, my attitude and my place in society, Lauren came galloping over. Fortunately, there was a song playing on the sound system with an accompanying video featuring luridly coloured cartoon characters, so not everyone had realised that I was being verbally attacked.

'Shut up, Liane! You can't talk like that in here.'

I was heartened by my friend's support, but it had absolutely no effect on Ms Bloomfield, who continued with her character assassination, liberally larded with swear words. Lauren indicated the porch as a suitable place to continue, and we duly marched out of the church. With Lauren as referee and translator, we faced up to each other.

'Where do you get off, trashing my sausage rolls? We haven't all got servants to do our work for us. And what's that pile of rubbish you brought along? It looks like roadkill.'

I had to hand it to her, she'd hit the ground running. Lauren gave a sharp intake of breath and turned her head to me. I decided to employ diplomacy.

'I'm sorry I said that. I'm sure your sausage rolls are delicious.'

It didn't work.

'Too right they are. I didn't even buy value ones. You come up here, swanning around with your posh clothes and your servants and looking down your nose at the rest of us. You should go back to where you came from.'

By which she meant West Brompton, I presume.

'I haven't got servants, actually. I've just got an au pair to help me out with the children. I do work full-time, you know.'

Liane Bloomfield put her hands on her hips and tilted her head to one side.

'Oh, you haven't got servants, *actually*! Get you, Mrs Posh! An *au pair*? What's that when it's at home? I work full-time too. Five kids, loads of cleaning jobs and trying to get maintenance out of my useless ex. You don't know what hard work is.'

Enough is enough. Isabella M Smugge has never been afraid of hard graft and has fought very hard to get to where she is today.

'I work all day, every day, thank you very much! I write, I take photos, I update my social media, I run a household and I still find time to build social relationships in the village. Lauren can testify to my success in that department!'

We both turned on our heels to gaze at Lauren, who was looking a bit ruffled. Before she could speak, the next batch of insults was being hurled at me.

'You take photos! You take *photos*! And you get paid enough for that to live in that huge great mansion? My boy went on your Insta and said it was all pictures of flowers and your fancy kitchen and your show-off swimming pool. Who do you think you are?'

Well! This was fighting talk. The gloves were off.

'If you spent a bit more time parenting your children and less shouting the f-word at people, you might be a better mother. You wouldn't believe the things your son has been saying to Finn. I'd be ashamed if a child of mine used that kind of language.'

She took her hands off her hips and jabbed her finger in my face.

'A better mother? You don't even bother looking after your own kids. You pay some girl to do it for you. I'll give you language!'

She duly did. I was a bit confused by some of the terms she used, but Lauren helpfully translated for me. The anger and resentment spewing from a woman who seemed to hate me would have floored a lesser person, but Issy Smugge is crushed underfoot by no one! As she called my parenting skills into question, I prepared myself to parry with some nifty debating, when she moved on to another area of my life.

'I bet your mum and dad were rich and posh and you went to a snob school and had big posh cars and servants. You should try living in a council house with rising damp and not enough room for the kids to play and nosey neighbours reporting you to the social. Look!' She pulled up her sleeve to reveal a scar. 'That's where I got between my mum and dad having a fight and he broke my arm with a chair. Ever watched your dad beating your mum to a pulp when he's nearly too drunk to stand?'

I hadn't, but I had a few traumas of my own. I pulled my hair back from my forehead to reveal the thin line where my twelve-year-old skin had been stitched back together. I could still feel the stinging pain and the tears that poured, unbidden, from my eyes. I'd sneaked into Mummy's room to borrow her perfume. I loved the smell and I wanted to feel more grown-up. Daddy had gone, Arabella had gone and we weren't allowed to see Penny and Minty any more. Nanny's warm, comforting arms had been snatched away from us and even our beloved ponies had been sold. It seemed that Mummy was punishing Suze and me, but we didn't know why.

'My mother hit me with a silver-backed hairbrush. I borrowed her perfume and she caught me. I had to pretend I'd fallen over and caught it on the door. Five stitches, as I recall.'

Lauren winced. 'That must have hurt.'

There was a brief silence while we all gazed at each other, then Liane Bloomfield revved up for the next bout.

'What's a silver-backed hairbrush when it's at home? That's nothing! Was *your* dad a drunk? Did he run off with your auntie?'

'No! He ran off with my mother's best friend, if you must know!'

We glared at each other. My heart was pounding, not with fear but with rage. I found myself yearning to hit Liane Bloomfield square in the eye.

Lauren chose this propitious moment to intervene.

'OK, girls, I think we should probably leave it there. Let's go and have tea.'

She was about half an hour too early with her diplomatic efforts. We still had a fair way to go.

'I hate people like you! Marching around in your fancy clothes, looking down your nose at us, posting rubbish on Instagram and sucking up to the vicar's wife. My boy's in trouble with the school because of you.'

'And *my* boy's in trouble because of *you*! If you've got nothing nice to say, you can keep your big mouth shut.'

'Don't you tell me what to do! I'll say what I like!'

There was a short pause, broken only by the sound of me gritting my teeth and Liane Bloomfield tapping her foot. I took a deep breath and applied my new mantra. What would Claire do in a situation like this? Unfortunately, it was fairly unlikely that she would punch anyone in the eye and move to the next county. I would have to try being nice.

'I sympathise, Liane. It must be hard to struggle with a difficult ex and lots of children. I can see that I must seem extremely privileged to someone like you, but I can assure you, my husband and I have both worked very hard indeed to get where we are today.'

I smiled, but from the look on Lauren's face, it was probably more of a grimace. Liane leaned forward.

'Let me ask you a question.'

It seemed that my diplomatic tone had worked. Hallelujah!

'You and your husband. You went to the local primary, did you? And then on to the comp?'

I felt a little awkward.

'Well, no, not exactly. We were both fortunate enough to have a private education, but I don't see what...'

'I knew it! You didn't have to work that hard to get a massive house and your big posh car! Money attracts money.'

I tried desperately to think of a suitable reply. The gulf yawning between this angry woman and myself seemed impassable. An insane thought suddenly flashed into my mind. What if I were honest? Things couldn't be any worse, surely, what with one of the village's most terrifying mothers on my case.

'You're right. I didn't have to work that hard to get what I wanted. Money was never a problem; I got a good education and I'm lucky enough to be doing what I love. But there's stuff I never talk about. I can't believe I'm telling *you*. My mother wanted a boy and blamed me for my dad running off with her best friend. She got rid of my nanny who was the only person apart from my father and my sister who was kind to me at home. She sold our ponies when we were away at school. When I see her, she spends her whole time putting me down. I don't think she even loves me.'

I'd never voiced this suspicion, although it had been nestling in my heart like a poisonous serpent for many years. As the words spilled out of my mouth, I felt my eyes fill with tears.

Liane Bloomfield was staring at me. I'd taken my gamble. Now let her say what she wanted.

'That's harsh. Did she chuck your nan out of the house? My mum made mine go and live in a home in Leiston.'

I realised that she thought Nanny was my grandmother, but to correct her would have been most unwise, so I nodded.

Lauren took advantage of the temporary cessation of hostilities to leap in.

'My mum gave my favourite doll and all her clothes to the charity shop when I was on the Year Six residential. She said I was too old for them but I cried for ages.'

'That's nothing!' Liane Bloomfield seemed to be possessed of an extremely competitive spirit. 'My mum microwaved my Girl's World head. Dad had just run off with my auntie and she'd gone loco. We had to ditch the microwave. She couldn't get all the melted plastic and hair off it.'

Lauren translated. It seems that this was some kind of head to which little girls applied make-up. Suze and I had never had one.

'Babes! That's rough. I thought losing my doll was bad!'

'Look, Loz, are you crawling all over her because you want to swim in her pool? Or is she OK underneath all the talk? Just be honest with me.'

Lauren swallowed and turned to me. 'No offence, babes, but when you first moved up here, I thought you were a bit up yourself. Claire told me I should get to know you before I judged you. You say stuff I don't understand and your house is like something off the telly, but you're really lovely underneath it all. I'd like you even if you didn't have the pool.'

To say I was taken aback was an understatement. I'd assumed that my gracious and friendly manner had won me friends by itself. I felt a stab of pain to think of Lauren having to be convinced by Claire that I was worth befriending. Tears rushed to my eyes again, and I blinked them back. All the anger seemed to have drained out of me, and looking over at my opponent, I saw that her body language had changed. She muttered something which I didn't catch.

'I'm sorry?'

'He died. My dad. He got killed when I was twelve. He was a miserable so-and-so, but he was blood. I've never felt the same about any of mum's boyfriends.'

My heart beat faster.

'What happened? If you don't mind me asking.'

'He was on his way home from work. He'd probably had a drink. He came off the road at Haughley Bends. Killed instantly.'

Haughley Bends, Lauren explained, was a particularly treacherous stretch of road a few miles north of the village. I swallowed hard and found myself reciprocating.

'My dad died too. He and Arabella, the lady he ran off with, were in Italy and their car came off the road and down a ravine. I lost two of the people who loved me most just like that and was left with my mother, who hated me.'

There seemed little more to say. We'd both lost our fathers at twelve, bore scars from warring parents and struggled to express our innermost emotions. It seemed that Liane Bloomfield and I were sisters under the skin, although I certainly wasn't going to tell her that.

There was a gentle tap on the glass porch. All three of us nearly jumped out of our skin. Claire was standing there, smiling and beckoning us in. Teatime.

The fight at Messy Church gave everyone something to gossip about for weeks. To my surprise, some kind of grudging respect had sprung up between Liane and me. When Mrs Jenkins summoned us for our meeting, the tension between us had eased considerably. Finn reported that Zach Bloomfield had laid off him at school, and when Liane and I crossed paths in the playground or the village, we exchanged brief nods.

It's funny, isn't it, how you think everything is fine and then suddenly it isn't? The row with Liane and Lauren's admission that it had taken Claire's comments to encourage her to be my friend had shaken my confidence. I found myself lying in bed that night crying until I could cry no more. My pillowcase was soaked with tears and I felt utterly miserable. I fell asleep at about three and woke at seven. My eyes were stinging and the face that greeted me in the bathroom mirror was not that of a successful and well-loved lifestyle blogger. I texted Sofija.

'Morning. I slept really badly last night and feel terrible. Could you do breakfast and the school run? Thanks so much! xx'

Back came the reply.

'Of course. I'll bring coffee xx'

God bless Sofija. Five minutes later, she tapped on the door and put a latte on my bedside table. I was lying back feebly on my pillows, like the lovesick heroine of a Barbara Cartland novel. By the time she returned from school, I was downstairs scrambling free-range eggs and toasting sourdough. #bestmealoftheday #gotoworkonanegg

I bunked off school for the rest of the week and buried myself in work. I considered having a coffee with Claire and chatting about it, but I didn't fancy revisiting the pain just yet. I took the children out on some bracing country walks to put the roses back into my cheeks. I got some lovely photos. Mimi would be pleased.

On the last Tuesday of term, my phone rang. To my amazement, it was my so-called friend Meredith. I hadn't heard from her since my disastrous trip to Freudian Sip.

'Hello, darling! How *are* you? It's been too long!'

Meredith lards her conversation with clusters of exclamation marks, making the simplest of utterances sound like a national emergency. I mustered up my sweetest tones and replied.

'I'm fine, thank you, and how are *you*?'

The chit-chat continued for a few minutes. I learned that Meredith's husband had given her a breast augmentation and eye lift for her fortieth. I would have been insulted beyond words, but she seemed delighted. Of course, she hasn't got my excellent genes and she's never used the right products.

After a bit more twittering, Meredith got to the point.

'Have you still got that sweet little Latvian working for you?'

I confirmed that I did.

'Well, I could have sworn I saw her walking along Piccadilly last night, hand in hand with Johnnie. I recognised that Balmain jumpsuit you wore to death last year. I know she lives in your hand-me-downs.'

I was a bit taken aback. Not that Sofija is still wearing the jumpsuit (although it was a great piece), but that Meredith could be so low as to try to plant seeds of doubt in my mind about my husband and my au pair. Why wouldn't my chivalrous husband take Sofija's arm to guide her through the London throng? He's such a gentleman!

'If you've just had surgery, your eyes might be a bit blurry, darling. And you are a couple of years older than me. They say it all starts to go downhill at forty.'

Bitchy, which isn't my style, but I say fight fire with fire. That shut her up. After a bit more gossip about the rest of the girls and some insincere good wishes for my health and happiness, she pushed off. Honestly!

I forgot all about Meredith's poisonous gossip until Wednesday teatime. I mentioned it to Sofija and she stared blankly at me.

'Don't look so shocked! Why shouldn't you and Johnnie meet up? What were you doing in Piccadilly?'

'I was going to Chinatown to meet friends for dinner. I ran into Johnnie and he walked me down there. He is such good English gentleman. He said he didn't want me to be in danger at night-time.'

Well, that made complete sense. Johnnie is chivalry itself. Just then, the man himself appeared, to the delight of the children and, of course, me.

We had a lovely evening. Finn was chatting away non-stop about what had been going on with Zach Bloomfield, Chloë and Elsie were telling him all about school and Sofija was clattering about in the kitchen putting everything away. I felt a twinge of guilt, but she does work for us, after all, so I enjoyed my Petit Chablis and let her get on with it. I needed to spend time with my husband. I had a cheeky little surprise planned for him! #keepingitfresh #blacklace

As we lay in each other's arms, just before we drifted off to sleep, I murmured in his ear, 'You are my perfect English gentleman.'

'What's that, Iss?'

'You were so sweet, walking Sofija to Chinatown on Monday when you ran into her. Most men wouldn't bother.'

He nuzzled my neck.

'You know me. Chivalry is my middle name. She doesn't look half as good in that jumpsuit as you did, you sexy beast!' #lovemyman #welcomehome

Thank heavens for the chalet. We arrived there late on Thursday night and slid the children straight into bed. Johnnie and I poured ourselves two flutes of champagne and fired up the hot tub. Is there anything more romantic than looking up at the stars in a frosty sky with the snow glinting on the mountains? I'd say not.

Sofija flies to Riga next Friday. She'll be back home on the Thursday morning, ready to open up the house and get something out for dinner as we return on Thursday evening. How do people manage without help? What with three children, a marriage to maintain and all my work, I'd be worn to a shadow without her.

I've got two weeks to capture heavenly images of the mountains, après-ski, stunning scenery and the little Smugges on the slopes. It's a gift for the internationally renowned lifestyle blogger. As Mimi says, relatable but just aspirational enough to be out of reach for most of my readers.

Finn was expressing embarrassment about my shots of him, so I've taken a few family photos with him in the background and have devoted most of my time to taking lovely pictures of the girls and the scenery. I built up a huge stock, so I scheduled the whole week right across my socials to give myself a break.

Midweek, we met for lunch. The girls and I arrived first and bagged a table outside. Johnnie and Finn joined us a few minutes later, stopping outside in a whirl of snow. I could see women staring at Johnnie as he took off his helmet and strode across the decking. In ski clothes, he looks even more devastatingly handsome than ever. He's got a tan and his eyes are as blue as the cloudless Swiss skies.

I greeted him with a long, lingering kiss, to the horror of the children. We ordered them sparkling apple juices while Johnnie and I got ourselves coffees. We didn't want to weigh ourselves down too much, so I had a salad Niçoise, Johnnie had veal piccata and the children went for *spaghetti alle vongole*.

After lunch, Finn and I chilled for a bit, while Johnnie took the girls off to try a red run. I told him about my altercation with Liane Bloomfield and we agreed that she must have told Zach to leave him alone since life in Year Five was now much better. It seems that some of Zach's gang have actually deigned to sit with my son for lunch. This, it seems, is a huge compliment.

I was a bit put out, to be honest. My lovely, handsome, gifted son, who has never wanted for anything, happy because some miserable little morons share their lunch table with him. I expressed my view. Finn shook his head.

'No, Mum, you don't get it. Being allowed to sit on the same table as them is a big deal. You don't get to sit there if you're not cool. Jake and I aren't. That's why Jake was so pleased when I joined Year Five. It was just him before, being bullied and left out of stuff. Now it's the two of us, it's loads better. He doesn't mind about me being posh, he says. It's just nice to have someone to hang out with.'

Well, I didn't see that at all! Jake seems like a very mature, sensible boy. So mature that he walks himself to school every day and back again and makes his own packed lunches. Finn put me straight.

'Jake's dad went off with Noah Ling's mum when they were in Year Two and now Jake's mum struggles with going outside the house. Jake has to do the shopping and his own lunch. Everyone takes the mick out of him because they say his mum's mental. And his dad hardly ever bothers with him. That's why he's mature.'

I sat back in my chair and digested this news. Sitting in my big, beautiful house on the hill, I had missed the fact that the village was a hotbed of scandal, gossip and heartbreak. And I thought the country was quiet and peaceful.

I switched the conversation to school. I needed to start thinking about getting Johnnie's old trunk down from the attic. Finn looked mutinous.

'About that. I don't want to go. I want to go to secondary school with Jake.'

I was gobsmacked. Three generations of Smugge men had gone to the same school, and while Johnnie had agreed to sending Finn to state school for his early years, he'd set his face against continuing the experiment once he left primary.

'But darling, think of the opportunities. You'll meet all the right people and have a far better education than you ever could at home.'

'I won't know anyone and I like it at home. I've only got one friend and he's going to secondary school, so I want to stay with him.'

I decided not to fight that particular battle right now. Johnnie would hit the roof, so I decided to soften him up with a session in the hot tub before I introduced it into conversation. As it turned out, I never got round to it. #romanceinthesnow

Johnnie and I promised the children we'd think about spending Christmas in Verbier this year. I love planning ahead. Sometimes I find myself gazing out of the window in my writing studio and thinking of all the years Johnnie and I have to make all our remaining dreams come true.

I nodded off in the car going to the airport, which is most unlike me, and woke up with a start in the middle of the most horrific dream. My palms were sweaty, my mouth was dry and my heart was beating like a drum. Do you ever have those dreams where you're falling and, just before you hit the ground, you wake up? I was in the car with Daddy and Arabella. I couldn't find my seatbelt and Daddy was driving very fast and kept looking over his shoulder at me.

'Slow down, Daddy!' I shouted. 'Please stop, I can't find my seatbelt.'

Arabella reached over and took my hand.

'Don't panic, darling. Your father is an excellent driver.'

I could smell her perfume and hear her husky, low voice. Daddy took his hands off the wheel and the car left the road and went tumbling down, down, down, towards the valley floor. I was shouting at the top of my voice, but no sound was coming out. By the time I woke up, my cheeks were wet with tears and Johnnie was saying, 'What's the matter with you, Iss? You nearly made the driver swerve, screaming like that.'

I'll be so glad to get home. #memories #mountainroads

May

I had a wonderful time in Verbier, but that terrible dream left me shaken and won't go away. I'm throwing myself into party planning for Elsie. Mimi loves birthday months.

'All those wonderful images, sweetie. Little faces lit by candles, cake and a golden opportunity to increase your reach. Are you quite sure you don't want a fourth child?'

Elsie wants a cake-baking party. I got the woman's number from Lauren and booked her. All the children get a personalised apron, there are three hours in which you make and bake cupcakes and there's time for them to eat and play in between. The kitchen's big enough to hold the whole class should it come to that. **#mybabyissix #GBBO #letsgetbaking**

Now that spring's here, it's a joy to get out into the garden. I've taken some gorgeous shots of the children playing which are getting lots of likes and comments. I'm back in my routine of writing, taking photos and thinking about my next project now that they're all back at school. That said, I am finding that walking in the garden and smelling the flowers is having a powerful effect on me. The gentle splashing of the fountain in the pretty pond has a soothing effect on my busy little brain, and occasionally we see large birds standing on the edge of it. I took some pictures early one morning and lit Twitter up. A heron, apparently, quite rare. **#whoknew**

At home in Kent, before Daddy left us, Mummy would be out in the garden as soon as spring came, haranguing the gardener and working on the borders. This morning, as I sat on the bench with my coffee in the sun, the gentle breeze blew the most intoxicating perfume across the garden and suddenly I was right back there, little Bella Neville playing hide-and-seek with Suze. I closed my eyes and heard again her piping voice calling, 'Bella, where are you?' and felt the ache in my legs as I crouched behind the camellia bush.

We inherited the gardener at the Old Rectory, a taciturn, elderly man who stumps about in old clothes and calls me 'Missus'. He certainly knows what he's doing. I tend to leave him to it. There's nothing worse than someone interfering when you're hard at work. We're permitted to pick flowers for the house, herbs for cooking, and fruit and veg when we need it, but the garden is very much his domain.

Sitting with my eyes closed and drinking in the intoxicating floral scents, I realised what a very real temptation it would be to stay on the bench, drifting off into idle reminiscing. This simply would not do at all! With my coffee drunk, I stretched and went for one last wander around my acres before returning to the studio. **#growyourown #kitchengarden #callmemissus**

Johnnie's little brother, Rafe, is getting married to his long-time girlfriend, Xenia, this month. She's from a very wealthy Muscovite family, and is tall, leggy, blonde and ferociously intelligent. Rafe's a sweetie. He's done very well in property development. They live in a huge glass house near Chislehurst which they designed themselves. I expect you've seen it on TV. One of the double-height glass window panels shattered in transit and the presenter nearly had heart failure.

Xenia went to the family yacht in Montenegro for her hen week. I was invited, but we were in Verbier. I was quite relieved, actually. Her friends are big drinkers and I'd rather be spending time with my family in the chalet than schmoozing with European royalty and B-list celebrities on her super-yacht.

I suppose I should be impressed that she's got a clutch of crown princesses on speed dial, but it all seems a bit shallow to me.

We haven't had a family wedding for yonks. The last one must have been Toby and horsey Davina. The girls are bridesmaids and Finn's an usher. Fortunately, Xenia has got nearly as much taste as she has money and isn't decking them out in hideous outfits.

Thank heavens Mummy won't be at the main part of the wedding. She was invited, but she's not a fan of Rafe or Xenia. To be honest, I'll enjoy myself far more if she's not there. I'd spend the whole time like Elizabeth Bennet at the Netherfield ball, blushing for her rudeness and failing entirely in getting her to be quiet. I wouldn't put it past Xenia's mother to have a contract out on her – she's terrifying. Eyes like lasers and a useful right hook, so Rafe tells me. My lovely mother-in-law Silvia will be there, of course, Toby and horsey Davina and Johnnie's oldest brother, Charlie, with his wife, Amanda, and their four. They've been out in Dubai for about fifteen years now. Their oldest is off to uni and the other three are at boarding school somewhere up on the Scottish Borders.

Unlike normal people who are content with just the one wedding, Xenia and Rafe are having a full Russian Orthodox ceremony one weekend then a traditional CofE one the next. They're holding open house until the Tuesday, when they fly off on their honeymoon. All a bit pretentious, if you ask me.

Mummy is making her grand entrance next Sunday. I know she's dying to have a snoop around the grounds and find fault with Xenia's planting scheme. We're heading home on Monday evening. There's only so much lavish living we humble Suffolk folk can take! #overthetop #weddingofthecentury

Speaking of divas, Mimi and I had a catch-up Skype booked. With the wedding coming up, plus the Blogging Awards next month, I assumed, wrongly as it turned out, that my agent would

be on top form, fizzing with excitement at the thought of so much lovely content.

'Darling! How *are* you? Wonderful stats, great content, my favourite client.' Mimi was an agent on speed, galloping through the usual conversational gambits to get to the point at hand.

We've worked together long enough for me to pick up the danger signs. The last time she was this rattled, my main competitor had scooped a book award, rocketed to the top of *The Sunday Times* Bestseller List and bagged a regular spot on a morning TV show. I know her well enough not to jump the gun. I took a deep breath and a gulp of coffee and waited for the revelation.

'Lavinia Harcourt. Do we know her?'

'Do *we* know her? *I* know her. We were at school together.'

Mimi sighed heavily and took a deep drag on her cigarette. 'Were you, now? And I'm guessing that you weren't the best of friends as schoolgirls?'

Well, that was the understatement of the century. There's absolutely no point in trying to second-guess Mimi or hide things from her.

'Now, sweetie, we seem to have made an enemy of Lavinia Harcourt. And we both know that that's a very bad thing. Imagine my surprise when I read the papers this morning. Please tell me you can think of something to shut her up.'

Unless you live off-grid, you'll recognise my old enemy's name. Her byline commands its own double-page spread in one of our country's biggest-selling tabloids. Her slightly narrowed eyes and wry smile sit atop the legend, 'Lavinia Harcourt Says It Like It Is' running underneath like a chemical spill. People love her, women in particular. I don't know why. She sells more papers than everyone else put together. Her editor is reportedly terrified of her, and so he should be.

I was experiencing just the merest touch of Mimi's famous whiplash anger. I didn't like it one bit. It's best to be direct with Mimi.

'Short of hiring a hitman, you can't shut her up. It's the old tall poppy syndrome, Mimi. They build you up, they cut you down. Best to ignore it, I'd say.'

This didn't go down well. Mimi's eyes narrowed to slits.

'Ignore it. Is that your advice? Well, why don't I read it to you and we'll see if ignoring it is the best way forward.'

I can spot a rhetorical question at a hundred paces, so I stifled a deep sigh and braced myself. Mimi was right. It was nasty stuff, vintage Lavinia.

Smugge by name, Smugge by nature: do we really care what Issy Smugge says? For nearly ten years, inspirational lifestyle blogger Isabella Smugge has told us what to wear, how to decorate our homes and how to bring up our children. And she's done very well out of it indeed. The so-called 'influencer' and her family, banker husband Johnnie Smugge and their three children, live with their staff in a sprawling old rectory in deepest Suffolk. If you believe the constant stream of saccharine content pouring from Ms Smugge's pen, you'd think her life was perfect. However, sources close to the blogger tell me that there's trouble in paradise. 'Issy never really wanted to move out of London,' says a family friend. 'She loved being queen bee in her social set, out every night with her husband while her children were cared for by the help. She doesn't even do her own housework.'

Ms Smugge's buzzword is 'relatability'. She likes to tell her followers that she's just like them, albeit living in a huge house with servants and not having to lift a finger. The first thing she did when she moved to Suffolk was to dig up a beautiful chamomile lawn which had been there for centuries. And why? So that she could build her own pool and gym. 'Issy's paranoid about her appearance,' another friend told me. 'She's pushing forty and she's terrified of getting old. Lifestyle bloggers are ten-a-penny these days and there are lots of younger, edgier ones coming up all the time. Johnnie's very handsome and charming and the word on the street is that he's got a roving eye.'

I'd heard quite enough. I was seething with rage. Pushing forty? Paranoid? Saccharine? Ignoring my stuttering response, Mimi took a swig of coffee and lit yet another cigarette.

'We have to deal with this. She can't be allowed to continue. If your brand goes toxic, we might as well forget it. Why's she doing this? And why don't I know about it?'

'It was all so long ago, Mimi. We were children. I can't believe she'd be so vile over a schoolgirl tiff years ago.'

This wasn't true. I could believe it only too well. Her words came back to me, ringing in my ears and making me break out in a cold sweat.

'I'll make you sorry.'

Mimi swung into action.

'I'm at a cocktail thing tonight with some editors. I'll have a word and find out what they've heard. We either maintain a dignified silence, in which case she'll keep going until she destroys you, or we mount a defence. Leave it with me.'

With a puff of smoke, she cut the Skype connection and was gone. I was left in my beautiful kitchen, the sweet spring air blowing in through the windows, my mouth dry, my heart banging and my palms sweaty. Was I frightened of Lavinia Harcourt? You bet I was! That clever, poisonous writing style had brought down a fair few people over the years. I certainly didn't intend to be one of them. #smearcampaign #issysmuggesaysgetlostlavvieharcourt

Knots of people scattered around the playground talking and laughing seemed sinister for the first time. Were they all talking about me? I walked over to a bunch of Reception parents with a big smile on my face. They were perfectly polite, but I could feel a subdued hum of excitement, and it wasn't good excitement. Nothing ever happens in this village. Me moving in was probably the most thrilling event since the church tower was struck by lightning back in the seventies and that hoard of Roman coins was discovered under the new housing estate. I could almost hear Johnnie's voice: 'What do you expect, Iss?'

Thank heavens for Lauren, who came marching over and threw her arms around me. I let my head drop on to her shoulder and felt a few tears roll down my cheeks. She had plenty to say about Lavinia Harcourt, most of it unprintable. I felt a bit better. Who cares what the miserable old moo says?

I invited Lauren and the girls back to our house and found myself telling her the story about the plait. Lauren nearly fell off her stool.

'You did not! You did not cut off her plait! Shut up!'

I might be 'pushing forty' (I most certainly am not) and producing 'saccharine content' (for which I have received far more awards than Lavvie Harcourt ever has), but I've got a family who love me and real friends who believe in me. And my followers adore me. I know they do. People don't buy merchandise and follow me on Insta against their will. No one's making them do it.

Lauren was agog. She sat with her eyes wide and her mouth open as I recounted the violence and threats that had characterised my relationship with my *bête noire*. As I went into the details of her vile behaviour to Suze and my fist fight with her, she sighed deeply.

'This is even better than Liane and the head in the microwave. I'm so glad you moved here, babes. It's like knowing a real live celebrity. Don't you worry about her. My dad always used to say today's news is tomorrow's chip paper.'

Since Lauren was a walking directory of village families, feuds and dynamics, I took the opportunity to quiz her about the sources in the article. The bit about me digging up the lawn was a complete fabrication. It was Johnnie who thought of the pool and gym and pushed it through planning. There was a scrubby bit of grass there with daisies and dandelions, but nothing special. I couldn't work out where Lavinia had got the idea from. Lauren speculated.

'That might have come from Ted.'

'Ted?'

'The old boy who does the garden at yours. He's a Ling.'

I frowned.

'And...?'

'Well, he's Liane's uncle through her mother's side, but his wife ran off with Pete the postie and got the kids, then he fought her for them and lost, so then...'

I drifted off a bit at this point, I must confess. What this had to do with my swimming pool was anyone's guess. I tuned back in as Lauren was saying, 'Although it wouldn't have been malicious. He's a nice old boy. Spends all his spare time at The Fox, so he might have had one too many and said something out of turn.'

The Fox is our local hostelry. Johnnie and I went in once when we first came here. No craft beers, only two types of gin and the kind of wine that comes out of boxes. It seems that my gardener spends most evenings there with his cronies supping ale and chewing the fat. I quizzed Lauren about the chamomile lawn but drew a blank.

'The whole place is centuries old. I can't see that you building the pool would upset anyone. That said, Ted is very protective of the garden. He doesn't like change. He might have said something he oughtn't down The Fox and that got back to someone.'

I wouldn't put it past Lavinia Harcourt to recruit a drove of villagers to spy on us and report back. The woman has no shame. I immediately thought of Liane Bloomfield. She's no friend to Issy Smugge, is short of money and would probably love to see me filleted like a turbot across the pages of Ms

Harcourt's rag. I put my theory to Lauren, who instantly refuted it.

'Liane wouldn't do that. She's hard as nails and doesn't take any nonsense, but she'd never go behind your back.'

We spent the next half hour picking through the article (if you can call it that) and analysing every last word. I laughed off the bit about Johnnie having a roving eye (jealousy, pure and simple. Lavinia never found her happy-ever-after as I did) and tried not to care about Meredith and whoever else it was from the old crowd who'd blabbed to her.

As I waved Lauren and the girls off, I turned back into my lovely house and thanked whoever was listening for the good fortune that allowed me to live such a blessed life. It could well have been God. I don't know. I'm in credit with Him thanks to fixing the church roof, so a quick thank-you prayer to make absolutely sure couldn't hurt.

The next morning, I woke up with a song in my heart and a spring in my step. Issy Smugge laughs in the face of difficulties. I headed downstairs to find Chloë slumped disconsolately on the sofa in her pyjamas. She's not usually an early riser so I was rather taken aback.

'Why are you up so early, darling? Do you want to come and help me make the breakfast?'

'OK.' She didn't seem particularly enthusiastic. My daughter is a bit of a puzzle to me sometimes. Getting information out of her is next to impossible, she has a terrible tendency to bite her nails and she suffers from sporadic nightmares. That said, she's no trouble, is very adaptable and is a sweet little thing. Sometimes I wonder if she's a victim of Middle Child Syndrome, but I don't quite know what to do about it.

I let Chloë get the eggs out of the egg bucket, break them and beat them in a bowl. She loves scrambled egg on toast. It was rather nice, sitting at the island with my daughter having an early breakfast. I realised that while I'd really bonded with Finn over the unfortunate goings on with Zach Bloomfield, Chloë and I hadn't talked, one to one, for I don't know how long. I tend to lump her in with the other two. Now was the time to rectify that.

'Did you have another nasty dream, darling? Is that why you woke up early?'

She shook her head and started gnawing her fingernails. For a heart-stopping moment, it was as if eight-year-old Suze was sitting there. I tried again.

'Is someone being mean to you at school, sweetie?'

She shook her head again. So far, this chat wasn't going terribly well. I was stumped. I took a mouthful of coffee.

'Are you and Daddy going to split up?'

A lesser woman would have choked on her sourdough.

'What? Why on earth would you think that?'

She looked down and chewed on her thumbnail.

'I heard you and Daddy shouting in your bedroom when Hannah's mum and dad came for tea. Tilly in my class says that's what her mum and dad did before they got divorced, and Amber says hers did too and now her dad sleeps on her nan's sofa. I don't want you and Daddy to split up. I talked to Hannah about it, but she says vicars aren't allowed to get divorced, ever. It says it in the Bible.'

I felt terrible. Here I was congratulating myself on my hands-on parenting and all the time my little girl was worrying herself sick over nothing. I put my arms round her and stroked her hair. I was determined never to let my children go through what Mummy put us through; I wasn't going to be that kind of mother to my daughter.

'Darling, Daddy and I are not going to split up. We love each other very much. Sometimes, grown-ups have little disagreements about things, but it doesn't mean they're going to get a divorce. It's healthy to talk openly about feelings. You mustn't worry about this any more.'

I felt her relax in my arms. We sat there for a while, her head nestled on my shoulder. Then she brought up her SATs, which were also worrying her, and we talked some more, then cuddled in silence.

After a few minutes, she gently disengaged herself and took a gulp of her hot chocolate. I didn't want this closeness to end. I picked up her hand and looked at her nails. They were chewed to the quick. Just like Suze. I vowed to be more perceptive from now on and spend more quality time with Chloë. She's such a quiet little thing that it's easy to forget that she must have her feelings and needs too.

We finished our breakfast and then went for a walk in the garden, both of us still in our pyjamas. I found myself chatting about our old garden at home in Kent and what Suze and I used to get up to. It was lovely. By the time we came back inside, she was smiling again. **#parentingwins #hearttoheart**

One of the very few things I regret about sending the children to our local primary is the difference in term times. Whit Week falls at the end of May, as usual, and that's when our three break up. However, all the private schools are off the week before, and that's when Rafe and Xenia's CofE wedding is scheduled. I had to go cap in hand and fill in various forms before I could take them out of school. When I got to 'Reason your child will be out of school', I was struggling a bit. The truth – 'Because my brother-in-law is marrying the scion of a Russian billionaire's family and my nieces and nephews are privately educated' – didn't really seem the right thing to put. In the end, I plumped for 'Family wedding' and left it at that. Smiley Mrs Hill raised one eyebrow when I handed her the form.

'Are you travelling abroad for the wedding, Mrs Smugge?'

I explained that, unlike ordinary mortals, Rafe and Xenia were having two lots of nuptials. She looked even more surprised.

'Well, I never! That sounds like lots of fun. Are the children going to be bridesmaids and pageboy?'

I ran through the make-up of the wedding party. Johnnie as best man, Toby and Charlie as ushers, along with Charlie's two sons and Finn, Charlie and Amanda's daughters as bridesmaids with my two and a squad of Russians filling in the rest of the positions.

'How lovely! It sounds amazing. I'm sure the children will have lots to tell us after half term. Have you decided on your outfit?'

Naturally, I had. I showed her a picture on my phone. She was gratifyingly impressed.

I walked out into the spring sunshine, the quiet murmurings of the children and teachers floating out of the open windows. I'm so glad we moved here. It beats London into a cocked hat. And that's something I never thought I'd hear myself say.

Johnnie and I were attending the Russian Orthodox wedding in London without the children. Sofija was happy to look after them at home, and they'd be with us for all the celebrations in Kent the following weekend. We felt that a long, elaborate ceremony would be too much for them.

We drove up to the flat on Saturday afternoon. We'd arranged to meet some friends for drinks and dinner later. I wanted to do a bit of digging and find out what they thought about Lavinia's scurrilous article.

It was a beautiful evening. We sat outside, sipping our drinks and watching as the world went by.

I told Johnnie about my chat with Chloë. He looked concerned.

'Poor little thing. What did you tell her, Iss?'

I gave him chapter and verse. I would have gone into more detail, but just then our friends appeared and it was forgotten in a round of hugging, kissing and catching up on all the news. The girls agreed with me that Meredith was behind a lot of it and promised to keep their ears to the ground.

The next morning, we got a cab, bracing ourselves for a long day. By the time you get to your late thirties, you're a veteran of Church of England weddings. Everyone dresses up, there are flowers everywhere, the groom looks nervous, the mother of the bride wears an unfortunate hat, the bride appears either looking wonderful or not, the bridesmaids are instantly forgettable, the vicar rambles on about love, someone does a reading, you sing the same old hymns then you leave for the reception. In the Russian Orthodox Church, this is not the case.

It takes quite a lot to impress Johnnie and me, but as we stood in front of the cathedral looking up at its towering façade, we were speechless. These Russians certainly know how to make a splash! Inside, the glittering interior, the smell of incense and the rustle of robes made the whole place seem like a temple of mystery. Silvia, resplendent in teal, jumped up and came over to embrace us.

'Isabella, you look wonderful, darling. Johnnie, my angel, how lovely to see you.'

I love Silvia. We went to sit next to Charlie, Amanda, Toby and Davina. Amanda and I have never really hit it off. She grew up in a castle, went to a much posher school than me, then did a ski season before she met Charlie. She's got that aristocratic hauteur about her and, try as I might, I've never been able to get close to whoever the real Amanda might be. She's lovely to the children, never forgets a birthday or Christmas, but there's no warmth there. At least none I can detect. She's followed Charlie around the world as his career's grown ever more stellar, and seems not to feel any pain at leaving her children in the care of strangers. A hundred and fifty years ago, she'd have been a memsahib with her husband in the pay of the Raj, bringing the little ones back to England at seven years old to live with their relations or in a boarding house.

Davina and Toby got up to greet us. She looked even more equine than usual, clad in a nondescript frock, clumpy shoes and an absolute fright of a hat.

It's not often that all the Smugge boys get together and I felt a rush of pride seeing them all sitting there. Rafe was off being sprinkled with holy water or whatever the Russian Orthodox crowd do before marrying someone.

The church was crowded with Xenia's family and friends. This was their turf, without a doubt. All the women were made up, coiffed and costumed to the nines. The smell of perfume and incense was blending, creating a heady mix. Davina was fanning herself and kept pressing her hand to her forehead. It was rather oppressive.

There were some clonking noises and all the Russians crossed themselves. A priest arrayed in a remarkable collection of vestments appeared with Rafe and Xenia walking slowly behind him. Silvia had been reading up on the traditions and kept us informed in a whisper.

'The priest is blessing their betrothal. He's going to hand them lighted candles.'

Sure enough, the candles appeared. More heat. Just what we needed. Xenia looked magnificent. Her dress was moulded to her splendid curves and she had a glittering diadem affixing her floor-length lace veil to her head. In one hand she carried a bouquet of crimson roses, in the other her candle.

Slowly, the three of them made their way to the centre of the church.

'Rose-coloured carpet,' whispered Silvia. 'The bridal couple stand on it for the reading of Scripture and the prayers.'

On our side of the church, none of us had any idea what was being said. Whatever it was, the Russians were lapping it up. There was chanting, murmuring and all kinds of strange noises. Xenia's parents rose to their feet and marched over to the bride and groom.

'Crowns,' Silvia informed us. 'Very important.'

And just like that, the priest produced two golden crowns and he and Xenia's parents placed them on the bridal pair's heads. I was a bit worried about the diadem, but my new sister-in-law is the most organised woman in the world, next to me, and no doubt had had everything measured well before the ceremony. If anything had gone wrong, I wouldn't have wanted to be in the priest's shoes. Xenia's mother has the build of a shot-putter, the face of a disgruntled pug and the social clout of our own dear Queen.

Next, the priest whipped out a wine glass and offered it to them. Well. You don't get that in the CofE.

'Wine,' whispered Silvia. 'They drink it then follow the priest around the lectern three times.'

Everyone trooped around in a circle for a bit, then they all came back to rest on the pink cloth. I was beginning to wonder if they were ever going to exchange rings, but this, it seemed, was the next part. Out they came and were put on the relevant fingers. Proceedings showed no signs of ever coming to an end as the priest produced a crystal goblet. Silvia was just leaning over to share the thrilling details of whatever this signified when Davina slumped forward. She was white as a sheet with a fine dew of sweat on her face.

She obviously needed some fresh air. I suggested this, *sotto voce*, and seized her arm. We trotted down the aisle and, just as we reached the door, the sound of smashing glass came from the centre of the church. I suppose even a priest makes mistakes sometimes, but I didn't fancy his chances with Xenia's mother.

I got Davina onto a bench, encouraged her to put her head between her knees and offered her water.

'Sorry, Isabella. I feel like such a twit.'

The colour was coming back into her cheeks. She now looked like a horse who's just come back from the gallops, rather than one heading for the knacker's yard.

'Don't give it another thought. Close your eyes and take some deep breaths.'

I leaned back on the bench and stared up at the sky while Davina puffed away like an ageing pair of bellows. Above me, all was intense blue with little white clouds scudding across the vast face of the heavens. Davina turned to face me and laid her hand on mine.

'Isabella, can I tell you something?'

Just then, Toby came cantering down the steps.

'Are you all right, darling? I couldn't rest till I knew you were OK.'

He leaned over her, gazing into her face and gripping her hand. I was a bit surprised, to be honest. He and Davina have always had one of those semi-detached marriages. Fond of each other, but devoted to their own interests.

Davina hauled herself to her feet and smoothed down her dress, which was wrinkling appallingly at the back. That's why I always say it's worth spending money sourcing really good clothes. You can relax, safe in the knowledge that you won't look as though you've just arrived from some kind of misguided backpacking odyssey. Poor Davina clearly wasn't listening when I advised her on her wardrobe.

Toby took Davina's hand in his and they trotted back up the steps. A terrible thought had just entered my mind.

Rafe and Xenia were safely married in the eyes of the Russian Orthodox Church, the Patriarch of Moscow and anyone else who had an interest in the whole business. Her parents were beaming, her brothers were towering over Rafe, embracing him and welcoming him to the family, and the rest of us were looking forward to the reception.

You need to know that my new sister-in-law is one of the leading lights in international event management. Anyone who's anyone uses her. I suppose it doesn't hurt to have insanely rich parents and an address book to die for (although those rumours were never proved, to be fair), but I have to say, she is a professional to her perfectly manicured fingertips. I think I speak for everyone when I say that we were dying to know what she had pulled off for the next part of the day's celebrations.

The woman is a genius. When we arrived at the venue, everything was decked out like a fairy-tale forest. Somehow, Xenia had managed to weave together Russian folk tales, English country garden and European glamour with a dash of whimsy. I can't think of anyone else in my social circle who could even begin to do something that audacious. She does have a huge team of minions to help her, but even so, organising a triumphant post-wedding lunch in style when you're the bride, *and* dressing the venue takes some doing. Had I been wearing a hat (so last decade), I would have taken it off to her.

The first thing to get through was the receiving line. Silvia was standing next to Xenia's father, looking a little flustered, as well she might. Xenia's mother was lit up like a Christmas tree. Huge, sparkling emerald and diamond choker, bracelets, rings and a brooch so large it could probably be seen from space. In comparison, dear Silvia was sporting only her wedding and engagement rings and a small, discreet pair of diamond earrings. Much less common.

After the obligatory round of hugging and kissing, we were released to go and quaff a range of exciting beverages. I was more than ready for some bubbles. Davina plumped for freshly squeezed orange and pomegranate juice, and Toby joined her. By now, I was observing my sister-in-law closely, and everything that unfolded as the day went on only confirmed my suspicions.

Xenia had managed the table plan with her customary brilliance. Johnnie and I were sitting with Davina and Toby plus three other couples. Davina was soon chatting away to the man seated beside her, an internationally renowned horse breeder, while his wife was deep in conversation with Toby about their boring careers. Johnnie and I had loads in common with the other four and our conversation simply sparkled. The food was wonderful, of course. Xenia has always been pro canapés. I won't bore you with all the details. You've probably read all about it by now in the society pages of the glossies.

Just before dessert, Xenia's father, Nikolai, rose to his feet and delivered a speech. I couldn't tell you what he said, as most of it was in Russian, but it went down a storm. At the end, he switched to English and welcomed Rafe to the family.

'We are so pleased that you have finally' (emphasis on the 'finally') 'taken our daughter as your wife. You are now our son!'

There was a storm of applause and banging on the tables and all the Russians started glugging shots. Never in my entire life have I seen so much vodka in one place. I predicted that there would be some sore heads in the morning.

I glanced across at Davina. She'd barely touched her food. Toby kept taking her hand and stroking it. I was sure that my theory was correct.

We took our leave at around seven and headed over to our favourite Korean restaurant for a light supper before returning to the flat. I didn't share my suspicions with Johnnie. There was time enough for that. Secretly, I was planning to have a heart-to-heart with poor Davina at next week's wedding celebrations. #lifestooshort #sadface

What a week! We were hardly back from London before it was time for my little Elsie's birthday party. It was marvellous. Nearly the whole class came, the cake-baking was a genius idea and the woman who ran it was a real find. I may start using her for my own cakes from now on. #shoplocal

It's nearly impossible to have too much content, but I found myself in the unusual position of wondering what to post first. What with the garden, spring, flowers, fruit, the wedding and the birthday party, I had to be careful not to bombard my followers with too much information. I needn't have worried. The posts of the wedding garnered me loads of new followers. Mimi was over the moon.

'People love that edgy glamour, sweetie. Such a shame they got rid of the Romanovs. So photogenic. Great job.'

Alas, Lavinia has really got her teeth into me. She's determined to bring me down. Most people would be worried, but I say bring it on! Mimi's come up with a ten-point plan to confound her evil schemes, including lots of content and images of me in my garden getting my hands dirty (figuratively speaking). We went through it and I suddenly had a brainwave.

'Listen, Mimi, why don't I start going to church for a bit? Lots of people do it, even famous ones. It wouldn't be so bad, I suppose, and it wouldn't be forever. Just till I can get her off my back.'

We agreed that this, along with everything else, might just do the trick. The key is to keep your followers engaged and to make them feel special. Yes, they want to see my life and feel involved in it, but it's a fine line when you become successful. What I don't want to do is seem out of reach to ordinary people. I need to build on my relatability. If Lavinia keeps on attacking me, they'll turn on her. Who says nasty things about a lovely, kind woman who goes to church? Only a miserable, perimenopausal old hag, that's who! In your face, Lavinia Harcourt!

I went outside to find Ted. I don't suppose he follows me on Insta, but I will have to find a way to explain why I've suddenly developed an interest in gardening.

At lunchtime, having crossed several things off my list, I texted Claire. *Do you mind if I start coming to church on Sundays? What time do you start? Do you have an approximate end time? xx*

Nothing. I would have thought she'd have been delighted to have another booking, but no. I had vast amounts of work to get through before I could take the weekend off for Rafe and Xenia's second wedding ceremony. Sofija was doing the school run for me every day. She's been marvellous about swapping her days off to suit me.

It wasn't until 4.30 that I got a reply from Claire.

'Hi, sorry for silence. Been up at hospital. Nothing serious, just an extra scan and some tests. Not as young as I used to be! Twelve-week scan in March showed up a few issues. Of course, we'd love to see you! We start at eleven usually all done by 12.15 then coffee and chat afterwards. Fancy coffee soon? xx'

I suddenly realised that I hadn't really chatted to Claire for ages and that I'd been so engrossed in my own life that I hadn't been thinking about my friend. My week was crazy, but Issy Smugge is nothing if not flexible and, actually, although I wasn't going to mention it to Claire, dropping everything to spend time with a friend in need would help in my campaign to keep that spitting cobra Lavinia at bay.

'Soz, I've been rubbish lately. Too much going on. Would love to see you – come for lunch tomorrow if you like. Need to chat re churchy stuff too xx'

What a fruitful week this is turning out to be! **#friendinneed #reachingout**

Claire doesn't look well at all. I insisted she sat on our most comfortable garden chair and made her a lovely lunch. Joel was at home with Tom so we had complete peace and quiet. She made light of her recent hospital visit, but it seems that her twelve-week scan a couple of months ago showed up some issues and they're monitoring her very closely. She's had to give up nearly all her church responsibilities for now, which is really bothering her.

I was going to tell her about Lavinia's article but it didn't feel like the right time. We ate our lunch and chatted about the children, school and our plans for the summer. I told her all about Rafe and Xenia's wedding and showed her the pictures on my phone. I popped back into the house to go to the loo and when I came back, she was fast asleep in the sunshine. There are dark circles under her eyes, and she's so pale. I left her in peace and texted Tom to say I'd pick up the children and bring them back to ours for tea. I think that's what normal people do. It felt like the right thing and it made me feel good.

In the grand scheme of things, what does it matter that my old enemy is prowling around like a lion? Maybe friendship and family and the little things of life are what matter. **#lifelessons**

Waving Sofija goodbye as we pulled out of the drive on Friday, I mused that her life is simple compared to mine. Reactive rather than proactive. Sometimes I yearn for a simple existence, without deadlines and the constant need to feed the marketing monster. Johnnie says that I wouldn't know the simple life if it bit me on the ankle, but I think that's a bit harsh. I can't imagine what it would be like to have the week mapped out in terms of cooking, meal planning, childcare and so on. Maybe I should try it some time. With my grandchildren. When I'm old.

As we drove south on the A12, I switched my thoughts away from the crazy week of work, Lavinia Harcourt and Claire's health, and started to focus on poor Davina. All the signs were there. Puffy face (steroids), thicker, glossier hair (obviously a wig), exhaustion, tendency to faint and Toby's sudden change of behaviour. I wondered when she was going to tell me. Issy Smugge is nothing if not empathic. We had three days together and I began to plan out what I might say.

As we joined the Friday evening queue on to the M25, I rehearsed the kind of conversation we might have and realised, with a pang, that I'd spent most of our relationship looking down on her. This was my chance to make all that right, and as I cut across three lanes of traffic, ignoring the beeping and hand signals from the other irate drivers, I vowed to be the sister-in-law poor Davina needed.

At the hotel, we had dinner and put the children to bed. I wondered whether to confide in Johnnie, but he seemed distant, somehow. I served a few conversational volleys over the net, but they fell at his feet and stayed there. He must be tired from work. Friday's never a good day for him, trying to switch off from a frantic week and morphing into family man. I gave up and had a long bubble bath and an early night. I'd need all my strength for the next day.

Another day, another wedding! I shoehorned the children into their outfits and herded them out on to the terrace for some photos. I ignored Finn's cries of, 'Mum! It's not fair! You promised!', pointing out it was all for the greater good. Which it was. Nothing says 'award-winning inspirational blogger' like a series of images of beautiful children in designer outfits in a landscaped Kentish garden. Johnnie strolled out looking unbelievably handsome in his suit and wearing the aftershave that gives me very naughty thoughts! I whispered some of them in his ear, which went down well. I'd selected a very on-trend floaty dress with nude heels and flattered myself I looked elegant and wedding ready. The car came for the children and we followed on behind. I squeezed Johnnie's hand as we drove, thinking back to our own wedding day all those years ago.

At the church, Xenia's touch was everywhere. I concede. She's even better at this stuff than I am! She'd managed to pull off country church meets boho meets spring bride. My expert eye spied shades of apricot, coffee and caramel while the beautiful fragrance rising from her arrangements told me she'd gone for the current trend of well-being flowers. Darn, she's good!

The children stayed in the porch with Silvia and their older cousins and Johnnie walked down to join Rafe. I took my seat next to Davina and Amanda. Poor Davina had chosen another ill-advised outfit and was looking very flushed in the face. She was fanning herself with her order of service while Amanda looked ready to organise a fundraiser while running a small republic. We made polite chit-chat while the Russian contingent clacked down the aisle to their seats on a wave of expensive French scent.

After a few more minutes, Xenia's mother, gorgeously arrayed and dripping with jewellery (mostly rubies this time; I believe she has an understanding with the caretaker at one of the museums in Moscow), walked down to the front of the church on the arm of one of her sons. An expectant hush fell over us all. Rustling in the porch and suppressed giggling alerted us to the bride's arrival. With a burst of organ music, the doors opened and she appeared.

We rose to our feet as one before she glided past on her father's arm. Last week, she was Russian through and through. Today, she was the quintessential English bride, her blonde hair caught up in an elegant chignon, discreet diamond and pearl earrings glinting as the light caught them, a plain crêpe dress with long sleeves and a fishtail train and an embroidered floor-length veil. She carried pale coffee roses, phlox, caramel carnations and a trail of greenery. As she reached Rafe, he turned, and the look on his face made me want to burst into tears. The love in his eyes as he gazed at her reminded me why I chose my wonderful husband in the face of such difficulties. Next to me, Davina was sniffing and scrabbling around in her bag for a tissue. Naturally, the efficient Amanda had one to hand, as well as Bach Flower Remedies, water and wet wipes, all of which Davina appeared to require. I am ever more convinced that my theory is correct.

The reception was all you would expect. If you read the society pages, which I'm sure you do, you can see all the details in there. I felt very proud. Finn looked so handsome in his suit and my girls were adorable. I found myself in the loo refreshing my make-up at the same time as Amanda. After a bit of a chinwag, I delicately alluded to Davina's condition.

'I thought you'd noticed. Poor girl, she's really suffering.'
Amanda is the only woman I know who can refresh eyeliner and

mascara while talking and not adopt that terrible slack-jawed look which ages a person so.

'I was hoping she might confide in me today.' I slicked on some more lipstick and touched up my brows. 'I see we're all seated together.'

'Yes, I'm so glad. We don't see enough of each other. I'd love the children to spend more time together, but Charlie's work takes us overseas and there it is.'

She clicked her powder compact shut and replaced it in her bag.

'Has she talked to you about it?' I felt that Amanda was avoiding the subject.

'Oh, yes. We chatted last week at the Russian shindig. I promised not to say anything, though. It's not fair on her. I'm sure she'll tell you today.'

I felt a little hurt, if I'm honest, but Issy Smugge knows how to manage an awkward social situation. We walked out of the loo and over to the bar where our husbands were deep in conversation with the Russian contingent. **#designersisterinlaw #sadnews #emotionalsupport**

June

May was exhausting! I'm glad June is finally here and I can focus on the work we're doing on the south wing. It's a bit of a rabbit warren, so we're knocking down some walls to give us two further guest rooms, both en suite. Sofija's bedroom and en suite is getting a makeover as well. She deserves it. There's some repointing work to do too, some carpentry and some rerooofing.

I've retained a local building firm to do all the work under my expert eye. I must say, the longer I live in Suffolk, the more impressed I am with the quality of tradesmen around here. My chosen firm are most professional. They quoted, gave me some decorative ideas and seemed very up on period properties. One of them is from New Zealand. I do like New Zealanders. Always so cheerful and willing. Colonials often are, I find.

I'm known for managing tradesmen. I've masterminded so many renovation projects in my time and Mummy has passed on her interior decoration genes to me. I don't suppose Kevin and Dave (for those are their names) have the privilege of working with someone like me that often.

I'm running away with myself. I'll have to take you back to the wedding for a little while. I was all prepared to be supportive and hear what Davina had to tell me. The meal and the speeches lasted for several hours, and after a little walk around the grounds with the children, I sat down on a bench next to her. The first dance was over and done with, but the French doors were open and we could see Xenia and Rafe whirling around surrounded by over-refreshed guests. Her father was doing a modified version of 'The Twist', all flailing arms and flushed cheeks.

'Doesn't Xenia look beautiful?' Poor Davina was gazing at our new sister-in-law, the early evening sunlight reflecting from her horsey teeth. 'I wish I could be like her.'

I patted her on the arm. 'You're lovely just as you are.' I smiled, encouragingly. Davina continued to prattle on about Xenia's dress, the flowers, the music and so on. I let her do so, waiting for the right moment. Issy Smugge prides herself on her sympathetic nature and her listening skills.

A spotlight appeared, illuminating the stage, and a girl walked on.

'Oh wow, this is the wedding singer Rafe told us about! Latara.' Davina was agog. I can't say I was that excited. If Xenia had managed to bag Gaga for her evening reception, I *would* have been impressed. However, as the girl started to sing, I felt tears pricking at the back of my eyes. Her voice was rich and emotional and she closed her eyes as she sang.

The whole atmosphere changed. Xenia and Rafe were dancing slowly, their faces close together.

Next to me, Davina burst into loud and extravagant tears.

'It's... so... beautiful!' she stuttered, blowing her nose noisily on the remains of Amanda's tissue. 'I love this song.'

Now was the time for Issy Smugge to offer her support.

'Davina, I've noticed that you haven't been quite yourself over the last two weeks. I just want you to know I'm here for you.'

The floodgates opened. She transferred most of her powder and eyeshadow onto the shoulder of my jacket in a burst of tears which showed no signs of ever stopping. Thank goodness for my dry cleaner.

'Oh, Isabella, you're so sweet! I've always looked up to you and thought how marvellous you are, working and having a family and all. Your life seems so perfect and I've never really felt good enough around you. I don't mean to be rude by saying that. You've got everything – your beautiful house, and your husband, and those adorable little moppets and your clever writing. I don't know how you do it. I only really know about horses.'

Talk about a stream of consciousness. I don't think I'd ever heard Davina string so many sentences together. I seized on her last statement as a good jumping off point.

'I used to love my little horse. Riding her made me forget about all my worries. I've often thought I should start again. Perhaps you could help me, Davina. There's nothing you don't know about horses.'

Davina wiped her eyes and gave a loud sniff.

'I haven't been riding recently. I do miss it terribly, but, well, my doctor has advised against it. You know, because of my condition.'

Here it was. I clasped her hand and put my head on one side in a sympathetic manner.

'How long do you think you've got – if you don't mind me asking?'

'Five months,' she replied.

This seemed incredibly specific, but it wasn't for me to doubt her doctor's prognosis.

'Five months! Is that all? Well, I don't know what to say. How are you feeling?'

At this, she burst into tears again, but the words that fell from her equine lips were not those I was expecting to hear.

'I'm just so happy! We've tried and tried, and I've lost so many, but this time everything is going well. I've never got past six weeks before. I don't care about not riding, or anything, really, just the thought of having my own little one to hold in my arms at last is almost too much. I've wanted to tell you for a while, but over the phone is too impersonal. Oh, Isabella, we are so happy! I've never seen my darling boy so overjoyed. We're not doing up the nursery yet – it seems like tempting fate – but I'm having all this wonderful care and I go up to the hospital for special clinics, and it's all going really well. I do feel so sick and tired all the time, but I don't care! It's all worth it to have my own little baby at last.'

Unlike my suddenly radiant sister-in-law, I was speechless. I could almost hear the neurons in my brain firing frantically as I tried to take this information on board. I had been ready to talk about palliative care, hospices, legacies and so on, and now here I was about to become an aunt again. Isabella M Smugge is rarely taken off guard, but Davina had achieved the impossible!

I found myself struggling to speak. I squeezed Davina's hand and made a series of inarticulate noises which she translated as congratulations.

'Oh, Isabella, thank you so much. I want you to be really involved in our baby's life. We'd love you and Johnnie to be godparents!'

I pulled myself together and managed to speak. 'Davina, honestly, I can't tell you how happy I am for you both. That's wonderful news! And thank you so much for asking. We'd be honoured.'

An alien emotion was creeping over me. I'd had absolutely no idea of what had been going on in Davina's life. Years of heartbreak and disappointment, all hidden, and my legendary empathy hadn't sniffed any of it out. What else was I getting wrong? Self-doubt is corrosive and I never give it house room, but those little icy fingers of doubt were prodding at my gut again. There would be time enough to ponder all that later on. For now, I concentrated on my ecstatic sister-in-law, beaming from ear to ear and consulting me on a range of indelicate matters. Cervixes, dilation, cramps, piles, excess perspiration, pregnancy wind – I suppose a lifetime spent in stables mucking out her noble steeds has fitted Davina for such honest conversations. I did my best to answer her eager questions, dredging my memory banks. It all seemed so long ago.

The singer was still pouring beautiful melodies into the mic. Later on, I would ask my husband for a dance, but for now, I felt it was the right thing to sit with Davina on our bench and listen to her talk, her face lit up with joy. I felt strangely moved.

I've been feeling a bit off ever since we came back from the wedding celebrations. I've got so much content that I'm able to be around the children a bit more, and I want to be, I find. Listening to Davina talking about her pregnancy reminded me of those early days where the years stretched out ahead of me into an endless, unknown future. Now, my little boy is only a year away from leaving primary school and the girls are shooting up. I won't get this time again. It's a sobering thought.

I wish I knew what was going on with Sofija. She's like a cat on hot bricks, jumpy, nervy and forgetful, quite unlike her usual efficient self. I've tried chatting to her, but she's blaming rampant PMT. Who has PMT for a fortnight? She had the whole weekend off while we were at the wedding and so I got her working on the Monday and Tuesday. It doesn't really matter which days she works as long as I get the support I need.

Johnnie promised me that he'd be at home all week, but a meeting has come up, as they always do. Sofija went to bed early, pleading a headache, and with the children upstairs in bed, I was left sitting in the family room by myself looking at Elsie's birthday cards. I should take them down really, but I like the children to enjoy them.

My eye fell on Suze's card. It's beautiful, hand-made as always, with swirling roses and daisies on the front and glitter everywhere. Suze always knows what the children like. I read the words inside and felt a dart of pain pierce my heart.

'To our dear little Elsie, with love from your Auntie Suzie, Uncle Jeremy and Lily. Have a wonderful day, my treasure.'

Suze used to be my treasure. I poured myself a large glass of wine. I had meant to do some work, but I just didn't feel in the mood. I was restless. I wandered outside and sat down on the bench by the herb garden. Everything in my garden looked lovely – but now I thought about it, there was a gaping hole where my relationship with my sister used to be.

The wine was going down terribly well. I walked back into the kitchen and poured myself another. I generally limit myself to one glass a night, if that, but tonight there was a pain inside me that needed to be numbed.

The kitchen clock told me it was well past my bedtime as I rinsed the wine bottle out and put it in the recycling. I felt woozy, yet strangely clear-headed. I got my phone out and composed a message. As I hit send, a feeling of peace washed over me. What was the worst that could happen?

The next morning, I woke up with a headache. Mummy's voice echoed in my throbbing head. 'A lady always knows when to stop, Isabella.'

I closed my eyes and groaned. I could stay in bed as long as I liked, safe in the knowledge that Sofija would do breakfast and entertain the children.

After a fitful doze, I swung my feet out of bed, drank down a pint of water and took a couple of painkillers. I dressed and looked at my phone. What had I been thinking? My message to Suze was long, rambling and sentimental. I had apologised again and again, begged for her forgiveness and abased myself in general. Quite right too, of course. I had betrayed the person who was dearest to me in all the world and I deserved to be punished. That's what Mummy said, anyway. I wished I hadn't written the message while over-refreshed. Suze had read it, but there was no reply as yet.

Sofija's moved into the guest suite. It's a bigger bedroom, and en suite of course, with nice views out over the garden. She seems happy about it and she'll have a wonderful, brand-new room and en suite once the boys are finished. Thinking about it, I wonder if she's finding life in the country a bit stifling. She used to have such a great social life back in town, and I suppose that even with her days off, she doesn't have that old flow and buzz. Mummy says it isn't natural for a young girl to live in with a family and look after their children, as it leads to trouble. I suppose that's why she hired Nanny, who although lovely and cuddly was by no means a raving beauty.

I can't bear the thought of losing Sofija, so I'll be chatting to her about the whole situation when the right time presents itself.

Nothing back from Suze yet. I keep checking my phone like a lovestruck teenager.

Half of me wishes I'd never sent that message to Suze, the other half hopes against hope that this might be the beginning of a bridge being built between us. **#thinkingofothers #bestaupairintheworld #renovationproject**

Back to school!

Kevin and Dave have started work. It's a hive of industry at the back of the house. I wander over a couple of times a day to take coffee and biscuits and make sure everything's going OK.

Still nothing from Suze.

On Wednesday, I ambled down to the veg patch to commune with Ted. He was bent over the courgettes, doing something with a trowel. He stood up slowly as I approached, rubbing the small of his back.

'Morning, Missus. Veg are doing well.'

We inherited a rather lovely Victorian greenhouse when we bought the house. Ted insisted on taking me in there and introducing me to each individual plant. I praised him extravagantly and asked after the health of the mangetout, which he had warned me had been Got At by something.

After a brief chat, I explained that I would like to do some weeding and garden maintenance. Ted looked blankly at me.

'But that's what you pay me for.'

I could see that this was going to take a while.

'Quite right, Ted, and you're doing a marvellous job. It's just that in my line of work, pictures are very important and my agent thinks it would be good if I could produce some shots of me getting my hands dirty.'

Ted pondered this. 'How dirty? Because the compost needs turning and the carrots could do with thinning out.'

I sighed. 'When I say dirty, I don't mean mud under my nails or anything like that. A little light weeding, maybe a bit of fruit-picking (gosh, those strawberries look delicious!) or even a little strimming. I don't want to take over in any way. It would just be a very good thing if I could have some photos of me doing gardening.'

'Hmm.' Ted scratched his head. 'So, what you're saying, if I've got this right, is that you want to look like you're doing the garden but without doing the actual work.'

'Yes. Exactly.' I was relieved that we'd reached an understanding. 'I can do it on your days off. I won't interfere with your work, I promise.'

'Well, no, we wouldn't want that. No offence, Missus, but amateurs messing around with the fruit and veg is what causes all the trouble. Ladyship always left the garden to me.'

'Ladyship' was the previous owner of the Old Rectory, a saint in human form, according to my gardener. After a few more minutes, the way ahead was clear. Ted had given me a list of jobs which were mainly decorative and would in no way impact on his precious fruit and veg. I thanked him and started to walk back to the house.

No reply from Suze.

It's my birthday! I'm thirty-nine, but thanks to an excellent diet and exercise regime, top quality skincare and good genes, I can easily pass for a much younger woman. The children came in at 7.45 with my breakfast on a tray and their cards. I felt so happy, sitting up in my bed with my lovely husband by my side and my beautiful children handing me their cards covered in protestations of undying love. Elsie had drawn a picture of me which left a lot to be desired in the matter of perspective, but was adorable just the same. After half an hour of cuddling and general bonding, they scampered off to get ready for school. I finished my coffee and had a shower. As I came out of the en suite, wrapped in a towel, I heard them walking down the drive chattering away to Sofija. Johnnie appeared.

'You're a bit overdressed, Mrs Smugge. Allow me to assist.'

Well, happy birthday to *me*! I had another shower, got dressed and ambled down the stairs. I felt totally loved, glowing, full of joy. Does life get any better than this? An amazing husband who understands and supports me 100 per cent, delightful children, the best staff in the world and a job I adore.

The door banged and Sofija came into the kitchen.

'Happy birthday, Isabella,' she said, giving me a kiss on the cheek. She handed me a card and a beautiful bunch of flowers. She's so sweet! I told her so and thanked her again for everything she does for our family. Her cheeks reddened and she looked at the floor. Funny. She doesn't normally get embarrassed when I compliment her.

I had coffee and cake booked with Claire, Lauren and some of the Reception girls, so after opening the post and reading all my cards (including one from Meredith, the two-faced old moo), I headed down to the vicarage.

I checked my phone before I went. Nothing from Suze.

What a blissful day! Issy Smugge is the luckiest girl in the world. The girls had clubbed together to buy me a hamper of local foods. Macarons, jam, honey, chocolates – I was so touched. We spent a lovely couple of hours together before I went back home. I shall have to do some extra lengths of the pool to compensate for all this eating!

Still nothing.

Johnnie had booked a table at a little seafood place up the coast. I felt like a teenager again, blushing, giggling and playing footsie under the table. My life is perfect! Well, very nearly. His phone rang during dinner. A breakfast meeting. Oh well.

No word from Suze.

I've got quite a few nods from the Bloggers' Awards. Best Photography (I've won that three years on the trot), Most Inspiring Influencer, Best Lifestyle Blogger and Best Content. You'd think I'd get bored with all the success, but I never do. Nothing beats that thrill of hearing your name read out.

Johnnie and I are staying at the flat until early Sunday morning. Sofija's in charge so there's no need to worry about anything. I originally told her we'd be back Saturday night, but she'll be fine with us being away for that extra night, I'm sure.

As well as the Awards, June is a busy month in the school calendar. We have school photos, the school fête and some kind of fun run. Sofija and I have divided it all up. I'm doing the fête, *en famille*, and she's doing the fun run.

I have received two begging letters via the book bags. The PTA, it seems, are struggling as they don't have enough volunteers, raffle prizes, tombola prizes, gazebos or cakes for the school fête. Back home, I ran our PTA like a luxury cruise ship, sailing elegantly through the limpid waters of fundraising with my Number Two, Nicki Hartington, at the helm. Yes, we lived in an affluent part of London, and yes, we had a higher than average number of stay-at-home parents of both genders, but really, how hard can it be to organise and run a successful event? I made a mental note to spend an hour with Sofija going through the cupboards to find a few bits and bobs to donate. I'm sure she won't mind making some cakes too.

I'm beginning to wonder if Suze will ever respond.

I was up early on Friday morning. I kissed Johnnie goodbye at 5.30 and then headed for the pool. I wanted to do double my usual morning swim and I did, too. As I towel-dried my hair, I heard my WhatsApp notification. It was Suze. My heart was beating fast and I felt suddenly terrified.

Hi, Bella. I didn't reply to your message straight away, not because I was ignoring you, but because I wanted to make sure I got the wording exactly right. I know you're sorry, but it isn't that easy to fix. The whole thing with Johnnie hurt me so badly, and when I went back to uni, I had to cope with seeing him around and people sniggering. I felt so stupid. When you got married, it was really tough for me, but I was honestly OK with it. I'd dreamt of having children with Johnnie. I know I was young but I fell so hard for him. We both know how charming he can be when he wants to. Bella, don't you realise you betrayed my trust, when I loved you more than anyone else in the world? You were the only one who was always there for me. Daddy left us, and Mummy sacked Nanny, and we weren't allowed to see Penny and Minty any more. Whatever happened, you were my champion. When I met Jeremy, he told me about him having mumps as a child and the chance we might never be able to have our own children. I had to sit by and watch as you and Johnnie had those three beautiful children with no trouble at all. I love them all so much, you know I do, Bella, but sometimes it felt that you had stolen my chance to have my own babies. I'd love our relationship to be mended, but I just can't see how. I've realised how damaging our childhood was and what an effect it had on us both. I know you think it didn't touch you, but it did. I do love you, Bella. Nothing could ever change that. Maybe next time we come over, we could get together and try to talk it all out. Happy birthday for yesterday and give our love to the children x

I doubled over in pain and burst into tears. I had one job to do, to look after and protect my little sister, and instead I betrayed her, stole her boyfriend and took away her chance to have her own family. I didn't deserve any of the good things that came to me. The only thing that made the pain slightly better was digging my nails into my thighs until I broke the skin.

I sat weeping and tearing at my skin for I don't know how long. Eventually, I gave myself a stern talking-to and took some deep breaths. I did a couple more lengths so that I could blame my red and puffy eyes on chlorine if anyone happened to see me. I wrapped myself in my robe and walked back up to the house.

Sofija was in the kitchen getting the breakfast ready when I came in through the back door. She did a double take.

'Isabella! What is the matter? Are you ill?'

I explained that I had overdone the swimming and played the chlorine card. She didn't look convinced and started fiddling with her hair.

'Isabella, I must talk to you. Is important. I need to tell you something.'

Her timing wasn't great. All I wanted to do was go upstairs and stand under a scalding hot shower and here she was confiding in me. I forced a smile and prepared myself to listen.

'This thing has been on my mind for a long time. I feel so bad...'

She broke off as Chloë appeared, hair tousled and eyes bleary.

'I had a bad dream, Sofi. It was the clowns again.'

She put her arms around Sofija and snuggled into her. My heart broke all over again. Not only a bad sister, but also a terrible mother.

'Tell me later, Sofija. I'm going to have a shower.'

By the time I came downstairs again, the house was empty. I made myself a coffee and walked over to my studio. Surely, I could find a path through my tangled relationship with Suze.

I wrote some content, did some editing and posted all over my socials about the Awards. I'd been so looking forward to going to town with Johnnie and glamming myself up. Now, it would take all my legendary self-control to present a smiling, confident face to the world.

Work done, I returned to the house. I had an appointment with my hairdresser and manicurist. My public expect, nay demand, to see me polished, immaculate and on top form. By the time they'd finished, the face that smiled back at me from the mirror was that of an internationally revered lifestyle blogger and writer. Whatever Sofija had to confide in me about could wait.

I worked non-stop in the cab all the way down to London. At the flat, I concentrated on putting my outfit together. I have to be classy, yet edgy; elegant, yet collected; proactive, yet composed. Writing all this down, I'm starting to understand why I get so tired sometimes. By the time Johnnie walked in, I'd managed classy, edgy and elegant, and was working on collected, proactive and composed.

He gave me a kiss then headed off for his shower. When he came out, fragrant and steaming slightly, it was all I could do to restrain myself from bursting into tears, pulling his towel off and asking him to wipe all those terrible memories away. I contented myself with putting on some more perfume and touching up my lashes. Though I say it myself, I looked amazing. The woman gazing at me from the floor-length mirror was a very different person from the weeping, distraught creature who had stood in the shower back at home that morning. I turned round and gave him a twirl.

'Do you like what you see, Mr Smugge?'

'I do, Mrs Smugge! You're a sight for sore eyes,' he retorted, splashing on some aftershave. 'Let's go and win some awards!'

So we did.

Lying in bed, while Johnnie slept beside me, I reflected on the evening. No one else has ever won the Best Photography award four years in a row. I lost out on Most Inspiring Influencer to the new kid in town, Vegan Megan. Hats off to her, she's a good writer and she deserved to win. I chatted to her afterwards, expecting to find her dull and preachy, but she was very sweet and touchingly star-struck.

I bagged Best Lifestyle Blogger, snatching it away from the avaricious clutches of my nearest rival, Bressumer Beams. (She lives in a seventeenth-century farmhouse which she's restored, brick by brick. Call me old-fashioned, but endless ramblings about lime plaster and oak beams leave me cold.) To my delight, I also won the People's Choice vote, largely based on my *Issy Smugge Says* book series. It was a triumph!

Mimi was there, of course, clad in black leather with scarlet nails. We posed for the usual publicity shots before I headed off to chat to the other bloggers. Bressumer Beams (real name Portia Waldegrave) came shimmying over.

'Isabella! Darling! You must be thrilled.'

I was, if only because the committee had seen sense and awarded the trophy to me rather than to the dullest woman in the blogosphere. It wouldn't do, however, to antagonise Portia, who was extremely well connected and rumoured to be a black belt in karate.

'Portia! Thank you, but of course, it's not about the winning for me; it's about being part of this wonderful blogging family.'

We both knew that this was a complete lie, but we continued to smile broadly and pretend that we liked each other. Portia quizzed me on the house.

'Georgian *is* lovely, such clean lines and a joy to decorate, but I have to say I find it just a touch predictable. How are you finding living in the space?'

I pretended to care and talked for several minutes about my plans for the south wing. She then bored the pants off me about her latest project, something to do with a well she'd uncovered near the dairy. While she droned on, I amused myself by picturing her falling down it. My eyes darted around the room, trying to find someone I hadn't spoken to yet. Portia stopped gabbling on for a minute. I smiled graciously.

'Now, do tell me more about your latest find. I was gripped when I read your last blog.'

I wasn't, obviously. Portia spends half her life scrabbling around looking for original features, and recently struck gold when she uncovered a bread oven while renovating her kitchen. I wouldn't have been surprised to find that she'd discovered a cottage loaf and a couple of meat pies in it. To do her justice, her research is meticulous and she does know her stuff, but she's such a frightful bore. If she'd stumbled across a couple of Shakespeare folios in the attic or Jane Austen's working notes for *Sanditon* in the buttery, I'd be a lot more interested.

I was nodding and smiling on autopilot when I felt a tap on my shoulder. It was Johnnie.

'Sorry to interrupt, Iss, but do you mind if we head off soon? Hello, Portia, how lovely to see you! How's Nigel?'

Portia simpered and giggled, an unattractive look in a middle-aged woman. After a few more insincere compliments, I was free.

Mimi was holding court at the bar. We air kissed and exchanged gushing farewells. Then I took Johnnie's hand and walked out into the balmy June night.

'Thanks, darling. I thought I was never going to escape from Broad in the Beam. If I had to hear one more story about her chimney stacks, I'd have screamed! Shoot me if I ever get that dull.'

'That's one thing you're not, Iss. You've always got something up your sleeve.'

It wasn't the gallant compliment I was expecting, but the poor man was running on empty, so I let it go.

Back at the flat, I sat on the balcony, looking out over the jewelled clusters of lights and musing on the day. I should have been on top of the world. But I wasn't. **#painfulmemories #mixedfeelings**

Next morning, we went out for breakfast to our favourite little Portuguese place. The concept of breakfast in Suffolk is very different from the one I knew when I was still the Queen of the PTA at Beech Grove, the primary the children went to back home in London. Call me a snob, but a bowl of mass-produced cereal with a cup of tea does not a breakfast make. A good slug of excellent coffee and a range of *pastéis de nata*, on the other hand, really gets Issy Smugge's day off to a great start. I decided to broach the subject of Suze's message.

'Listen, darling, I've got something on my mind.'

Johnnie looked concerned and his eyebrow went up. He's so in tune with my feelings.

'Fire away, Iss. I'm all ears.'

I gave him a brief rundown. There was silence. He was frowning and fiddling with his tart.

'What do you want *me* to do about it? I'm sorry, you're sorry, she knows we're sorry. And?'

I felt a cold shiver run down my spine. How could Johnnie be so callous? He knows how much I love Suze and how I yearn to mend our relationship. This was a new side to my husband, and one I didn't care for.

My feelings must have shown on my face, because he reached across the table and took my hand.

'I don't mean to be harsh, Iss, but we've been over this so many times. Even if we hadn't done what we did, she and I wouldn't have lasted. I was getting bored before I met you. I'd have probably called it a day in a few months anyway.'

His words stung me like a whiplash and I jerked my hand out of his.

'What? You were going to dump Suze and break her heart? How come I don't know about this? I've always taken all the guilt on my shoulders and all the time you were planning to ditch her? Don't you know how in love she was with you?'

He sighed. 'That was the trouble. She was so needy. She always wanted to be sure of me and I wasn't ready to be tied down.'

'But when I came along, you were? Great! I hope *I'm* not boring you – we wouldn't want that, would we?'

I put a twenty under my coffee cup. Issy Smugge pays her way, thank you very much.

'Don't be like that, Iss. You're overreacting.'

That was the final straw. I jumped up and gave him the rarely seen death stare.

'Get lost, Johnnie Smugge! I don't want to see you again till tonight. You think about what you did.'

And with that, I turned on my heel and marched off down the street. I was furious, tingling all over and with my heart beating in double time. It was only just after ten and the whole day stretched ahead of me. I had planned a lovely, lazy day with my husband, but he could whistle for it. Issy Smugge was having a rubbish morning, but Bella Neville was massively excited about the thought of wandering around some galleries and enjoying her own company. **#metime #artandculture**

I'd forgotten how much I love galleries. I took in a couple of interesting exhibitions (surrealism and photography) then headed out for a well-deserved lunch. When I checked my phone, there were three messages from Johnnie, apologising and offering to take me anywhere I liked. I ignored them. Issy Smugge cannot be bought.

Back at the flat, a contrite husband awaited. Say what you will about Mummy, she was a strong female role model for Suze and me growing up. OK, she spent a lot of her time shouting at Daddy and ordering the help around, but she was never content to do what she was told. Her generation were supposed to marry well, raise a family and throw successful dinner parties. She started her own business, survived a catastrophic break-up and ran her own show. Somewhere along the line, she forgot about being a nice person, but you can't have everything.

In similar circumstances, Mummy would never have caved in and apologised for her behaviour. In that respect, I am certainly made in her image. Johnnie rose from his chair and came towards me, arms outstretched.

'I'm so sorry, Iss. I should never have said what I did.'

I allowed him to embrace me, then gave it to him straight between the eyes.

'You're right. You shouldn't. I've been thinking about it all day and you need to make amends. You've allowed me to carry a huge burden of guilt all these years that wasn't all mine. And while we're at it, there's some other stuff I want to sort out.'

Strike while the iron's hot and all that. I told him how disappointed I was that he spent so much time away when he had been the one to convince me to move up to Suffolk. I pointed out that the burden of parenting and emotional support for the children was falling squarely on my shoulders. I berated him again for his behaviour to Claire and Tom and told him he was a snob. Which he is. And I finished off by telling him that I was going to start going to church when I felt like it and that was down to me, not him.

Bosh, as I believe some sections of society say. He looked aghast. I fixed him with a steely glare and told him to chew it all over while I got ready. And with that, I turned on my heel for the second time in twelve hours and retired to the bathroom. #empoweredwoman #callaspadeaspade

Back at home on Sunday, I felt like a new woman. I'd texted Sofija on Saturday morning to say that we were staying over an extra night and her reply was not exactly forthcoming. And quite right too! What was I thinking, playing fast and loose with her life like that? On Sunday morning, I walked into the house, hugged the children and invited her to come and have a coffee with me in the garden. She looked absolutely terrified. Have I become such a monster?

'Sofija, we need to talk. I think we both know what's going on here.'

The poor girl fiddled with her hair and went as pale as an Egyptian cotton Oxford pillowcase.

'Isabella, I don't know what to say. Please…'

I interrupted. 'I realise that I've been selfish. I've assumed far too much and done my own thing without thinking of you and your needs. I want to apologise, from the bottom of my heart. I don't know what we'd do without you. We all love you and you're part of our family.'

She burst into tears and said something in Latvian, which wasn't going to move the conversation on one jot. After a few minutes, she calmed down. We chatted for about half an hour and when we came back indoors again, I felt that I had done a truly good thing. We'd agreed on a pay rise and a weekly meeting to discuss everything in an honest and open fashion. Seeing us walking back in together, Sofija's eyes red and her cheeks pale, Johnnie stood up and looked horrified. My tirade at the flat had clearly had quite an effect on him.

I gave him the gist of the conversation and left it that. He looked relieved and offered to take us all out for lunch. We went to a gorgeous little bistro near the beach and had the most wonderful meal. Afterwards, the children played on the beach and the three of us sat on the sea wall watching them in a companionable silence.

Johnnie couldn't have been more charming for the rest of the weekend. He took the children out for a long bike ride and told me to do whatever I wanted in their absence. That's a bit more like it.

On Monday morning, I received a nasty shock. Brygita, my cleaner, is taciturn to say the least, but boy, can she clean! My taps are always shiny, my porcelain gleaming and my floors immaculate. She's a woman of few words (English ones, anyway) and always seem to have something against the world. Sofija is the only person who can get through to her. I gave up long ago.

On Mondays, she works from nine o'clock to one. I had come back into the kitchen to make myself some lunch when I found her texting with a scowl on her face, the smell of bleach hanging heavy in the air.

'Hello, Brygita! You've done a wonderful job. Thank you so much.'

Mummy drilled the importance of good manners into us from the egg, and when even confronted with a face that could stop a clock, something prompted me to be as charming as possible. A complete waste of time, as it turned out.

'Isabella, I am leaving. I have found other job. I give you month's notice.'

Like Sofija, Brygita struggles with her definite articles, which gives her rare utterances a strangely prophetic quality. I've often heard her speaking in Polish on her phone and wished I could understand what she was saying.

'Oh, gosh, Brygita, really? I am sorry. Can I say anything to change your mind? A pay review, perhaps?'

'No. I have other job. I tell you this. I work four weeks and I go.'

That seemed fairly clear. Expressing my regret one more time, I smiled charmingly and double-checked that she wasn't leaving my service because of some deeply buried grudge or inadvertent insult.

'I do hope that you've been happy working here. We've loved having you…' (a massive exaggeration). 'Are you quite sure there isn't anything I can say to encourage you to stay?'

She looked at me as though I were an inadequately seasoned bowl of *rosół*.

'I have boyfriend. He move to London. He say to me I go with him. So I not work for you any more. Goodbye.'

I watched her stride across the kitchen, heard the door slam and realised I'd better find a new cleaner double quick. Perhaps it was the Omega Three in my smoked mackerel salad, but as I sat at the island, so recently vacated by my cleaner, a brilliant thought popped into my mind.

With my new agreement with Sofija, and Brygita going, I needed to create a new position: someone who would clean, do all the washing, ironing and bed-making and jobs too menial for Sofija. I googled local employment agencies and came up with three. Half an hour on the phone secured me four interviews. All I had to do now was tell Sofija the glad tidings.

Sometimes, I wonder how I keep all my plates in the air. Hard on the heels of the news of Brygita's departure, I got a call from Kevin.

'I hate to tell you this, Isabella, but we've found woodworm in the floorboards. There's also some rising damp and some kind of infestation. It's going to take a fair bit of work before we can even start thinking about painting and carpeting.'

I asked him to give me an idea of costs and timings. Both were fairly depressing. It's not that we don't have the money – we do, and this being such an old house, you've got to expect to invest in repairs and improvements. I gave him the go-ahead and off he went to magic some more workmen out of the ether.

I was just about to head back down to the studio to do some more writing when my mobile rang again. It was Dave this time to tell me that we needed to think carefully about reroofing as we had to comply with listing regulations. No sooner had I finished with him than I got a call from the school. Chloë had been sick. Could I please come and fetch her? Obviously, I was going to get no work done today. Sighing to myself, I headed off to pick her up. **#awomanswork #busybusybusy #multitasking**

My poor little girl was in a terrible state. We walked home and I installed her in the family room. Her hands were burning hot, as was her forehead, and her eyes were bleary.

'Can you stay with me, Mummy?' she asked in a weak little voice. 'I don't want to be by myself.'

What mother could resist such an appeal? As she laid her hot little head against my shoulder, I remembered my vow to spend more quality time with my children. I texted Lauren to ask if she could bring Finn and Elsie home for me. Sofija had gone to Ipswich and wasn't going to be back until teatime, so I was flying solo.

Thank goodness for Lauren! Back came her text.

'Of course, babes. Poor little Chloë! Wish her better from me xx'

I love Lauren. I turned on the TV and, at my daughter's request, selected the children's channel (the one without adverts) and resigned myself to an afternoon of manically grinning young people dressed in luridly coloured separates singing songs about anthropomorphised animals. After twenty minutes, Chloë was asleep. Thank heavens. I found a documentary on early medieval European art and immersed myself in it.

Chloë was sick three times in the night. Elsie wet herself (most unusually). By morning, Sofija and I were hollow-eyed shadows of our former selves. We had four sets of bedding to wash, plus a heap of towels. Sofija, God bless her, had put the first load on at two in the morning and the second at five. I volunteered to do the school run while she stayed at home to keep an eye on Chloë and hang out the wash.

Claire was in the playground looking very tired. I wanted to give her a big hug, but decided against it, just in case I passed the sick bug on. I contented myself with waving and smiling, while miming copious vomiting. That made her laugh. It also put smiles on the faces of the Year One and Two teachers who, I realised too late, were standing right behind her.

Walking out with Lauren, I thanked her again for her sterling support. I expressed concern that I might have infected her and her entire household.

'You're all right, darling. Nits, yes. Worms, yes. Throat infections, yes. But the girls are hardly ever sick and we seem to miss it every time. How about I take Elsie home with me for tea and she can sleep over tonight? Give you a bit of a break.'

Lauren is the kindest person I think I've ever met. I felt it incumbent upon me to share the news of Elsie's bed-wetting.

'Don't worry about it. The little ones rinse themselves on a regular basis! That's why God invented washing machines.'

Nothing seems to faze Lauren. I returned to the house of pestilence to find Sofija grimly scraping vomit from Chloë's duvet cover and firing up the carpet cleaner. There had been an eruption in the family room. Wordlessly, I turned on the coffee machine and went upstairs to strip Elsie's bed. Today was a day that only strong coffee, and plenty of it, could fix.

By lunchtime, we'd done another three loads of washing and Chloë had been sick twice. I'd drunk so much coffee that my eyelids made a scratching noise when I blinked and my hands were twitching slightly. Poor Sofija looked exhausted.

My mobile rang. What now? Had Finn been sick? Was Elsie suffering from rampant nits? Had Kevin discovered deathwatch beetle in the walls? It was only Charlene, Jake's mum, asking if Finn would like to come back to theirs for tea. I shared the news of our current state of health.

'I'll take the risk. Jake's hardly ever sick. He's got guts of iron. Is Finn OK to walk back from ours around seven?'

I confirmed that this was fine and thanked her from the bottom of my heart. I passed the news on to Sofija, who sighed and clapped her hand to her heart.

'Thank goodness! I cannot take much more today.'

I knew how she felt. Strangely, surrounded by vomit and urine-soaked sheets, sleep-deprived and over-caffeinated, our relationship seemed back in place. When the noise of Chloë gagging floated in from the family room, she rolled her eyes at me in the old way and joined my vomiting daughter with a stack of towels. I trotted outside with the washing basket and filled it with freshly laundered duvet covers, pillowcases and sheets before hanging out the next load. It was strangely soothing.

Returning to the house, I found Chloë slumped over a large metal bowl, dry heaving. It was going to be a long day.

Sofija and I braced ourselves for another hideous night. Thank goodness, Chloë eventually stopped being sick and fell asleep under her beloved blanket on the sofa in the family room. She looked so peaceful that we decided to leave her there. Sofija offered to make up a bed next to her, but I sent her upstairs to sleep. She looked quite peaky, so I told her to sleep in. Finn could take himself to school if I overslept. I wrote a note to him on a piece of kitchen roll with a discarded felt-tip pen.

'In family room with Chloë. If I don't wake up in time for school, can you do breakfast and take yourself? Love you! Mummy xxx'

It took me five attempts. Naturally, we only buy the very best brand of kitchen roll and it's so absorbent that the ink from the pen disappeared as fast as I could apply it. **#firstworldproblems**

I betook myself to the blow-up bed, which was slightly too short for me. Once I'd contorted myself to fit, I tried to go to sleep. This was no mean feat. Sofija and I drink a lot of coffee between us, but we usually have our last cup at around four o'clock. We were still knocking back double-strength lattes at eight and now I was paying the price.

At some point during the night, I must have lost consciousness. In my dreams, I was searching for something which kept slipping out of my grasp. The kitchen was crawling with huge worms which were threatening to eat us, while Mimi banged on the window, shouting, 'You're down to five followers, Isabella! I'm going to have to let you go.' I kept pleading with her to give me another chance, but then she turned into Mummy and started chasing me with a hairbrush. As I cowered under the coats in the boot room, she dropped a huge stack of interiors magazines on my head. The noise of them hitting the floor woke me up with a start.

I had no idea where I was for a minute. My nostrils were full of the smell of carpet cleaner and I had rolled off the bed and was now curled up on the floor. I pride myself on my flexibility, but the Issy Smugge who creaked her way into a sitting position was more like a woman in her seventies than the still young and extremely fit Best Blog Photographer of the Year. After a minute or two, I rubbed my burning eyes and realised that the noise that had awoken me was the post landing on the mat. Chloë was still fast asleep and the clock on the wall told me it was gone ten o'clock.

I staggered into the kitchen. My note to Finn was still there, but there were signs of a hasty breakfast and the front door was unlocked, so I assumed he'd made it to school. I rang the office and got the ever-cheery Mrs Hill.

'Yes, he's here, no need to worry, Mrs Smugge! How's Chloë this morning?'

I gave her the update, accepted her good wishes for our health and happiness and eyed up the coffee machine. The very notion of putting another drop of caffeine into my body repulsed me, so I made myself an extremely milky hot chocolate and sat there sipping it, gazing out into the garden. I hadn't felt this rough since Elsie was first born.

I drained my mug and tiptoed upstairs to check on Sofija. Her door was ajar and I could see that the curtains were still closed. I was glad she was catching up on her sleep. I pulled on some clothes and ambled back downstairs again. I checked my socials, posted a couple of photos and left it at that.

I picked up a novel and curled up on the big chair in the family room to get started on it. I'm not a great one for fiction. I read on holiday, of course, but the rest of the time I'm too busy. Today, however, Isabella M Smugge was giving herself permission to switch off. After a couple of chapters, the words began to swim in front of my eyes and I nodded off to sleep again.

I woke up with yet another start to see Sofija folding up the blanket on the sofa. I gazed blearily at her for a second.

'Where's Chloë?'

'She is having shower. Her temperature is back to normal, and she wants to freshen up.'

I was delighted. I stretched, yawned and uncurled myself.

'Thank you for letting me sleep this morning, Isabella. I feel better now.'

Sofija was smiling her old smile at me. I grinned back.

'Me too. Coffee?'

She stared at me for a moment, then we both fell about laughing. It wasn't that funny, but you know when you just can't stop? Finally, we started to calm down and wiping the tears from our eyes, made our way into the kitchen to face up to what was left of the day. **#laughtertherapy #coffeenocoffee**

On Wednesday evening, Johnnie returned from London looking disgustingly fit, healthy and well rested. I'd texted him the news of Chloë's sick bug and he'd sent me a series of encouraging messages which were of absolutely no help at all. Sofija and I could hardly keep our eyes open and neither of us felt particularly hungry. Since no dinner was forthcoming (we were both too worn out to cook), Johnnie suggested a Chinese, which was met with cries of rapture by Finn and Elsie. Chloë burst into tears and wept copiously all down her clean pyjamas.

'What on earth's the matter now?' Johnnie wasn't being very sympathetic.

'It's so unfair! We never have Chinese and I can't eat it in case I'm sick and they're going to have it and I'm not.'

She dissolved into wracking sobs and put her head down on the island in a theatrical fashion. I mouthed, 'You go, I'll deal with this,' at Johnnie and mustered what was left of my natural empathic mothering style to comfort my weeping daughter. The door banged behind the three of them as Sofija and I tried to calm Chloë down. After extravagant promises of as much Chinese as she could eat in the near future, she calmed down and consented to be put to bed with her favourite book.

Half an hour later, the kitchen was filled with the fragrance of the mysterious East. Sofija, looking pale and tired, declined to eat anything and departed. I nibbled on some prawn crackers and then excused myself. The moment my head hit the pillow, I was out like a light. I presume Johnnie did bedtime. If there's any justice in this world, he'll be doing it for the rest of the week. **#equalparenting #sauceforthegoose**

I woke with a start. This was becoming a habit. Checking my phone, I found it was a quarter past nine. I jumped out of bed, pulled on my dressing gown and ran downstairs. The dishwasher was whooshing away contentedly to itself, there were crumbs around the toaster and someone had left the butter and jam out. Finn and Elsie's book bags had gone and the door was unlocked. I texted Johnnie.

'Ru on school run? Just woke up xx'

Back came his reply.

'Thought I'd let you both sleep. What do you fancy for breakfast? Go back to bed, I'll bring it up. Xx'

I winced. Far too much had been brought up in my household over the past few days, but the sentiment was charming.

'Pot of lapsang souchong, two slices of rye toast on medium setting with butter and hedgerow jelly please. Love you. xx'

He did ask!

Chloë was pretty much back to normal by Thursday teatime and managed a bowl of Sofija's chicken soup, made to her mother's recipe. Sadly, by that time, the bug had got its deadly tentacles wrapped around the internal workings of another member of the Smugge household. Sofija brought up her lunch (*borscht,* so unfortunate) in the cloakroom and staggered up to bed, clutching her stomach. From what I could ascertain from regular visits to her room, she spent most of the next twenty-four hours with her head down the loo in the en suite. That messed up all the poor girl's plans for her long weekend away in London, but I can make it up to her once she gets better.

165

I encouraged Johnnie to throw himself into parenting duties, which he did with good grace. We had a quiet weekend, recovering from the vicissitudes of the previous few days.

Ted, incandescent with joy, shared the news that the gooseberry bushes were loaded with fruit and ready to pick. I sent Johnnie and the children down to the fruit cage and they returned with four huge baskets of little green globes. Gooseberry bushes guard their treasure jealously with spikes and thorns, as evidenced by the scratches all over Johnnie's hands and arms. He weighed their haul and discovered it was a whopping 18lbs. I had no idea what I was supposed to do with so much fruit. Nanny used to make jam, and I do believe gooseberry crumble is delicious, but I certainly didn't fancy spending hours topping and tailing the darn things with nail scissors.

Our gooseberry problem was solved by Ted on Monday morning.

'Ladyship always froze some of her fruit and gave the rest to the ladies at church. They made jam for her and sold the rest. For charity. Babies in Africa.'

I duly froze several ice-cream containers full, put the rest in the outhouse and texted Claire.

Do you want 15lbs of gooseberries? Ted says the church makes jam and sells it for Africans. Do not understand. How are you feeling today? xx'

Back came her answer.

'Not personally, but thank you! Lady H used to give a lot of her fruit to Mary, Sue and Wendy at church. They're the jam makers. We sell it to help a charity which works with young mums and babies in Kenya. Still a bit rough. How ru?? Xx'

That explained it. I could tell that I was coming out of the sleep-deprived fog which had robbed me (albeit temporarily) of my usual acuity. Jam! Of course! This was yet another way I could give back to my community and build on my social responsibility. That would be one in the eye for Lavinia. Graciously giving of my resources while helping those less fortunate than myself in far-off lands. Smiling to myself, I sat down to compose an email to Mimi.

My campaign to add to my everywoman relatability, become a better person and get one over on Lavinia Harcourt began in earnest on Monday afternoon. Sitting in my studio gazing out over the garden (which was looking picture perfect thanks to Ted's efforts), I planned out the many philanthropic activities that would shield me from Lavinia's spiteful prose.

At school, I marched up to Claire to chat through my church attendance. What was the dress code? Was there an after party? Should my phone be switched to silent throughout? Was I expected to sing? How would Tom feel if I photographed portions of the proceedings?

Claire chewed her lip for a moment then replied that I could wear anything I felt comfortable with, that they gathered for coffee, biscuits and chat after the service which she supposed could be described (loosely) as an after party, that Tom would prefer it if I muted my phone, that I could sing or not as I wished and that if I needed photos, it might be best to come along on a weekday and take them.

I enquired if I could book a space at her Friday group. The lip chewing gave way to a broad grin and then a noise I can only describe as a chortle.

'You're so lovely, Isabella! I'm not laughing at you. You don't need to book a space. It's just a bunch of girls sitting in my front room drinking coffee and chatting. It's a safe space where we explore different aspects of faith, ask questions and get to know each other better.'

I assured her that she could count on my support for this week's session and we walked out of the playground, passing several knots of earnestly chatting parents. Several of them were holding clipboards and frowning. I was puzzled until I remembered that the school fête was coming up. These must be the PTA members. We'd never had any trouble getting help and support for our events at Beech Grove. I wondered where this school was going wrong. I made a note to find out more about the committee and see if they needed my expert help. Looking at the furrowed brows and set jaws, I was fairly sure they did. #fundraisingfun

Armed with a list of phone numbers supplied by Claire, I rang the jam makers and offered up my abundant fruit harvest. This was met with rapture by all three. The whole thing was a bit of a time suck, to be honest, as I had to listen to them telling me how marvellous Lady Hamilton had been, what a difference the jam made, how much they loved being able to use local produce and what a transformational job the people in Kenya were doing. I made the right noises and told them I'd text when the next batch was ready. I decided to contract out the job of fruit picking to the children. The blackcurrants were close to fruiting, according to Ted, and their juice is ruinous to the nails.

In an idle hour (and it's not often that I have one of those), I spent some time looking back over my diary entries. I suppose it is just possible that I come across as a little venal in parts. In fact, nothing could be further from the truth. I'm as charitable, altruistic and philanthropic as the next woman. Ever since I relocated up here, I've reached out to my community, given of myself in my limited spare time and stepped out of my comfort zone. London Issy Smugge would never have set foot in a church except for weddings and christenings. I'm sure God understands. It was fine in the old days when people had nothing better to do than toil in the fields and go to church twice on a Sunday. I have such a full life, and if I'm to reach that holy grail of three million followers, I need to put the hours in.

The week shot by in a whirl of writing, photographing, editing and child-related activities. Completely restored to her former self, Sofija took her time off and I was alone at home with the children for four days on the trot. Either they're getting older and more responsible or I'm becoming a better parent. That familiar feeling of terror that has dogged my footsteps ever since I gazed at my first positive pregnancy test seems to be receding.

On Friday, having a done a last-minute check on hair and nails for the children (school photos this morning), I headed off to the vicarage. I wasn't quite sure what to expect, but I'd foreshadowed the whole thing for my followers with a series of little teasers. Claire had explained that it wouldn't be appropriate for me to photograph the group, but Issy Smugge is an old hand at delicate allusions so I found a way round it.

The grey-haired woman from Messy Church was sitting on the sofa, gazing earnestly at a pile of Christian paperbacks. Claire introduced us.

'Sue, this is Isabella, my friend from school. She's joining us today. Isabella, this is Sue who runs the group with me.'

I enquired if she was the self-same Sue to whom I had recently spoken about soft fruit and she admitted that she was. She seemed perfectly friendly, although I stand by my view that a decent haircut and getting her colours properly sorted would have done her the world of good.

After a few minutes, the rest of the group started to arrive. Sue announced that we would be talking about forgiveness again. It seemed that the previous week the group had explored this concept and it had been a lively and thought-provoking session. For my benefit, Sue ran through the main takeaways. Apparently, we need to forgive others, especially those who do us wrong; forgiveness is a choice; just because you forgive someone doesn't make what they did to you right; and it's a lifelong process sometimes. I had questions immediately.

'But that doesn't make sense. Why should I forgive someone who's done a terrible thing to me? Surely getting revenge is better.'

There were murmurs of agreement from the rest of the group, Lauren excepted.

'As humans, that's our natural inclination. If someone hurts us, we want to hurt them back. Even if we don't get revenge, resentment can build up and the other person doesn't even know we're feeling that way. Anger festers and it's not good for us.'

I chewed this over for a bit. I could see her point, but I certainly couldn't imagine how on earth you could truly forgive someone who had done something appalling. What about murderers? A few more questions popped into my mind, but as the new girl, I didn't want to dominate the conversation.

The two hours shot by and, before I knew it, it was half past eleven and everyone was off. Sue came over and touched me on the arm.

'How did you find that, Isabella? We've thrown you in at the deep end a bit.'

I couldn't agree with all of it and I didn't understand above half of it, but I wanted to find out more. Now wasn't the time, though, as Sue was off to some meeting or other with a batch of assorted vicars and I had to get back home to work.

I was about to take my mug into the kitchen when Claire let out a sound that was halfway between a groan and a scream. She was bending over in her chair, holding her stomach and watching a dark red stain spread over her trousers. Sue and I stood frozen for a second, then we leapt into action. Sue rushed to the bathroom to find towels and I changed my plans in an instant and offered to take Claire to hospital. Tom was out at a meeting and Joel was having his nap. Lauren came out of the kitchen, tea towel in her hand, looking horrified. Within seconds, we agreed that she would stay to look after Joel.

The journey to hospital was short and terrifying. It's only about fifteen minutes down the A12, but it felt like the longest quarter of an hour of my life. When we got there, Claire was whisked away and I was left sitting in the waiting room with a pile of bloody towels. At this time of day, I would usually be on my phone, working, but this morning, my mind full of new thoughts, and fear and concern for my friend, I couldn't have cared less if I was trending or had new followers. And that's not something I thought I'd ever hear myself say. **#truefriendship**

Claire's been admitted and stabilised. The baby's fine, but they're going to keep her in over the weekend to do scans and monitor her. Turns out her placenta isn't playing ball. I texted Lauren, and between us and the rest of the Friday group, we worked out a meal and childcare rota to make it easier on the vicarage household. I think this is what normal people do. It felt pretty good, I have to say. Sofija is still off, so I'll be doing all the cooking myself. I found it strangely grounding. I'll be making jam and wearing a ruffled pinny at this rate! Perhaps I could add baking and patisserie to my specialities. I can see my grid now, full of crème patisserie and croquembouche. **#mercimadame #mangezvous #queenofthetent**

I was exhausted. The baking blogger idea was stupid. I was so accustomed to having unlimited headspace to get on with my work that having a few days of cooking, looking after children and performing mercy dashes to hospital was sapping my strength. How do ordinary people manage? I wondered.

At pick-up time, Lauren and I stayed in the playground for a good half hour, answering anxious questions from other parents about Claire. Everyone seems to love her. I hope she won't be in hospital for too long.

Over on the field, the PTA parents were rushing about in a frenzied manner, laying out chairs and tables, humping boxes around and generally making a bit of a mess. I was sorely tempted to go over and offer my assistance in streamlining their activities, but I was just too tired. Plus, Lauren warned me not to as several of them are apparently on the edge. It seems that running PTA activities in rural Suffolk is not at all the same as it was back home at Beech Grove.

When I walked into the kitchen, Johnnie did a double take.

'Whoa! You look worn out, Iss. What's going on?'

I thanked him for his tactful greeting, gave him a kiss and wondered if it was too early for gin. The girls rushed at him, demanding horsey rides round the garden, and Finn gave him a sideways grin. It was a beautiful day, not a cloud in the sky, so I brewed us a coffee and we went and sat on the garden bench and watched the children bouncing on the trampoline. I gave him a brief rundown of the week's events. He shook his head.

'Dear me. Should I pop round to see Tom?'

I wasn't sure how helpful a visit from Johnnie might be, but it was a nice thought. We lapsed into silence, drinking in the birdsong, the fragrance, the breeze sighing through the trees. It's not often I stop and look and listen, but today seemed like a pretty good time to start. You just never know what's around the corner. Sometimes I think of Johnnie and me, retired, perhaps with grandchildren, looking back over rich, satisfying lives, and I don't want to have any regrets.

I had a brilliant idea.

'Why don't we go to the beach and have fish and chips? It's a beautiful evening. I'm too tired to cook and it would be a lovely way to round off the week.'

So we did. It was brilliant. Hot, salty chips, crisp batter and meltingly soft fish. Does it get any better than sitting on a Blue Flag beach with your amazing family, gazing out to sea? No. It doesn't. That was a rhetorical question.

Back home, we put the children to bed and poured ourselves a nice, crisp Chablis. Tomorrow, I'm giving myself the day off to go to the school fête. Isabella M Smugge is the luckiest girl in the world. **#lovemyfamily #winningatlife #suffolkshores**

I woke late on Saturday morning. When I rolled over in bed and peered at my phone, I was amazed to see it was gone nine. Johnnie's side of the bed was empty. I stretched and yawned. The previous night had gone very well. Friday evenings have replaced our old date nights back home in London. Absence, however short, does seem to make the heart, and a few other body parts, grow fonder! As I lay back on my pillows, I heard the rattle of china and Johnnie appeared with a breakfast tray. Is there a greater treat for a hard-working woman than to be brought breakfast in bed by the best-looking man in East Anglia? I think not. Another rhetorical question.

Johnnie knows I try to keep my carb intake low, but I do love bread, and from time to time it can't hurt. He presented me with a latte and a pile of toast with butter and a china dish of pinkish jam. It seems that upon going downstairs to get the post, he opened the front door to find the jam sitting on our doorstep with a little note. The first of the church jam makers past the post was Wendy, who had turned our gooseberries into the most delectable preserve ever to pass my lips. Johnnie hopped back into bed and we sat in a companionable silence, crunching our way through the toast and jam and sipping our coffee. The curtains were open and I could see the trees waving gently in the breeze, and beyond to the church behind the hedge. Idyllic.

For weeks, the PTA had been sending out a constant stream of letters in the book bags, their tone becoming increasingly desperate. My conscience was clear as I'd donated a shedload of unwanted gifts and samples. I certainly wasn't going to sacrifice my own precious time running a stall.

When we walked on to the field, I was impressed. There was colourful bunting everywhere, the field was packed with inflatables, games, stalls and tables and the playground was covered with exciting-looking vehicles. Johnnie and I strolled around hand in hand gazing at trucks, tractors, classic cars and motorbikes.

Everywhere I looked, there were harassed-looking women clutching clipboards and hissing instructions at each other. Each wore a badge saying 'Supporting Play with the PTA'. I had no idea what this meant.

Johnnie took the girls down to the far end of the field where they could ride around in a pony cart.

I took a seat by the tea tent and surveyed the scene.

Lauren appeared. Her daughters were hanging off her, demanding money for ice creams. She sank down on to the bench beside me.

'Will you shut up! I don't want you getting ice cream all down your fronts before your performance. Honestly, they've been nagging me for money since we got here! Where are your kids?'

'Finn's on the inflatables with Jake and the girls are having a pony ride with Johnnie.'

This set Lauren's three off.

'Pony ride! Pony ride! We want to go on the ponies with Chloë and Elsie!'

With a sigh that seemed to come up from her boots, Lauren dug a crumpled tenner out of her pocket and gave it to her eldest. With yelps of excitement, they ran off down the field towards the ponies.

'I'm going to be broke by the end of the day. They keep on at me for money for food and sweeties and plastic tat. Poor Scott's been roped in to helping with the barbecue so I'm in charge.'

Scott is Lauren's husband.

There was a sudden burst of screechy feedback from the sound system which stopped everyone in their tracks, and Mrs Tennant, the head teacher, addressed us all in mellifluous tones.

'Good afternoon, children, parents, friends and families. Welcome to our school fête. Before we begin, I'd like to say a huge thank you to our PTA, who have been working very hard to put on this amazing day for us.'

There was a ripple of applause and the PTA ladies stopped dashing around for a minute. Mrs Tennant gave us a full rundown of the day's activities, reminded us to buy our raffle tickets and burbled on for a while about new play equipment. Just in case we didn't know, she informed us that play is most beneficial to children's learning and that she believes that child-driven activities in a safe and open environment help with the emotional, social, physical and cognitive development of primary school children.

Once the lecture was at an end, she exited and was replaced by the beleaguered nursery teacher and a ragged crocodile of tiny, confused children. We were then treated to something calling itself a dance. Some of the children hopped on one leg, others whirled round and round, several stuck their thumbs in their mouths and stared into space and one stole the show by announcing, 'I need wee wee,' and urinating lavishly on the grass. This would never have happened at Beech Grove.

At this point, Johnnie appeared with the girls. We made our way over to the barbecue. A long queue had formed and delicious smells were wafting our way. I quizzed Lauren about the PTA badges.

'It's because they're fundraising to replace all the old play equipment. Mrs T is very keen on play-driven learning. They raised enough to do the gym trail last year and this year it's a play fort and a kick wall. They're struggling because that kind of stuff is so expensive.'

A marvellous thought was forming in my mind. Mimi had been nagging me about social action and this seemed to be the ideal forum. What could be better than a brand-new selection of play equipment bought and paid for by a caring, philanthropic member of the community? Nothing that I could think of.

We reached the head of the queue. Lauren introduced me to Scott, who was furiously cooking burgers. He seemed nice. I whipped out a fifty and paid for everyone's lunch before

Lauren could protest. It's the least I can do. **#summerbarbie**
#sustainablelunch

The day wore on. I paraded around, buying raffle tickets,
winning myself a selection of tinned goods in the tombola and
guessing the name of a slightly sinister cross-eyed teddy bear.

In between the children's performances we were treated to a
display of taekwondo, some majorette marching and a troupe
of belly dancers. Clad in glittery black and white costumes and
fluttering veils, they gyrated around seductively, waving little
sticks and drawing the eye of every man in the place with their
undulating hips. As I stood watching, a flustered-looking
woman came over, clutching a walkie-talkie.

'Maddie – it's Kate. The urn's blown again. Can you get Scott
to have a look? I know. Yes, I know he is. No, I haven't. Yes, I
will. No, I haven't yet, but I will.'

She ran her hand through her already ruffled hair. Her
walkie-talkie bleeped.

'What now? She can't! No! She didn't! I'm coming up.'

I was intrigued. I'd seen the woman around in the
playground but had no idea who she was. I followed her up past
the tractors where a group of PTA ladies were leaning wearily
against the wall. Feigning interest in a collection of motorbikes
and classic cars, I eavesdropped shamelessly.

'If anything else goes wrong, I'm resigning. Have we covered
the gaps in the volunteering, Maddie?'

'Scott's going to man the inflatables when Andy goes home.
I've calmed the WI ladies down and the urn's working again.
The face painters are happy now I've moved them under the
tree and the earring woman packed up and left after the fight
with the garland people. I won't ask her back next year.'

A miserable-looking woman, with a pair of overgrown
eyebrows in desperate need of work (don't these people
subscribe to beauty blogs?), piped up. I moved closer to
scrutinise the interior of a Frogeye Sprite.

'We ran out of loo rolls, Kate. I told you we should have
ordered more. One of the toilets blocked, the generator broke

176

three times, half the volunteers didn't turn up, someone was sick by the pagoda and I've had loads of complaints about how much everything costs. I'm resigning.'

This kind of slipshod organisation was never tolerated when Nicki Hartington and I were running the show at Beech Grove. Sensing a golden opportunity, I walked over and introduced myself. These people clearly needed me. #helpinghand

Issy Smugge doesn't let the grass grow under her feet. By the end of the fête, I'd agreed to take over the role of secretary when the new term starts, replacing the woman with the eyebrows. I'd also had a confab with Mrs Tennant and the PTA chair, Maddie, and agreed to make a charitable donation to cover the remaining costs of the play equipment. This offer had been received with dazed rapture. The PTA seemed exhausted and beaten down. Wait until I sprinkle a little of my magic dust upon their ragged ranks!

Clutching a bag of assorted tinned goods and the teddy bear (blast!), I ambled back up the hill to our house. Johnnie had taken the children home earlier as they were exhibiting signs of poor behaviour brought on by too much sugar. I felt it had been a most fruitful day. #newbeginnings #reachingout

Sofija's taking most of this week off to visit friends in Hertfordshire. I'll be OK on my own. I've arranged to meet up with Mrs Tennant on Friday to firm up the details of my offer. She is most gratifyingly appreciative.

On Monday, Claire was discharged. I have to say, I thought they would have kept her in for longer than that. I went straight round to see her at the vicarage and found her propped up in bed, looking pale and tired. I can't tell you how delighted I was to see her. We sat and chatted and I made her lunch. I don't know what I'd do without her friendship and I told her so. For some reason, I felt quite tearful. I caught her up with the goings-on at the fête and told her I was joining the PTA.

'You're a powerhouse, Isabella. I truly don't know how you do all you do. Just remember to give yourself some time. I'd hate to see you overdoing it.'

I laughed. As if.

On Monday afternoon I had interviews for the new housekeeper. The first three candidates were all good, but number four stood out from the off. Very well presented, polite and proactive, which is what I'm looking for. I ran through the list of tasks and gave her a brief tour. Upon our return to the kitchen, I noticed her eyeing up my spice cupboard and twitching slightly.

'Mrs Smugge, I hope you won't be offended, but I can't leave your spices in that formation. Do you mind?'

With that, she moved over and started putting them all in alphabetical order. When she'd finished, looking slightly abashed, she explained that she suffered from OCD. I hired her on the spot. Bingo!

On Tuesday, I got to work on the next batch of content and images. Kevin and Dave were busy with their squad of workmen down at the south wing. Today was the day they would take up the carpet and floorboards in Sofija's old room as they suspected there was a leaky pipe, causing damp. Occasionally, I wish I'd never gone down the road of remodelling, but you can't stand still in this life.

I finished work at three. I ambled down to have a look at the fruit cages and was pleased to see that the blackcurrants are ripening nicely in the sun. Breathing in the pure Suffolk air, I gazed up the sky and thanked whoever was listening for my lovely life. This year is going so quickly. I can't believe tomorrow will be 1st July.

As I served tea, there was a knock on the window and Kevin appeared.

'OK, Isabella, that leak is fairly extensive, but I think we've got it under control. One of the lads found something under the carpet and didn't like to throw it away in case it was important. Here you go.'

He handed me a little plastic bag and waved goodbye.

Once the children were in bed, I pottered around, tidying up. It felt good doing these little normal chores. I noticed that I'd filed black pepper and cumin in the wrong order. Oops.

By ten o'clock, I was ready for bed. I stretched, yawned and prepared to ascend the stairs to my room when I remembered the little plastic bag.

I couldn't understand what I was seeing at first. What were my gift cards from Johnnie's flowers doing under the carpet in Sofija's room? I read the first one and blushed. I didn't remember Johnnie using quite those words in the past, flattering though they were. The second one was even more passionate.

Then, suddenly, like a bolt of lightning from a clear blue sky splitting a tree clean in two, I realised what I was looking at. My heart leapt violently and painfully in my chest.

How could he? And with Sofija, under my nose, the woman I thought was my friend. I dropped the cards as though they were burning coals. I started to look back over the last few months and everything dropped into place. I'm the most stupid, short-sighted woman in the world.

Meredith and her sighting of Johnnie and Sofija walking along hand in hand. Sofija's strange behaviour of late. Johnnie's horror when he saw me at the airport. Those flowers in the flat that weren't my favourite but were clearly hers. The eyebrows and the lashes.

The clock told me it was half past ten. There was only one woman I could call at this hour. I hit speed dial. She answered on the second ring. #betrayal #rage #heartbreak

Isabella M Smugge, loser, betrayed wife, rubbish mother, terrible sister.

I thought I led a charmed life, but torturing myself by reading and rereading Johnnie's words, I was confronted with evidence I couldn't deny. As the moonlight streamed through my kitchen window and the harsh cries of a fox echoed round the garden, the stark, uncompromising truth hit me right between the eyes. Everyone I love leaves me.

I laid my head down on the cool counter top and sobbed as though my heart would break. The anguish of the betrayal was unbearable.

I wiped my eyes, blew my nose and tried to marshal my thoughts. My instinct was to get in the car, drive to the flat and catch the two of them red-handed. But did I really want to see their guilty faces together on the pillow, her hair spread out on my 500 thread count Egyptian cotton slate-grey sheets?

Thank heavens for Mimi. She's not a good person, but she's a top agent. She was on to it the minute she answered the phone last night.

'What do we do when we face a crisis? We stay calm and collected and we think.'

Her rasping tones were the only ones I wanted to hear as I stared at the incriminating words on the cards.

'If you two split up (and that's up to you, my darling), Lavinia will find out. And she'll make capital out of it. Put your feelings to one side and think brand. Isabella M Smugge is family, togetherness, unstudied naturalness, affection. Your readers want to believe in your perfect life. If that comes to an end, we've got a lot of work to do.'

Having Mimi in your corner is like being harnessed to a hang glider on the edge of a Swiss Alp. Danger and uncertainty might be just around the corner, but she never lets go (as long as you keep paying her, of course). The trouble was, my emotions and my business sense had split in two and one was refusing to give the other house room. The obvious thing to do here was to take some deep breaths and have a little chat with Johnnie at the weekend. Plenty of people in our social set have discreet affairs and carry on with their marriages perfectly happily. The trouble was, I didn't seem to be that kind of person.

I didn't sleep that night. At one, I put my pride in my pocket and rang Suze. She sounded anxious.

'Bella! Is everything all right?'

Hearing her voice was the final blow. I dissolved into helpless tears and cried and cried. More than anything in the world, I wanted to see her, for her to hug me and tell me that everything was going to be all right. After a few minutes, I managed to tell her what had happened in a shaking, hoarse voice that didn't seem to be my own.

Suze is such a great listener. I'd forgotten that. She didn't interrupt once, apart from making sad, sympathetic noises when I broke down in tears, which I kept doing. When I'd finished, she didn't leap in and start saying all those awful things people do:

'It could be worse.'

'At least you've had twenty happy years.'

'Plenty more fish in the sea.'

The great thing about talking to your sister is that you don't have to go into all the ins and outs of the whole sorry business. Partly, of course, because he dumped her for another woman (me), which is a tad embarrassing, but mostly because, for years, it was the two of us against the world.

Once I'd finished crying, Suze stopped making sympathetic noises and started talking.

'Bella, I can't tell you how sorry I am to hear all this. I'd do anything to take the pain away for you. What are you going to do?'

All I wanted was for everything to go back to the way it had been. Naturally, I also wanted to give Sofija a good kicking, but at the same time I wanted to ask her why. Haltingly, and with none of my usual eloquent style, I tried to explain.

'Mimi made me promise not to do anything silly. She's really worried that Lavinia will find out and splash it across her column. I kind of don't care, but I do. Do you know what I mean?'

Well, of course she did. At that moment, Lavinia trying to destroy my reputation and my brand paled into insignificance beside the huge smoking hole into which I was gazing.

'When are you going to tell Mummy?'

'I don't know. I'm not feeling strong enough to face it. I can hear her now.'

I put on Mummy's loud, penetrating voice, which has a certain buzz-saw quality at the best of times.

'Good heavens, darling! If you'd listened to me in the first place, none of this would have happened. You've only got yourself to blame. Hang on, I'm just pouring gin on my cornflakes (hic!). Now, what was I saying?'

Peals of laughter echoed down the line as Suze joined in.

'Why don't you girls listen to me? If you'd gone to Château Hautain instead of running off to that silly college with all those dreadful common people, you could have bagged a decent husband with a title.'

'And as for your children! Well! If you'd only shipped them off to a high-achieving boarding school once they were out of nappies, they'd be far less well-adjusted than they are now.'

'I can't believe you've only got two acres! And no moat. I can barely hold my head up at the Golf Club.'

Laughing and chatting like this with the person I loved most in the world was utter bliss. I took a deep breath and blurted out the words I'd been longing to say.

'Suze… I know I sent that message when I was drunk, but I meant every word. And I'm not just saying sorry because of what Johnnie's done. I'd give anything for us to be friends again. I've got no right to ask you after what I did, but please, can you forgive me?'

'Oh, Bella. I'm working on it, I really am. I know I've been holding on to the pain and the resentment for years now and I need to let it go. I'm sorry I said all those things to you.'

My voice wobbled and cracked. 'I just want to be friends again, like we used to be. I've missed that so much, Suze.'

I could hear her crying. 'Me too. More than anything.'

I burst into tears again, this time of mingled happiness and grief, and cried loudly down the phone. Knowing that Suze and I were friends again slightly mitigated the anguish of uncovering Johnnie's treachery.

We talked for hours until, looking out of the window, I saw the first pink streaks of the sunrise across the inky sky.

'The Neville girls are back in business! Watch out Johnnie Smugge!' **#lovemysister #backtogetheragain**

July

There's a lot to be said for a lifelong habit of denial. You do get terribly good at wearing a mask. Sashaying into the school playground holding my daughters' hands and watching my son rush ahead of me, you'd have thought I didn't have a care in the world. I worked the Reception line, chatted to the teachers, kissed the girls and gave of myself without stinting.

I couldn't waste any more time stewing at home while my husband and au pair got up to goodness knows what in London. I needed to have concrete proof and get our lives back on track. Ambling out of the playground with Lauren, I asked if she would be able to take the girls home for tea that night and have them for a sleepover.

'I know it's a huge ask on a Wednesday, with it being a school night. A big family issue has come up unexpectedly and I have to go down to London. Sofija's off and my mother-in-law isn't around to help. Obviously, I'll make it up to you.'

Lauren was all concern. She's such a lovely girl. I invited her back to mine, apologising for the mess. She stared at me.

'You think this is messy? I lost the phone the other day and found it in the cat's litter tray! That's messy. Scott ran out of pants last week because I couldn't keep up with the washing. I wish I had a beautiful big house like yours.'

It occurred to me that Lauren probably didn't have flowers sent to her very often, so when she'd left, I got in touch with my florist and ordered a bouquet to be sent to her that very afternoon with a warm message of thanks from me. I don't know what I'd do without her, and that's the second time I've said that about someone in a week.

All I had to do now was sort out Finn. I texted Charlene who, thank goodness, agreed to have him overnight. I ordered her some flowers too and then, since I was on a roll, I asked for a basket of fragrant summer blooms to be sent to the vicarage. I don't know why it hadn't occurred to me before. I get fresh flowers for the house every week, on account, from my little woman in Ipswich, but how often do ordinary mums have a delivery like that?

The children sorted, I began work on Operation Husband. Naturally, I'd take Johnnie back, but on my own terms. I needed him to realise that playing away and cheating on Issy Smugge was not acceptable. I'd clicked into business mode. No more tears or self-doubt for now.

Step one was texting Sofija.

'Hi, Sofija, how are you doing? Are you having fun? See you Friday! xx'

'Hi, Isabella. Thank you, having lovely time xx'

'Whereabouts are you? Anywhere near St Albans? xx'

There was a short pause, presumably while she googled towns in Hertfordshire.

'No, my friend lives in place called Ware xx'

I felt a pang. Before the appalling revelations of the night before, I would have texted back, *'Where? xx'*, and there would have been much merriment. Not now.

'Have fun! See you Friday xx'

It was time to move on to my cheating pig of a husband.

'Hi, darling. How's work? All good here, children missing you, work going well on south wing. What time are you home Friday? xxxx'

There was a long silence. Eventually, my phone beeped.

'Hi, Iss, flat out with work, board meetings back to back, working late tonight. Will grab quick dinner and work through. Send kids my love. Back teatime Friday. xxxx'

I suspected that he would indeed be grabbing something at the flat, but it would not be of a nutritional nature. I needed to catch the two of them coming home together, one of them in a place they had no business to be. Ware indeed!

At three o'clock, I shimmied out of the front door to climb into my taxi, smiling at the admiring glance the driver gave me. I used the first hour of the journey to write and post on my socials and the second to think. Surprise was of the essence.

I told the driver to drop me and wait. I'd booked into a boutique hotel overlooking St Katherine's Dock. Once I'd confronted Johnnie and Sofija, I had no intention of hanging around. I pictured myself turning elegantly on my heel, leaving them grovelling behind me as I looked forward to a night of child-free luxury.

It was just gone five and I was gambling on the fact that the two of them were probably enjoying a drink after work. I walked into the flat, my eagle eye noting the signs of occupation. There were several pairs of shoes neatly lined up on the hall floor, all size four, all Sofija's. As I walked into the front room, signs of her were everywhere: her make-up bag, her hairbrush, her favourite jacket. I took a deep breath and pushed the bedroom door open.

Our bed was unmade, the sheets rumpled, the indentations of two heads on the pillows. Clothes were hung neatly over the bedside chair and the shutters were closed. In the en suite, two toothbrushes sat cosily in a glass together and there was a clutch of shampoo, conditioner and bodywash bottles in the shower.

The fridge yielded half a dozen oysters and two Dover sole. I swallowed a sob. We always had Dover sole on our anniversary.

Half past five. I needed to get myself ready for the showdown. I poured myself a large glass of wine and settled myself in a chair facing the door on to the hallway. I could wait all night, if need be. As it turned out, I didn't have to.

At six, the key turned in the lock. I heard their voices in the hall. She laughed, musically, and his deep voice said something I couldn't quite hear. I glanced down at my feet, feeling that I was intruding on something private, but unable to move. I took a deep breath, folded my hands on my lap and looked up.

They were gazing at each other as they walked through into the living room. Then they turned to face me and stopped dead. If it hadn't been so terrible, it would have been funny. Like two marionettes dropped back into their box, their eyes stared straight ahead, locked on to mine.

I studied them both intently. I could have no doubt now as I saw the unmistakeable signs of a couple anticipating a night of passion.

Johnnie broke the silence.

'Isabella. What are you doing here?'

The last time he called me Isabella was when I was standing beside him in a church fragrant with spring flowers and we were exchanging vows binding us together for a lifetime.

'Oh, I fancied a change so I thought I'd pop up to town to see what was going on. Country life can be so dull.'

I was rather proud of myself. My voice was clear and steady and my hands were hardly shaking at all.

Sofija hung her head, as well she might.

'Isabella, I am so sorry. I have done bad thing and I know I am hurting you. I wanted to tell you...'

I interrupted. Terribly rude and not something a St Dymphna's girl should ever do, but really, under the circumstances, I think I was entirely justified.

'Did you, indeed? You're fired. I'll give you a day to come back when the children are at school and I'm out so that you can pack up your stuff. I'll write you a reference, then I never want to see you again. Now perhaps you could leave so that I can talk to my husband in private.'

It was as though another Isabella was hovering above the real one, watching the proceedings with interest. I was as cool as a freshly picked ridge cucumber sliced into a crystal jug of iced water.

I waited for her to scuttle out of the room, but then Johnnie seemed to come to life.

'She's not going anywhere. Sit down, Sofi. We need to talk.'

Since when does my husband call my au pair 'Sofi'? That's the children's pet name for her. The balance of power in the room shifted. This wouldn't do at all. I fixed my husband with a limpid stare.

'We do need to talk, Johnnie. I agree. How about you tell me how long this has been going on?'

He sighed. 'Does it really matter? The fact is, it *is* going on. I'm sorry you had to find out like this, but it's probably just as well it's all out in the open.' He turned to Sofija and took her hand. 'The three of us need to work out how this is going to go. The children's welfare is paramount, and the house is in your name, so I don't expect you'll want to move. That would be another trauma for the kids and we don't want that.'

I held my hand up.

'Who's we? I've just found out that you're cheating on me with – her – and I'm waiting for a sorry, at the very least. It's not ideal, especially with the school holidays coming up, and we'll have to find another au pair, but we can get through this.'

'Iss, there's no easy way to say this. I haven't behaved well, and I'm sorry for hurting you. We were going to tell you, but it never seemed to be the right time. It's over between you and me. I'll always love you and I'll be there 100 per cent for the children, but Sofija and I are making a new start together.'

I felt a splinter of ice being driven into my heart. We stared at each other for what seemed like an eternity while I took in every familiar and well-loved feature. Could it be that I was losing him?

I moistened my lips and spoke in a quavering voice.

'But – I don't understand. I can forgive you. We can work through it. Surely, you're not turning your back on me for *her*? I thought she was my friend. I thought you were always going to love me.'

To my shame, my voice wobbled and I felt tears filling my eyes. Johnnie leaned forward and spoke in the gentle voice he used when one of the children had hurt themselves.

'Things don't always work out, Iss. We'll arrange regular visits, and it's not as if I'll be living with a strange woman. The kids know Sofija and they love her so it won't be much of a change for them.'

I sprang to my feet. 'You don't seriously expect me to agree to you shacking up with her and having my children seeing you two together? Have you lost your mind?' All my intentions of being cool, calm and collected were swept away in a white-hot torrent of rage. 'You're very quiet, Miss Sofija. Anything you'd like to say?'

She blushed and gazed at her feet.

'Isabella, I am so sorry. I never meant for this thing to happen. You are friend and employer and you are so good to me. I didn't want to lie to you all these months. I don't want you and the children to hate me.'

I snorted. 'It's a bit late for that. You betrayed my trust. All the time I thought we were friends and you were sleeping with my husband. How could you?'

She looked down and burst into tears. To my horror, my husband started comforting her, his arms around her, and whispering sweet nothings in her undeserving, cheating little ear. I tried to wrest back control of the situation.

'Johnnie, I'm prepared to forgive you. I need you to end it with her, once and for all, and commit to building up our relationship again. I won't say anything to the children. Hopefully, they won't notice anything amiss. They hardly see you anyway.'

Bitchy, but who could blame me? I prepared for my dignified exit, but Johnnie interrupted.

'No, that's not how it's going to go, Iss. We'll talk about it properly, I promise.'

'What about this weekend? I assume you're coming to spend it with us as you usually do?'

Johnnie sighed. 'You're emotional and I don't want lots of embarrassing scenes this weekend. We need to think about the kids. Sofi will have to stay here for now until we can find a place together. I'll FaceTime lots and maybe the kids can come up and stay for a week or so in the holidays. That's only three weeks away.'

Well, I wasn't having that. Emotional? Embarrassing scenes? I turned on my heel (as previously planned) and marched into the kitchen. Issy Smugge is not a violent woman, but this was Lavvie Harcourt and the plait all over again, with an added helping of betrayal and deceit.

The Dover soles were nestling together on a plate. I took them out, along with the oysters, and went back into the front room. It was with a calm demeanour that I took the oysters from their bowl one by one and hurled them at my swine of a husband and my two-faced cheat of an au pair. One of them grazed Johnnie's cheek and drew blood. Ha! Another missed Sofija altogether and exploded on the floor, spraying her foot with juice and pieces of shell.

While they gazed at me, frozen in horror (much like the petit pois I'd found in the freezer), I took advantage of the element of surprise to slap them around the face with the soles. How good it felt to see their staring, glassy eyes and pallid flesh. The soles didn't look too good either.

With their romantic dinner ruined, seafood and fish scales on the carpet and myself well and truly on the moral high ground, I picked up my bag, ground the fish into the floor with my heel (try getting that out, Sofija!) and left. #illgiveyouromanticdinner #revengeissweet

I didn't feel up to dinner out, so at the hotel I rang room service for half a bottle of red wine, a steak (rare), kale, buttered spinach and French beans. Seafood was very much off the menu that evening.

Settling myself down in a chair on the balcony, I realised with a jolt that no one knew where I was. I could do anything, be anyone. If I wanted to go out dancing, minus my wedding ring, I could. Getting blind drunk was also an option, although so unattractive in the morning. I contented myself with going to bed and crying myself to sleep, having exfoliated and moisturised first.

The next morning, I woke up with a start. I hadn't set my alarm, but the sun streaming through the French doors must have teased me awake. I squinted at my phone. Nine o'clock. The children would be at school already, and who knows what Johnnie and Sofija were up to. I didn't want to think about that, so I sat up in bed, rang room service and ordered breakfast.

The traces of tears were still on my cheeks and my eyes were red and puffy. I hadn't cried this much since Nanny went. I'd been doing so well until I realised that there was no one I could talk to. All I wanted was a friend, but there was nobody. I could have rung Claire and poured out all my troubles, but saying the words, 'My husband has left me for our au pair,' made it all seem too horribly real.

I packed my case, cleaned my teeth and tried to repair the facial damage. Patting under-eye cream onto my dark circles, moisturising and brushing my hair, I pondered the next step. I've always tried to be open and honest with the children, but I'd have to think up some convincing lies on the way home. #homejames

As the taxi pulled on to the drive, I found I was glad to be home. I always used to think of London as the place I belonged, but looking back over the events of the last year, it occurred to me that it was a hotbed of vice and depravity. With a few honourable exceptions, of course. I smiled to myself, grimly wondering if Sofija had managed to get the fish out of the carpet yet. We'd selected a particularly deep, thick pile, so I was guessing not.

At school, I thanked Lauren profusely and promised I would always be there if she needed me. Jake and Finn were dashing round the field playing some kind of violent game and there was no sign of Charlene, of course. What a life, trapped in your home, unable to move on. I must see if there is something I can do for her.

Back at home, I realised that I was the responsible adult. I could tell my children the truth, or protect them. I went for protection. I whipped up a quick tagliatelle carbonara and dug some frozen yoghurt out of the depths of the freezer. Then I ran a deep bubbly bath for the girls and stayed with them, listening to their excited chatter while Finn took a shower in the privacy of the family bathroom. When they had their pyjamas on and had brushed their teeth, I read each one a story (Finn excepted) and went straight to bed myself. I was exhausted. How do ordinary people manage? I wasn't sure how I was going to make it through the next week. **#hardtimes #lonely**

On Friday morning, I walked around to the front of the school to have my meeting with Mrs Tennant. Liane Bloomfield was running down the path, pushing the baby, while Zach and her little girl dashed ahead. She was clad in a bright pink smock that clashed unattractively with her hair. I smiled graciously, and was rewarded with a breathless, 'All right?' as she galloped by. Whatever the vicissitudes of my life, I would never allow myself to become so disorganised that I was late for school. Neither would I wear a shocking pink smock with peroxide blonde hair. No doubt Lauren would fill me in later.

Mrs Tennant received me in her office, where we chatted about the play equipment. I agreed to transfer the money that very day. I explained that I would need some images and content to post on my socials.

'You know, pictures of the play equipment being installed, some shots of the school and the grounds, the children enjoying it. My agent will be over the moon. She's all for social action.'

Mrs Tennant looked a little puzzled, but concurred. 'We'll have to be careful about photographs, Mrs Smugge. We've got several looked-after children here, plus some complex family situations, and I'll have to check on permissions. However, I'm sure it will be fine. Let me take this opportunity to thank you again for your generosity.'

I took my leave. Friday group started at 9.30 and I would just about make it. **#ladybountiful**

The topic this week was prayer (boring!), but I'd enjoyed the stuff about forgiveness the previous week so much that I asked a few leading questions and before too long, we were back on that topic. It seemed all too appropriate, given my situation. Once again, I was baffled as to how one forgave those who had done terrible things. What about Hitler?

'Sometimes, we have to leave those huge questions to God.' Sue seemed to have things well in hand.

'As humans, it's impossible for us to be able to comprehend everything. God has His perfect plan, and one day we will see it in all its glory.'

One day? Perfect plan? I wanted all the answers now, but equally, didn't want to rock the boat. As we went round the circle, listening to stories of anger and resentment, I wondered what I should say. I certainly wasn't going to share my shameful behaviour towards Suze, my loathing of Meredith or how I really feel about Mummy. Suze had begun to forgive me, but had I ever managed to do the same for anyone else?

Lauren finished speaking (she'd told us that she had to forgive her parents, her uncle and her grandfather every single day and it still didn't always work), and the spotlight was on me. I thought quickly, then it came to me.

'I was at school with a girl who was really mean to my little sister. I hated her for it and I wanted to get revenge on her. It wasn't just to make me feel good (although it did); it was to stop her bullying Suze.'

'Ooh, is this the girl with the plait?' Lauren was beaming from ear to ear. 'I love this story!'

As the tale unfolded, I could see that I had my audience's rapt attention. I played down some of the details (the lacrosse pavilion – I didn't want to come across as an entitled snob), but I painted the picture with every narrative brush stroke I could think of. Lavinia's gang of sycophantic hangers-on. Her shimmering golden hair. Her sweet smile which masked a dark heart. The fact that I waited for suet pudding night to strike. As I recounted my silent entrance into the dorm, I could see that I held the room in the palm of my hand.

'Did she wake up? What did you do with the hair?' asked one of the girls, who before my tale had been fairly offish but who seemed intrigued with this revelation of the naughtier side of Isabella M Smugge.

I recounted the entire story, right up to me stowing the plait under the loose floorboard. There was a brief silence while I took a drink of water.

'Did she find out it was you? Did you get told off?'

'No, I didn't. The teachers tried everything they could to find out who'd done it, but they never worked out it was me. I suppose I should have felt bad about it, especially when she had to get her other plait cut off and she looked like she'd just escaped from an institution.'

I laughed heartily at the memory. Even now, thinking of the miserable little worm minus her shining golden hair makes me feel good inside.

'We had a fight one day, proper fisticuffs. A teacher came along and stopped us before it really got serious, but getting the chance to beat her up made me feel great.'

Sue was frowning slightly. 'That's a very interesting story, Isabella. Thank you for sharing it with us. So, did she ever forgive you for what you did to her?'

I was baffled. Had the woman not been listening?

'She hates me. You must know who she is. "Lavinia Harcourt Says It Like It Is" in that trashy paper. She wrote some horrible stuff in her stupid rag and keeps dropping little acid remarks in her column. They're obviously about me. But I don't care.'

Sue was still looking confused. The other girls were laughing and looking at me admiringly.

'There's a lot to think about in that story, isn't there? Why do you think you felt so angry with Lavinia, Isabella?'

I stared at her. I'd told a corking story, and now she seemed to be trying to take the wind out of my sails.

'I was sent away to school, leaving my little sister and my parents and nanny behind, I didn't know anyone, I got bullied and had to work out how to become popular all by myself. And my father died tragically. Don't you think that's enough to make a person angry?'

It was a rhetorical question, but Sue seemed determined to answer it.

'Leaving home at such an early age with little or no support must have been incredibly traumatic for you, and losing a parent when you're a child must be extremely painful. It's admirable that you wanted to protect your sister, but I'm interested in the fact that you still seem to feel just as angry now as you did nearly thirty years ago. Have you ever thought of trying to forgive Lavinia?'

Only my unfailing politeness and good breeding stopped me from laughing in her face. Forgive that miserable little toad? It seems to me that these religious types all go around being weak and wobbly and pretending they don't mind when someone's vile to them. I couldn't say that, obviously, so I paraphrased my thoughts in a socially acceptable fashion. Claire, who had been listening intently, joined in.

'Isabella, before you joined us, we talked about forgiveness being unnatural. As humans, we want to get our own back, to hurt those who hurt us. But as Christians, we're able to forgive people who have done us wrong with God's help. That doesn't mean that what they did was right, or that we forget about it. Still, deciding for ourselves that we're going to cut ourselves free from the chains that bind us is a difficult but liberating experience.'

A lightbulb switched itself on in my brain.

'Hang on – so is this something to do with trespassing?'

I must have mumbled the Lord's Prayer hundreds of times, at school and various church services, but I'd never connected the trespassing bit with forgiveness.

'We can ask for forgiveness every time we make a mistake and know that if we're sincere, we'll receive it. But we have to forgive those who hurt us too. It's a two-way street.'

Claire has such a good way of explaining things.

'So what you're saying is that I should try to forgive Lavinia Harcourt? What if she writes more horrible stuff in her stupid column about me?'

'Think of letting go of all that anger you've been dragging around with you for years. Imagine how good that would feel.'

'Hmm.' I couldn't begin to imagine *how* that would feel. I needed to spend some quiet time pondering it at home. I addressed Sue, who seemed to be the woman with all the facts.

'How would you suggest I let go of the anger? Where would it go?'

Sue explained that God (Him again) wants to take all our burdens and asks us to trust Him with our issues and pain. Well, I didn't see how that was supposed to work!

'Think about your father, Isabella. How was your relationship with him?'

Well, Daddy was kind and loving and thought that everything I said was hilarious. Surely Sue wasn't implying that the good Lord was like him?

The spotlight had been on me for too long and I was starting to feel uncomfortable. That's the trouble with these religious people. They look at you so intently and talk about things that are best left unsaid. I smiled, graciously, and said I'd think about it. By which I meant I wouldn't. I ask you!

I walked down the road with the girls towards the school nursery. Something had shifted. Whereas before they had been polite but stand-offish, now they seemed positively fascinated by me.

'We've never had an Instagram influencer in the village before,' one of them said. 'Now we've talked to you, you don't even seem that up yourself. No offence.'

It was rather charming to be looked up to like this. At the nursery gates we parted, me to walk back up the hill to my house, them to pick up their children, go home and feed them whatever people without staff cook.

Later, in the playground, everyone was sharing their weekend plans. I was going to be alone – no husband, no au pair, three children asking awkward questions. What I needed to do was fill my days up.

'I'm usually very busy at the weekends, but I've got a window tomorrow – my husband's been called away on a conference. It's going to be glorious weather. Would anyone like to come over for lunch and spend the afternoon in the pool?'

Well, you'd have thought I'd chartered a private jet and offered to fly them all to Antigua. Everyone seemed terribly excited. Lauren, of course, is an old hand, having lowered herself into the swirling waters of my Jacuzzi on a number of occasions, but the others seemed quite taken aback by my invitation.

'Are you sure?' This was Kate, one of the PTA ladies I met at the fête. 'If everyone comes, you'll be overrun! Please let us bring some food.' The chair, Maddie, agreed and promised to bring her signature dish, chocolate crunch. She's known for it, according to Lauren, and it always sells out at school fundraisers. I must ask her for the recipe.

I accepted their offers and we divided up who would bring what. I texted Charlene and invited her and Jake.

That's so kind of you. I'm sure Jake would love it, but I hope you'll understand if I don't come. My anxiety is very bad at the moment x'

Poor woman. What a life, being dictated to by your internal issues. I don't know how she gets through the day. I texted back.

Would Jake like to have tea and come for a sleepover tonight? Sorry for short notice x'

My impulse was largely altruistic; however, if Finn had a friend over, I hoped he would forget about his father's absence.

That left Sunday. I invited Claire and her family over for lunch. **#busyweekend #reachingout**

At home, even with Jake present to ameliorate a difficult situation, things weren't going smoothly. I'd explained that Daddy was held up at work and would be Skyping them. When I told them another big fat lie, namely that Sofija's mother was very ill and that she had to go and look after her, their faces became set and mutinous. Elsie's bottom lip protruded (always a terrible sign) and Chloë glared at me.

'But what if we run out of food? We'll starve to death!'

My daughter is such a drama queen. While this sort of thing will stand her in good stead for school productions, there's no place for a prima donna in my kitchen.

'I can cook, you know! You love my food.'

They didn't look convinced.

'You do make very nice toast, Mummy,' conceded Elsie. 'But Sofija does all the real food. When is she coming back? I miss her.'

'Soon, I hope. We'll see. We've got a lovely new lady starting on Tuesday. Her name's Ali. She's going to keep our house all clean and tidy and do lots of jobs for Mummy so I can spend more time with you.'

My cheerful voice and positive attitude were fooling no one. The girls continued to frown and a sense of gloom hovered over the kitchen. It was too early for bed, so I suggested a nice walk or a hearty round of Scrabble. Both were met with stony silence. It went against my principles, but furnishing both girls with a bag of organic popcorn (a Friday treat), I allowed them to sit and stare at the TV while I got ready for the next day's pool fest. #notaseasyasitlooks

My pool party went amazingly well, as did Sunday lunch. I had decided to do a barbecue for the girls, gritting my teeth and using some of the marinated steaks, ribs and chicken thighs from the freezer made by Sofija. It pains me to say it, but she really does have an amazing palate. No taste, clearly, if she thinks running off with other people's husbands is acceptable, but a real talent for mixing up the right herbs and spices.

Kate, Maddie and their children were lovely. They would have fitted in well on my team at Beech Grove. We chatted about the PTA and how hard it is to get volunteers. I can't wait to get my teeth into a new project. I need to keep my mind occupied. And do good in my local community too, of course.

It's always lovely to see Lauren and her girls, and all in all, the day was a great success.

Sunday was equally delightful. It was so lovely to spend time with Claire and Tom. I told them I'd try to get to church the next Sunday. I really do mean to – it's only an hour of my life, after all. I just wish the poor girl was a bit better. She's still so pale and wan-looking. September can't come soon enough.

Which reminds me. I must call horsey Davina and see how she's getting on. I was so good at maintaining relationships when I had proper help. Staying in touch with everyone plus cooking and running a household is exhausting work. And that's before you even think about your career. No wonder so many of the women in the playground look so rough. Once Ali joins the team, I should be up and running again. What with her OCD and my excellent taste, everything should be back to normal in no time.

On Monday morning, the children safely packed off to school, I Skyped Mimi.

'Well, sweetie, how are we doing? Lavinia's still scattering her column with acid drops, but nothing too major. We could even turn them into good publicity with a bit of work.'

Eyes narrowed, Mimi squinted at me through a cloud of smoke, her nails painted the colour of venous blood. I shared the good news about the PTA and assured her that once I got Johnnie into the safety of the master bedroom, he would be back in the fold.

'I hope so, darling. Men do stray at that age. My third cheated on me with a traffic warden. He loved authority. Something to do with the uniform and the little notebook. Took my eye off the ball for a second and there it was. Johnnie won't stay with your little nanny. You're a power couple, one of the best there is.'

I was rather hoping that Johnnie loved me for more than my status and achievements, but I let it go. We moved briskly through our agenda. Lavinia had vented her spleen twice over the past week with nasty little snippets about me in her stupid column.

'What well-known blogger is rumoured to be doing her own cooking and cleaning of late? She says: It's so grounding.'

I've always cooked! And what is loading the dishwasher and wiping down the surfaces if it isn't cleaning? I ask you!

Stay at Home Mums versus Working Women: Why the Debate Won't Go Away. With her perfectly groomed hair and nails and expensive outfits, this woman has made a career out of making *you* feel bad about yourself. If *you* had a cleaner, housekeeper, nanny and gardener, wouldn't you look just as good as her? Lavvie Harcourt Says: Stop Showing Off.

Mimi advised me to ignore it. 'She can't possibly know about Johnnie and whatshername. Hit her where it hurts, with your new play equipment.'

With a final racking cough, she blew me a kiss and was gone. #stopshowingoffindeed #whodoyouthinkyouare

On Tuesday, Ali appeared five minutes early for her first day working with Isabella M Smugge. Anything less like the dour Brygita couldn't be imagined. Back in the kitchen, I made us both a coffee. It seems she's a huge fan of one of my closest competitors, the cleaning blogger.

'She's so inspirational. She deals with her anxiety by cleaning and organising. I've got all her books. Do you like her, Mrs Smugge?'

Like her? Her books and mine had been leapfrogging up the charts together ever since she burst on to the scene. She's a sweet girl with some very good ideas. I conceded that she was jolly good at what she did and dropped some names. Ali's eyes widened.

'Wow. You're an inspiration too, Mrs Smugge. I started following you a while back. All your design suggestions work so well. I got my mum *Issy Smugge Says: Let's Refresh the Kitchen for Christmas* last year and she's never looked back.'

This was all going terribly well. A devoted follower of my work with OCD and a work ethic not unrelated to my own. Leaving Ali with her list of jobs, I departed to the studio to get on with a whole heap of content writing. **#gleamingsurfaces**

I returned to the house at three and sniffed the air appreciatively. The kitchen was imbued with a delightful spring fragrance, the surfaces were gleaming and Ali had cleaned out the fridge, something that Brygita had rarely done. Upstairs, all the beds were made with hospital corners. The girls' rooms looked immaculate. Ali had put the toys away, neatened up the bookshelves and generally dressed the space as though she were about to put my house on the market. I complimented her lavishly and she blushed.

'I suffer from anxiety a bit, Mrs Smugge, and I've found that cleaning and tidying really helps me. This house is so beautiful that it's a joy to work here.'

Better and better. We'd already had the chat about increasing her hours, and now a question popped into my busy little brain.

'How do you feel about cooking, Ali?'

She beamed. 'I love it! I batch cook at home and fill up the freezer so that my husband and the boys always have a home-cooked meal.'

I could have wept with joy, but managed to restrain myself. A cook! A cleaner! A woman who understands how to dress a room! All my Christmases have come at once.

The rest of the week, the children were rude, sulky and uncooperative. They were never like this when Sofija was around. I grounded Finn for two days for bad behaviour and had to speak sharply to the girls several times. Hearing my own voice, I got an uncomfortable echo of Mummy shouting at me and Suze. What have I become?

I braced myself for Johnnie's return. I was determined to be cool, calm and collected. When he appeared with the children at pick-up time, I greeted him with a kiss, for all the world like a devoted little wife. I let him spend time with the children while I pottered around upstairs. There was really nothing to do. Ali had left everything clean, tidy and ordered. I found myself idly rearranging the towels in the airing cupboard for want of something to occupy myself with. Then I put my perfumes into alphabetical order twice, once by fragrance, then again by manufacturer.

With the children in bed, I braced myself for the inevitable conversation but, to my horror, he announced that he had a room booked in a hotel.

'I beg your pardon?' My tone was as icy as a perfectly chilled Muscadet.

'I'm here for the kids. That was the agreement. If we start rowing tonight it'll upset them, and we've still got the rest of the weekend to get through. It seems far more sensible for me to sleep elsewhere and spend time with the kids when they're here.'

'And what should I say when they ask where you are tomorrow?'

'Say I got up early and I've gone for a run. They won't ask. They're just delighted to have me back. Sort out sleepovers for them on Saturday night so we can have the house to ourselves.'

And with that he was off. I ask you! **#rude #hellhathnofury**

Friday slid by in a haze of work. Johnnie was as good as his word, picked the children up and devoted himself to their entertainment. Without consulting me, he ordered pizza and informed me we were having a family movie night. The children were ecstatic, of course. Pizzas consumed and movie watched, he packed them all off to bed and left me once more to my own thoughts, which were far from saintly.

The next day, I slept in (all that emotional turmoil) and came downstairs to find Johnnie presiding over breakfast. He'd made the most terrible mess, and Ali doesn't work at weekends. I departed for an extra-long swim and fantasised about Sofija being deported as I glided gracefully up and down. When I came back, glowing from the exercise, it was to find a note on the table.

'Gone to the cinema with the kids. See you later, I'll sort dinner.'

Johnnie was clearly going for Father of the Year. By the time he deigned to return, I'd made a batch of bread (so grounding), taken loads of outdoor and interior shots, gone for a five-mile run and sorted through the clothes in my dressing room. I'd also organised sleepovers for the girls but had been unable to find anywhere for Finn to lay his head for the night. Jake's dad was making a rare attempt to fulfil his paternal duties and had taken him away for the weekend. It occurred to me that my son doesn't really have any other friends, which is not good. I need to spend some time sorting out his social life for him.

As the evening wore on, my stomach began to twist itself into knots. Finn said goodnight and ambled up to bed at nine. I shut the kitchen door, poured myself another glass of wine and faced up to the most difficult conversation of my marriage.

'So… Johnnie. When are you going to stop all this nonsense and come home?'

'Iss, it's not nonsense. I love Sofija and she loves me. I never meant for this to happen, but I was in the middle of it before I realised. Like I said, it won't be too traumatic for the kids because they know her and love her. It'll be like having two mothers for them.'

Rage burst into flames in my stomach and roared out through my mouth.

'Two mothers? One is more than enough. I'm your *wife*. I moved up here even though I didn't want to, I've coped alone while you did goodness knows what in town and now you think you can waltz in here and tell me you're leaving me for *her*?'

'Maybe that was tactless of me. What I mean is that they don't have to get to know someone else from scratch. They can spend the weekends and some of the holidays with us and the rest of the time here. My mother will help and I'm sure you'll want to spend more time with Davina and Toby once they've had the baby.'

I stared at him. Isabella M Smugge, award-winning blogger, writer, photographer and influencer does not intend to go scampering around the countryside cuddling babies and asking her mother-in-law to help around the house. I made this abundantly clear. We carried on, voices getting louder, wine disappearing at an alarming rate. I tried hard to remain calm, but it was impossible. At last, I blurted out the question I'd been wanting to ask ever since I opened that little plastic bag.

'We were happy, weren't we? What has she got that I haven't?'

He looked down at his hands and had the grace to colour.

'I didn't see this coming any more than you did, Iss. When we were in London, we were on the same page. You were fun and edgy. You were always the coolest girl I'd ever met. I admit it, moving up here was a mistake. You lost your edge. You were always working and I didn't feel part of your life any more. One day, I looked at Sofija and saw someone else, not the au pair, not part of the furniture, but a woman. There was a spark and I shouldn't have pursued it, but I did.'

Lost my edge? Against my will, my eyes filled with tears. Johnnie was speaking quietly, his eyes cast down and his whole demeanour crestfallen. I should have been furious. But instead

I felt like putting my head down on the cool quartz counter top and crying until I had no tears left.

Johnnie got up and took another bottle of wine out of the fridge. I could feel myself cascading out of control, my heart beating fast and my hands cold with fear. Surely this wasn't the end of our marriage?

'Maybe moving up here wasn't the best thing we ever did, but we can make a fresh start. I think you'd like it here if you gave it a chance. We're going to retire in the next ten years anyway and then we can do whatever we like. I love you.' My voice wobbled, and I swallowed hard. 'I gave up so much to be with you. You know you're the only man I've ever loved.'

Long ago, I learned that letting your slip show is a dangerous business and not to be encouraged. I was so far out of my comfort zone that it was merely a tear-filled blur in the distance. I reached out my hand and took his. He squeezed mine, then pulled away.

'Iss – I don't want to hurt you. I'll always love you too. Thing is, I'm not *in* love with you any more. That excitement we used to have, that spark, it's gone. I'll always respect you and support you as much as I can, but it's time for the parting of the ways.'

I fixed my eyes on his face. The deep blue eyes, the crisp dark hair, the chiselled jaw, the lines round his eyes – I knew them as well as I knew myself. It all seemed like a bad dream. Surely, I'd wake up in a minute to find myself in our bed lying in Johnnie's arms, Sofija still my friend and right-hand woman, the children happy and well adjusted.

'You and I are grown-ups, Iss. We'll work it out. It's perfectly possibly to have a civilised arrangement that doesn't affect the children too much.'

Anger bubbled up in me again. 'I'm a child of a broken home. You don't know anything about it. It tears you apart. Suze and I were convinced it was all our fault. Do you know what that kind of guilt does to a child? We both dragged it around with us for years, and when Daddy died we knew there was no way it would ever leave us.'

'Oh, come on, Iss, you're being a drama queen. I can see where Chloë gets it from.'

Maybe it was the wine. I rose to my feet, walked deliberately over to him and slapped him round the face, hard.

'Don't you dare, don't you *dare* ever call me that again, Johnnie Smugge! You're sleeping with our au pair, the person I thought was my friend, and you're telling me not to overreact? I think I'm being remarkably calm under the circumstances.'

His face reddened with anger as he jumped to his feet. I jabbed him hard in the chest with my finger.

'Too much of a drama queen for you? Take this and stay cool, you two-faced, cheating pig!'

I hurled my limited-edition acrylic pepper mill at him. It ricocheted off his shoulder and crashed to the floor, spraying hundreds of organic pink peppercorns on to the floor. Flushed with anger and coated in peppercorns, he banged his hands down hard on the quartz counter top.

'You're proving my point. Chucking things and raising your voice. Look at yourself.'

I used to be pretty good at track and field at St Dymphna's. The matching salt mill struck him squarely on the side of the head before bouncing off the dishwasher and discharging its payload of organic flaked sea salt all over the floor.

I felt something give way, and all the anger and resentment that had been bubbling away inside me came pouring out. My carefully guarded suspicion that I'm an unlovable person had been awoken by Johnnie's words. Daddy left, Nanny left, Mummy never loved me and now my own husband was dumping me. I opened my mouth and out came a torrent of angry words at top volume. I won't shock you by quoting them. You can imagine.

I don't know how long we stood there screaming at each other. It could have been five minutes; it could have been an hour. My throat was raw, my face was hot and it felt good. We'd always had an equal marriage. However, with the hurling of the condiments and the moral high ground, I'd pulled ahead.

As I've said before, I'm not a violent woman, but some of Johnnie's comments were so incredibly annoying that we were soon three wine glasses, an entrée dish, several spice containers and an olive oil jug down. I've spent my whole life doing the right thing and being a Nice Girl and now I was turning into a shrieking harridan, as Mummy would say.

I was telling Johnnie exactly what I thought of him as he brushed ground ginger from his hair when the sound of the kitchen door creaking open interrupted us. We turned around to see Finn's white face staring at us. There was silence for a few seconds, then we both hurried towards him, our feet crunching on crushed spice, broken glass and shattered tableware.

'Finn, darling, it's OK, there's nothing to worry about. Daddy and I are just having a little chat.'

His eyes took in the scene. He said nothing.

'Finn, listen, buddy, Mummy and I are a bit cross with each other, but it's nothing to do with you. I'm sorry we woke you up. Grown-ups get angry too, sometimes, just like you and the girls do. Come on, I'll take you back to bed.'

Finn nodded, his face pallid and his eyes dry and wide. I watched as he slowly ascended the stairs, Johnnie behind him with a protective hand on his shoulder. My eyes filled with tears once more – what had we done? Suze and I had witnessed any number of fights between Mummy and Daddy, but we were always too scared to intervene. I could only hope that the sight of his son had brought Johnnie round.

A few minutes later, he returned.

'Port, Iss?'

'Oh, go on, then.'

Johnnie produced a bottle of white port, my personal favourite, and we sat sipping it in silence while the candles guttered in the slight breeze from the open window.

'Remember the night Finn was born?' Johnnie's face had softened. 'We sat there holding him and telling him all the wonderful things we were going to do together. We were besotted. He's growing into such an amazing person. My old school will be the making of him.'

I was pretty sure it wouldn't, but now wasn't the time to open that can of worms. We sat and talked about the children and reminisced about holidays and birthdays and parties and times past. I was too afraid to shatter the fragile calm between us and, judging by his diplomatic refilling of my glass and his smile, so was he.

'You're a great mother. And I admire you more than I can say, Iss. I haven't told you that enough. You're a brilliant writer and photographer and you never let anything get in your way.'

'Thank you. That means a lot. I don't, do I?' I took a huge gulp of port and returned the compliment. 'Mummy always said that at least you were a good provider.'

He grinned. 'At least? That's a double-edged sword. Your mother never liked me, even with us being a Good Family. If I'd been Lord Smugge of Somewhere, she'd be singing a different tune.'

I giggled. 'She certainly would! Lord John de Smugge!'

'The Earl of Smugge!'

'The Duke of Smuggeville!'

'Baron von Smugge!'

'Viscount Smugge!'

'The Marquess of Smugge!'

We were both shaking with laughter, tears pouring down our cheeks as we hurled made-up titles at each other in Mummy's voice. Johnnie rose to his feet and made me an elaborate bow.

'Would milady Smugge like to accompany the Baron to the bedchamber?'

'She would, your Eminence! She very much would!' I made a slightly off-centre curtsey in return, belatedly realising that I had actually said 'mush' rather than 'much'. Arm in arm, we walked deliberately up the stairs towards our bedroom, both rather unsteady on our feet.

At the door, we stopped and gazed at each other. Johnnie took my face in his hands. He leaned forward and kissed me, so gently, so lovingly. Within seconds, we were in the bedroom, entwined like a pair of lusty teenagers. **#marriedbliss #nightofpassion**

I woke up in a pile of rumpled bedclothes feeling happier than I had in months. Rolling over, I saw that Johnnie's side of the bed was empty. A pleasing fragrance of shower gel and aftershave wafted from the en suite. He must have showered and tiptoed downstairs to get me breakfast and coffee. I felt a little seedy, not surprisingly considering the amount we had drunk, but at least our marriage was back on track. That alone was worth a bit of a head and a queasy tum.

I could hear the church bells ringing, summoning the faithful to prayer. I wasn't going to be one of them this morning, but I was sure that Claire would understand, and, by association, God. I heard Johnnie's footsteps on the stairs and my heart leapt.

In he walked, holding a mug of coffee, bless him, and a packet of aspirin. I drank him in. Even after all these years, never had I seen a better-looking man.

'Thank you, darling! Just what I needed.' I pulled the sheets back with a seductive smile. 'Do join me.'

He sat down on the edge of the bed.

'I won't, Iss, if you don't mind. I need to get back to London. I've cleared up downstairs and made Finn his breakfast. We had a chat. He's OK about it, but be aware he might be a little upset later on today when it sinks in.'

'OK about what?' I was mystified.

'The whole separation thing. I'll ring tomorrow after school and chat to all three of them. Perhaps they can come up to London when school breaks up.'

I clutched the sheet to my chest.

'What... what do you mean, Johnnie? Surely you aren't going back to town, to *her*? Not after last night. You can't be.'

He leaned forward and took my hand. Either his was extremely warm or mine was as cold as ice.

'Iss, last night was great, don't get me wrong. But I'm with Sofija now. I told you that. Here's your coffee and your painkillers. I've got a bit of a head myself.'

He kissed me on the cheek and straightened up. If you were to see me lying naked in my bed with the bells ringing in the background, staring up at the most handsome man in the world, you'd think I lived in paradise. But the jaws of hell were opening up before me, the smell of brimstone in my nostrils, as my husband casually ended all my hopes and dreams with a few words.

He turned and walked away. I heard his footsteps on the stairs and his voice calling out to Finn. I jumped out of bed, pulled on my dressing gown and ran downstairs. He was walking out of the front door, Finn standing in the hall staring after him.

'Johnnie! Please don't go. We can talk about this.'

He looked over his shoulder, shook his head and got into the car. With a throaty roar, it started up and moved slowly down the drive, tyres crunching on the gravel. I ran after him, careless of who saw or heard, calling, 'Johnnie! Johnnie! Come back!'

But he was gone, a dot in the distance dancing before my tear-filled eyes. I turned and walked slowly back to the house, towards my son and the realisation that my life as I knew it was over. I would never give up on the fight to get my husband back, but it was going to be a long, hard road.

I reached out to hug Finn, but he pulled away, shouting, 'It's all your fault! You made him go! I hate you!'

He ran up the stairs and slammed his bedroom door, leaving me in the hall, alone and remembering with a jolt the words I'd shouted at Mummy when we came home for the holidays after Daddy left.

'I hate you! You drove him away and I'll never forgive you!'

I never had. And now I had to face up to the fact that my own son blamed me for this debacle. **#heartbreak #pain #anguish**

Someone punched me in the stomach and now I can't breathe. Huge waves of grief and rage keep knocking me to the floor and it's so hard to struggle to my feet again. My life is over. I'm a loser. No one loves me, not really.

For the rest of Sunday, Finn stayed in his room. I tapped on his door several times, but was greeted with either a stony silence or a muffled, 'Go away!'

I walked around the garden, eyeing up the pond and wondering how hard it was to drown. I could put stones in my pockets, like Virginia Woolf, but the only dress I had with pockets was one of my favourite Scandi ones and the full skirt would make me too buoyant. Also, where would I find that many stones? It would take me ages to pick up enough gravel from the drive.

As the church clock struck three, I remembered that I was meant to be picking up the girls from Lauren's. I pulled out my phone. Two missed calls and a whole heap of texts.

'Hey, babes, I couldn't get hold of you, so have taken the girls to church. Hope you don't mind. We're going to the park after lunch. Want me to drop them back to yours? xx'

I wondered what possible response I could give.

'Do what you like. My husband has left me for my Latvian au pair and my life is over xx'

'Don't whatever you do let the girls come anywhere near the pond. Try to remember me as I was xx'

'Goodbye, forever! Thank you for your friendship xx'

Johnnie's words rang unpleasantly loudly in my head. 'Oh, come on, Iss, you're being a drama queen.'

That's the trouble about being a mother. You have to put your children's needs before your own. And there's always something they need. Reluctantly, I conceded that a dead and martyred Issy Smugge would be no good to anyone and replied thus:

'Hi, Lauren, of course that's all right. I hope they enjoyed it. Would you mind dropping them back here? Thanks for being such a good friend and having them for me xx'

I hit send and burst into tears. What on earth was I going to tell Lauren? **#awfultruth**

What have I done to deserve a friend like Lauren? As soon as she arrived, she sent the girls off down the garden to play, took me indoors, brewed me up a strong coffee and listened as I sobbed out the whole sorry story. Most people would have started telling me that at least I had the house and didn't have to worry about money and was young enough to start again, but not Lauren. She sat there holding me and gently stroking my hair.

I don't know how I'm going to get through the rest of the term. I have to make an appearance at Sports Day (thank heavens for oversized sunglasses) and do every single school run, thanks to Sofija's defection. At least I don't have to worry about the cleaning and cooking. That's something, I suppose.

Once Lauren had gone home, promising that she was there for me and would tell Claire so I didn't have to go through it all again, I took a deep breath and asked the children to join me in the family room. I didn't know what I was going to say to them, but I did know that at least they would hear the news from their mother's own lips, unlike Suze and I who had to find out second-hand.

'Darlings, there's something we need to chat about. Everything is absolutely fine, but there are going to be a few little changes in our lives.'

Finn cut across my soothing tones.

'Mum and Dad have broken up. Sofija's living with him in London.'

The girls stared at me with open mouths and wide eyes.

'But you said you and Daddy weren't going to split up, Mummy. You promised.' Chloë's lip was trembling.

'I know I did, but sometimes things happen that even grown-ups don't have any control over. Daddy and Mummy have decided that, just for now, it would be better if we lived apart, but you three will always be the most important people in the world to both of us. It just means that you get to live here with me and see all your friends and have fun, then spend time with Daddy back in London. Mummy and Daddy are going to keep on talking and I'm sure he will be back before too long.'

I thought I was doing rather well under the circumstances. Finn was glaring at me and the girls looked utterly bewildered. Elsie was sucking her thumb and gazing at me while Chloë chewed savagely at her fingernails. I wondered what on earth I should say next.

'Where's Sofija? When is she coming back? I miss her.' Elsie's little face was downcast.

'Sofija has decided that she will live in London from now on. A nice lady called Ali is helping Mummy with the cooking and cleaning and you'll be seeing a lot more of me! That's good, isn't it?'

My voice was becoming increasingly screechy. If I carried on like this, I'd be donning luridly coloured separates and singing about talking animals on children's TV.

'Sofija and Dad are living together because he loves her and not you. You've ruined everything! I hate you!'

For the second time in twenty-four hours, Finn ran up the stairs and banged his bedroom door behind him. I was left with two trembling, tearful little girls.

'Why has Sofija gone away, Mummy? Is it because we were naughty? Please can you ask her to come back so that we can say we're sorry?'

I could feel my heart breaking. People say that, don't they, and I always put it down to cheap sentiment, but it turns out that it's an actual thing. I reached out and gathered my little girls close to me and told them that they were the most precious angels in the world and that I loved them more than I could say.

'You haven't been naughty at all. You're lovely. Sofija has decided to stop working for me and to live in London instead.'

I struggled to say her name. How could she and Johnnie put me through this? Looking down at Chloë's red-gold hair and Elsie's thick blonde curls took me straight back to Suze and me cuddling up together in my bed and conversing in whispers about what we'd done to drive Daddy away. Right there and then, I vowed that I would never do to them what Mummy had done to us. I would be honest and open and adult in all my dealings with them.

'But Mummy, you said that Sofija had gone home to look after her mum.'

I sighed.

'Yes, I did, darling. I told you a little fib. Sofija is in London and so is Daddy. She's living at the flat for now but I expect she will try to find her own place to live soon.'

'Why did you fib? When can we talk to Sofija? When can we see her?'

Being honest and open and adult was proving to be harder than I thought. I felt exhausted. All I wanted to do was drink several bottles of wine, go to bed and sleep for a week.

'Now, it's getting late and we've got to be up for school tomorrow, haven't we? Come on, let's go and put our pyjamas on and have a lovely bedtime story.'

Even to my own ears, my voice sounded forced and shrill. We walked upstairs, Elsie sucking her thumb furiously and Chloë chewing her fingernails. I supervised teeth-brushing, read them both a story and turned out their lights. I walked down the hall to Finn's room and rapped smartly on the door.

'Go away! I don't want to talk to you.'

Issy Smugge didn't bring a child into the world to speak to her like that. I turned the handle and walked in. My son was sitting at his desk, scowling at me.

'Finn, I know this is a shock for you, but you have to understand I'm just as upset as you. I'm sure Daddy will come back at some point, but in the meantime I can't cope with you having tantrums and crashing around the house. I need all the help I can get.'

He folded his arms and glared at me. 'So, it's all about you. What about me? Everyone's going to find out at school and laugh at me. I wish we'd never come here. I hate it.'

Great. All that hard work on my part and this is the thanks I get.

'Tough! You live here now and you'll just have to suck it up. You can talk to Jake, can't you? He's in the same boat.'

'Not really! His dad ran off with someone else and his mum is too scared to go out of the house. He has to have free school meals and everything. All his uniform comes from the second-hand shop and the other kids laugh at him. We've got this massive embarrassing house and you keep sticking your nose into other people's business and joining groups and making me look stupid. Why can't you be like the other mums? No wonder Dad left. You're so lame.'

Something snapped inside me. I lunged forward, seized his shoulders and shook him hard. I wanted to hurt him and make him feel as bad as me. A voice I didn't recognise came out of my mouth.

'Shut up, you ungrateful little brat! You don't know how lucky you are. While you're at school playing football and having fun, I'm working my fingers to the bone so you can have nice things. I don't ever want to hear you speaking to me like that again.'

He stared at me, white-faced. What had I done?

'Finn – darling. I'm sorry. I didn't mean any of that. Please forgive me.'

'Get lost! I hate you and I want to live with Dad.'

He jumped up, pushed me hard in the chest and fell into his bed, covering himself with the duvet. I stood there uncertainly, wondering what to do next. I patted the bedclothes, trying to work out the rough location of his head.

'I love you, Finn. I'm sorry. I'm a bit upset. Let's talk again tomorrow. Goodnight.'

I turned off the light and tiptoed out of his room. I'd assaulted both the men in my life and traumatised my daughters. And yet the people who had caused this disaster were happily shacked up in London, probably sipping champagne and nibbling on smoked mussels, holding hands and laughing while Isabella M Smugge struggled on alone.

I wandered aimlessly downstairs. I was too wired to go to bed, but couldn't think what to do. I picked up my phone and texted Johnnie.

'That went well. Finn furious, says he hates me and wants to live with you. Girls very upset, think they've done something wrong. You've done a great job of ruining my life. And remember I own 50 per cent of the flat.'

A text had come in from Claire.

'Hi, Isabella. Lauren has told me the sad news about you and Johnnie. Tom and I are both so very sorry and we want you to know that we're here for you, whatever you need. We're praying for you. See you at school tomorrow morning. xx'

I texted back.

'Thank you both, that's so sweet. How are you feeling? xx'

After a bit more chit-chat, we signed off. I can't imagine that two people in a shabby vicarage talking to someone who may not exist will mend my marriage.

I walked back into our room. I hadn't made the bed and the sheets smelled like Johnnie. The towels in the bathroom were still damp and smelled of his aftershave. Like a pathetic, lovelorn teenager, I lay in my bed, holding his pillow with my face buried in it. What have I become? **#badmother #sleeplessnight**

The dreams are so hard to bear. When I finally cry myself to sleep, I wake calling out his name. In that strange country where we go when we lose consciousness, I see him running towards me, arms outstretched; I smell his aftershave and feel his strong arms around me. It was all a mistake. He's here. But he isn't.

I'm alone.

I woke up to the sound of my alarm going off. Could I really be bothered to drag myself out of bed and do forty lengths of the pool? No. I could not. Even if I developed rampant cellulite and what I believe is called a muffin top, did it really matter? Such self-pitying and frankly defeatist thoughts do not usually go through the mind of Isabella M Smugge. I hit snooze and went back to sleep.

I was jerked into wakefulness by Chloë shaking me and shouting, 'Mummy!' in my ear. It was not a pleasant awakening.

To my horror, I realised that it was 8.20 and we had less than half an hour to sort out packed lunches, breakfast and uniform.

I came downstairs to find Elsie stuffing her urine-soaked bedding into the washing machine. I gave her a quick cuddle, dried her tears and told her it didn't matter one bit. There was no sign of Finn.

I called up the stairs. Shouting at the girls to get their book bags and do their teeth, I ran up to his room and knocked before going in. He was still in bed.

'Finn! What are you doing? Come on, get up and get dressed. We'll be late.'

He stared mutinously at me.

'I'm not going to school today.'

'Oh, yes, you are!'

I took hold of his arm and tried to pull him upright. He shook himself free.

'Get off me! If you make me get up, I'll tell Dad you hurt me last night.'

We stared at each other for a long minute.

'You and I are having a serious talk the minute I get back from school!'

I marched downstairs, rang the school and told them Finn had a cold. Another lie. The girls just made it in before the doors closed. I couldn't face talking to anyone, not even my friends, so I watched the girls go in then blew kisses to everyone, turned tail and fled back home. Finn stayed in his room for most of the day, emerging only to drop crumbs on the floor and leave a mess on the worktops. At least, that was my assumption when I returned from a hard day's work in my studio.

Johnnie's phone call to the children after school only made things worse. I was left to pick up the pieces. Great.

I'll draw a veil over the rest of July. Sports Day was a blur, Finn went in three days out of five and I had to have a chat with Mrs Tennant about the trial separation (as I'm calling it). Now I have to spend the summer holidays with a surly, uncooperative son and two miserable daughters, one of whom has unaccountably started wetting the bed. **#nightmare #schoolrefuser**

August

August began with more terrible news. Just as I thought things could get no worse, Mummy rang and announced she was coming to stay while we Sorted Things Out. A visit from Vlad the Impaler at his most bloodthirsty would have been more cause for celebration. Just as I was considering moving to Albania, Suze rang. Her timing was perfect. I'd had a hideous day with the children, all of whom lay around the house demanding food and refusing to do anything fun. I had got virtually no work done (why do children have such ridiculously long summer holidays?) and was starting to feel a creeping sense of panic.

'Listen, Bella, Jeremy and I have been talking. I've got some annual leave to use up and I want to come over and see you. What do you think?'

What did I think? I thought goodbye Albania and hello a fortnight with my favourite person in the whole wide world. I could have wept with joy. I shared the news of Mummy's impending visitation.

'Oh, my goodness! Can you imagine what she'll be like?'

'You can't say I didn't warn you.'

'Of course, no one ever listens to me.'

'Mummy knows best.'

'I told you so.'

I couldn't help but laugh. Suze does a wicked impression of Mummy. I knew the children would be over the moon to see their auntie. After much to-ing and fro-ing, I had agreed that the three of them could visit Johnnie in London for a week in August and then see how the weekends panned out. I was loath to let them go, but I was sick to death of all the moping around and weeping and wailing.

'When are we going to see Sofija? We miss her,' was the constant refrain which grated on me more than I could say. I would have thrown myself into my work to get away from it, but with just me and Ali in the house, it seemed that I was the responsible adult and I was struggling to find the time to parent and work at the same time.

Before all this happened, I saw myself as a multitasking full-time working parent with all my boxes ticked. Now, I was sad, lonely, unsure, apprehensive, tired, unmotivated and resentful. These are not adjectives that Isabella M Smugge has any truck with, but they were bedfellows all to Bella Neville. I thought I'd left that pathetic little girl behind, but still she dogs my footsteps, whispering in my ear as I lie sleepless in my bed and trotting around after me as I try to be a good mother and a successful career woman. **#whathaveibecome #horriblememories**

Johnnie rang or FaceTimed most days. I couldn't bear to be in the same room and left the children to it. I listened outside the door the first couple of times. They fired the same questions at him as they had at me and, to do him credit, he was calm, consistent and reassuring. We had agreed that we would take the line of assuring them that nothing major was going to change, that we were still friends (a big fat lie) and that nothing was their fault. This didn't seem to be sinking in. Elsie wet the bed four nights out of seven, Chloë's fingers were raw and bleeding and Finn's attitude stank.

I was embarrassed for Ali to see the way we now lived. She'd been employed by a woman at the top of her game and now I could hardly bear the look of pity on her face as she hung out Elsie's bedding day after day.

One morning, after a particularly trying exchange between myself and Finn, I walked upstairs to find a particular pair of earrings that I wanted to feature in a fashion-based post. Ali was dusting the cornices and singing quietly to herself (why do spiders and cobwebs adore the country so? It's like living in a haunted mansion!).

'Ali, are you free for a quick coffee and a chat?'

She looked concerned. I reassured her that she was doing everything right and that this was merely a review and feedback session. Earrings located (in the wrong place – what is happening to me?), I ran downstairs and fired up the coffee machine. For some reason, since Johnnie had left, every time I smelled coffee it made me want to cry.

I love that machine. I used to call it Mother's Little Helper and make Sofija laugh. Sometimes I called her that too. She didn't understand at first until I explained the cultural reference. Then she laughed.

I made myself a latte but left out the extra shot. I hadn't been sleeping well and, although I hated to admit it, my coffee habit probably wasn't helping.

We sat down together on the bench on the terrace.

'I'm delighted with the standard of your work. You're proactive and I like that. I think you've got a great eye for interiors, too – you changed those teal and oatmeal cushions around in the snug and it looks much better. How do you feel it's going?'

A huge smile spread over Ali's face.

'Oh, Mrs Smugge, I'm so happy to hear you say that! I didn't even realise I'd moved the cushions around until I went home on Friday and I was up half the night worrying that you'd be angry about it. My husband told me not to be silly, but unless you've got anxiety, you can't really understand how little things can make you feel. This house is so beautiful and your taste is impeccable. I hope I'm working in the way you want.'

What a treasure. I took a sip from my latte and recoiled. It tasted rather bitter. I would have to ask Ali to give the coffee machine a deep clean. I'd clearly taken my eye off the ball when it came to giving the kitchen appliances the once-over. I assured her I was delighted with her work and, pouring the rest of my coffee on to a slightly bedraggled viburnum (Ted would never know), I led the way back into the house.

Misery loves company, as Nanny used to say. Hard on the heels of the coffee machine malfunctioning, Lavinia took the opportunity to gun her engines and drive at my brand like a freshly tuned Harley Davidson.

'*Not So Smugge Now*' read the banner headline in her column. I can hardly bring myself to quote her Machiavellian prose, but for the sake of veracity, I shall.

> For what seems like forever, so-called aspirational lifestyle blogger Isabella M Smugge has posted nauseating content about her seemingly perfect life. What *does* the M stand for? Could it be Me, as in 'It's All About Me'? Certainly, Ms Smugge does love to talk about herself. Whether it's her immaculate home, her picture-perfect family or her designer wardrobe, she's bombarded us with images of her life for years through Instagram, Facebook and Pinterest. There's no escape from Ms Smugge, even at Christmas, when she entreats us to Fill Our Stocking with Isabella M Smugge. Those who have given in to her pleadings over the years report that in return for their hard-earned cash, they receive something that can hardly be called good value.
>
> One disgruntled customer told us, 'I ordered the *Festive Issy Smugge Says* set for my elderly, housebound mother. Our Christmas was ruined! She read them all cover to cover and immediately started pestering me to register her for Pinterest. She's eighty-five, partially sighted and has never had any idea of style. Even now, she's still going on about the pair of brass table lamps I

wouldn't let her buy. I caved in on a reclaimed Regency card table and she kept barking her shins on it. I laddered two pairs of tights in one week alone! Thanks, Isabella M Smugge, for your completely impractical ideas!'

And she's not the only one. The self-centred blogger is constantly preaching her gospel of style, trends and family values to her followers. You won't need to add sugar to your tea when you read one of her outpourings. Saccharine? You be the judge.

'Issy Smugge doesn't like to boast, but I just had to share these adorable snaps from my daughter's third birthday party. I threw together a little on-trend gathering with an Edu-tainment theme. The little ones were having such fun, but they were also learning! **#smartparenting #soblessed #mumofthree** While the children played, I was in the kitchen knocking up a batch of healthy vegan cookies and dips. **#noneedforsugar #lovingourplanet** Happy smiling little faces round the party table and happy parents in the kitchen. If you want to be a cool, party-throwing mama, buy my latest book by clicking here: *IssySmuggeSays: Let's Have a Party.* **#lifegoals** Love you all! Issy xx'

And there's more. Ms Smugge bombards her followers with pictures of her perfect house, her interiors, her clothes and her children. You'd think she lived in paradise. But there's trouble in the garden. Someone took a bite out of Isabella M Smugge's apple of happiness. You read it here first – **#bragstagram**.'

The cheek of it! So-called? *So-called?* I shall bide my time and consult Mimi. **#illgiveyouappleofhappiness #justyouwait**

All the stress was causing me to exhibit some very inconvenient symptoms. I was tired, craving carbs (so unlike me!) and terribly snappy. Claire came over with the children and I took some much-needed me time.

Being with Claire soothes my soul. She doesn't judge and she's such a great listener. I poured out my heart to her and she sat like a beautiful, pregnant Madonna in the sunshine, nodding and holding my hand as I sobbed. I don't know what's come over me. I never let anyone see my innermost feelings. Maybe it's because she's a vicar's wife (they must train them in some way). All those sleepless nights are playing tricks on my mind.

Claire thinks my symptoms are all linked to my emotions.

'When I'm stressed or anxious, I turn to carbs too. My go-to snack is a huge chunk of white bread with loads of butter.'

I tried not to wince. Each to their own, but who eats white bread in these health-conscious times? I conceded that she may have a point, however. I was absolutely fine before I found out about Johnnie and Sofija. I hardly ever ate carbs, drank coffee round the clock and was chock-full of energy.

'Grief and bereavement can do that to you, Isabella. A split like this is a huge trauma.'

She was right there. I'd found a jar of Sofija's homemade beetroot relish at the back of the fridge the night before and the sight of her handwriting on the label had reduced me to tears. No sooner had they dried than I was overcome with rage and hurled the jar at the dishwasher, where it shattered into a thousand pieces. Have you ever tried to remove beetroot juice from white goods? Hard on the heels of trying to explain why quite so many organic pink peppercorns had rolled under the fridge, I then had to try to convince everyone that the beetroot incident had been an accident.

I shared my concerns about the children and their behaviour. Claire sighed.

'It breaks my heart to hear that. Poor little things. Their whole world's been turned upside down. Thank heavens they've got you.'

She wouldn't be saying that if she knew about me shaking Finn. I felt ashamed, but I wasn't going to tell her the truth. Instead, I shared the glad tidings that Suze was coming to stay.

'Oh, how wonderful!' Claire seemed delighted. 'I so want to meet her!'

I wanted to introduce the two of them as well. I was sure they'd get on like a house on fire. Mummy, on the other hand, is to cosy girlie chats what white vinegar is to a finely chased silver cake fork. A conversation with her makes me feel that someone has been running a cheese grater over my soul without cessation. I was a bit worried that even Claire's radiant good nature might be dimmed by Mummy's acidic quips. However, she seemed keen to plan a summer holiday day out.

'I'm feeling better now I've had all this bed rest, so do you fancy joining a group of us next Thursday? We thought we'd take a picnic and go to the country park. Lauren's up for it and most of the Friday group are coming. I even asked Liane and she's agreed. I wonder if your sister might like to come?'

Well, that sounded brilliant! I offered to take the people carrier which meant that I would have two spare seats. As for Liane Bloomfield, I would just have to take a deep breath and be charming. I hope she doesn't read Lavinia's column.

'Do you think I could invite Charlene, Jake's mum?' I asked. 'I don't know if you know her.'

'Not really,' said Claire. 'I know of her. She's the lady with the anxiety, isn't she?'

'That's the one. She's been brilliant the last few months, helping me out with Finn. I think a day out would do her the world of good.'

Claire smiled. 'You've got such a kind heart, Isabella. What a lovely thing to do.'

I felt ridiculously pleased. Now all I had to do was to persuade Charlene to leave her house. If anyone can, Issy Smugge can! **#livingyourbestlife #reachingout**

Once I had finally wrestled everyone into their pyjamas and got them packed off to bed that night, I sank onto the sofa and closed my eyes. For two pins, I could have nodded off right there and then. What on earth have I become? I'm keeping up with work, but only just.

The next thing I knew, I was waking up with a snort and wiping dribble from my chin. The clock said half past ten and my body said it was time for bed. Yawning and rubbing my eyes, I slowly climbed the stairs for another night of bad dreams and broken sleep. **#timeforbed #disturbedsleep**

My campaign to coax Charlene out of the house began in earnest the next day. I invited myself over for coffee and tried to behave like Claire. I listened, I nodded, I didn't judge, even when she offered me a frankly undrinkable cup of coffee and a piece of cake that had the consistency of sawdust. Appearing to be interested in other people's lives is exhausting! I listened to her tale of woe and immediately diagnosed a severe case of self-pity. Her husband departed five years ago!

I floated the idea of a nice day out and offered myself as chauffeur. She looked horrified.

'Oh, no, I couldn't do that. You don't understand. I'd be fine in the car, but getting out and not knowing where I was…'

Here she broke off, shuddering. Issy Smugge loves a project and I decided right there and then that rehabilitating this poor, terrified woman would be my next one. So what if my own husband has run off with the help? Who cares if a perimenopausal chequebook journalist has got it in for me? It was ridiculous to see a fellow parent cowering in her cramped little house in high summer when she could be filling up her diary with exciting engagements. Back home in London, parents in the playground at Beech Grove had vied for my attention. A coffee with Isabella M Smugge was roughly equivalent to receiving an MBE. Charlene didn't know how lucky she was.

As Nanny used to say (the woman was a veritable goldmine of aphorisms), fine words butter no parsnips, so I went for it.

'You're doing an amazing job with Jake. You so obviously want to do the very best for him and he's a credit to you. I truly don't know what I would have done without your help. You've been so kind.'

I read around my subject constantly, so I know all about the kind of thing you're meant to say to get people to open up. Prior to Sofija's departure, parenting was a snip, but my recent struggles had led me to suspect that perhaps it was a little more complex than I had previously thought. With my legendary empathy, I'd found exactly the right gambit to get Charlene talking. Which she did. For ages.

Two hours later, I was in possession of all the tawdry details of her ex's goings-on (most of the early part of the relationship had played out on the back seat of his car), her feelings of anger and guilt, what her mother had said, how she felt everyone in the playground was laughing at her, how her former best friend from high school had sided with the woman in the case and what her concerns were about Jake and his emotional well-being. I can see why Claire sometimes looks so worn out. Really listening to someone is a very tiring business.

Having invested so much time in Charlene and her problems, I needed to use my people management skills. Only a few months ago, I would rather have died a slow and painful death than reveal that I suffer from panic attacks. However, living up here has changed me. I took the leap.

'Charlene, there's something I need to tell you which may surprise you. I suffer from panic attacks and very slight anxiety myself.'

She looked amazed, as well she might. My immaculate appearance and God-given talent for sharing the details of my lovely life don't suggest a woman with the same kinds of issues as normal people. She started sniffling and wiping her eyes.

'Oh, Isabella, I feel so honoured that you've shared such a personal thing with me. I had no idea. I look at you and feel so humble. If you're brave enough to open up to me, then I will really try to do this for you. And I know Jake would love it.'

Once I decide I'm going to achieve something, I don't let anything get in the way. Of course, it will take more work, but I seemed to have got Charlene on the road to recovery in only two and a half hours. I assured her I was there for her and left, texting Claire on the way.

'Charlene coming to country park with us. How good am I? xx'

Once I'd hit send, I wondered if I sounded a little smug. Probably not. Now to go home and start getting ready for my visitors. **#helpingothers #lifewins**

Sometimes I think there may be a God. Sometimes not. This week, I'm pretty sure there is and I visualise him as a benign old chap sitting on a cloud, bestowing blessings on Issy Smugge with both hands. The news that their Auntie Suze was coming to stay lifted the children's moods no end. Elsie only wet herself twice, Chloë occasionally took her fingers out of her mouth and Finn laughed several times before realising what he was doing and assuming his usual scowl. They were disappointed to hear that their cousin wasn't coming, but agreed to help me get Suze's room together, and even came up with some ideas to beautify it. The old Isabella M Smugge would have told Sofija to entertain them while I did all the dressing and embellishing. The new me gave them free rein with flowers, cushions and handwritten cards welcoming their aunt to our home. It was rather sweet, actually.

By some miracle, we had a meal without any eruptions. I took advantage of the relative peace to break the news that we were expecting another visitor. Predictably, their faces fell. Granny is not a popular member of the Smugge extended family.

'How long is she staying, Mummy?' Chloë was shredding her thumbnail.

'A week. It'll soon be over. And we're out with Auntie Suze at the country park one day so we won't see her for at least eight hours.'

I became aware that this probably wasn't the best way to promote good interfamily relations.

'Not that I'm sad that Granny is coming! It'll be such fun! She won't believe how much you've all grown.'

Clearly, I hadn't convinced anyone.

'But she always looks cross when we talk and she nags us about homework and stuff. Can't she stay in a hotel?'

I laughed before I could stop myself. 'That wouldn't be very hospitable, would it, Chloë? And anyway, Auntie Suze will be here. She's very good with Granny.'

Gloomily, we all cleared the table and started to load the dishwasher and scrape the food scraps into the compost bin. The unwonted harmony continued as we all repaired to the family room. Finn normally stalked up to his room straight after dinner. I decided to try a new tack.

'You choose what we watch. You're in charge.'

To my amazement, it worked. After a slight tussle between Finn and Chloë, we settled down in front of some kind of puerile game show. It was frightful, and as far as I could tell had absolutely no educational content, but I settled down to eat organic popcorn, sip strawberry lemonade and let the girls cuddle up to me. Actually, it felt pretty good. Perhaps this is what people mean when they talk about family time. My phone was on the island in the kitchen, but you have to believe me when I tell you that I left it there. All evening.

I must have nodded off, because when I awoke, the girls were gone and Finn was picking up the popcorn bowls and brushing the crumbs from the sofa into his hand. I yawned and stretched.

'Thank you, Finn. That's so kind of you. I must have gone to sleep.'

He grunted and walked out to the kitchen. I waited for him to mutter 'Night!' over his shoulder as he ascended the stairs, but to my surprise, he came back in and sat down. The peace between us was fragile and I didn't want to do anything to shatter it. The memory of the shaking and the harsh words we'd shouted at each other still hung over us like a toxic cloud.

'Mum, now that Dad's gone, do I still have to go to his old school? I really don't want to. I know I said I wanted to live with him, but I didn't mean it.'

Tears rushed to my eyes. My instinct was to embrace him, but I restrained myself. Ten-year-old boys are allergic to the fond caresses of their mothers.

'Dad and I will be having lots of conversations over the next few weeks and your future is one of the things I want to nail down. I'll certainly be talking to him about school.'

I was rather proud of myself. Isabella M Smugge was being flexible, listening to her child and meeting his needs. What excellent parenting.

'Is he ever coming back?'

Finn looked suddenly young and vulnerable. I swallowed hard, and looked at my lap.

'I don't know, darling. I hope so. I really hope so.'

Suze arrived on the Monday. I was ridiculously, ludicrously excited. We hadn't seen each other in the flesh since Elsie's third birthday and she'd never been to our new house. The children were almost as agitated as me, rushing to the window every time they heard a car. They'd insisted on making a banner which hung lopsidedly across the bay window at the front, reading 'Welcome to our home Auntie Suzie' in large, uneven letters, liberally embellished with gems and stars from the craft box.

Just after two, we heard the crunch of tyres on the gravel and there she was. I forgot that I was a revered influencer, wife and mother in my late thirties and hurled myself at her, shouting,

'Suze! Oh, Suze!' To my astonishment, I found that I was sobbing uncontrollably. The taxi paid off, we stood in each other's arms, our heads resting on each other's shoulders, crying and laughing simultaneously. Goodness only knows what the taxi driver must have thought.

The children, Finn included, forgot all pretence of dignity and leapt up and down, seizing their aunt's hands and insisting she come in at once and have the grand tour. Feebly, I tried to intervene, suggesting a cup of a tea and a sit-down, but the children pooh-poohed such nonsensical adult notions and dragged her off to see every nook and cranny.

Suze brought all the joy back into the house. The children were their old selves, I felt so much better and we started to enjoy all the wonderful things about living in the country again. We went on walks and bike rides, I introduced her to my friends and we sat and talked until well into the night once the children were in bed. I was worried that bringing up the subject of Johnnie would be awkward, but in fact it was completely natural. Now that both of us had been let down and betrayed by him, it was yet another bond between us. Even the thought of Mummy's visitation couldn't dull the sparkle. #impendingdoom #mummyknowsbest

After two blissful days with Suze, we braced ourselves for the Royal Visit. Neither of us could face picking Mummy up from the station, so it was with some trepidation that the five of us stood at the front door watching as a beleaguered-looking taxi driver came to a halt on the drive. No one rushed forward to greet her. No banner hung drunkenly from the window. Like the Queen Empress, but a foot taller and minus the Hanoverian profile, Mummy emerged, handbag clutched firmly to her side, lips pursed and eyes narrowed.

'And *that's* more than you deserve!' She pressed a note into the driver's hand and waited while he unloaded her suitcases from the boot. He leapt back into the car and did a wheelspin off the drive without a backward glance. Oh, yes. She's still got the old magic.

After the requisite double-cheek kisses and remarks on how pulled down I looked (thank you so much), we moved indoors so that she could look over the children, find things to criticise and park herself majestically at the island. The children released to their own amusements, I made her a coffee ('None of your fancy concoctions, thank you, Isabella, just plain black for me') and braced myself for the inevitable.

'You can't say I didn't warn you. But does anyone ever listen to me? I'm not at all surprised. That impertinent little chit was just waiting to get her claws into him. I did tell you, Isabella, don't let the help get too familiar.'

Suze weighed in; God bless her.

'Why don't you think about Bella's feelings, Mummy? She's still in shock. Johnnie hasn't behaved well, but there are the children to think of and you talking like this isn't helpful.'

Mummy bristled, as only Mummy can.

'I do beg your pardon, Suzanne. This is a nice welcome for a mother to get from her daughter. I've hardly got my foot in the door and already you're telling me off.'

Suze seemed to be quite immune to our parent's towering rage.

'Put yourself in Bella's shoes. She's been kind enough to invite you up here when she's got a huge amount on her plate. The very least you can do is show her some compassion.'

There was a short silence, and then, with an outraged sniff, Mummy rose to her feet and marched out into the garden to scatter fag ends around the shrubbery.

'Wow. I don't know what to say.' I was temporarily lost for words.

'Don't mention it! Too early for wine, Bella?'

It's never too early in my book. By the time Mummy came stumping back in, Suze and I had cracked open a bottle of Pinot and were a glass down. **#chinchin #cheersbigears**

Until very recently, I'd have told you that getting my Instagram blue tick was the best thing in my life. Now, though, having Suze back in my life has overtaken it. I watched her taking Mummy on at breakfast, lunch and dinner with a song in my heart. The children were happier too. They love their Auntie Suzie. I was fascinated to see that her positivity diluted Mummy's venom. The two of us versus Mummy was just like old times.

At breakfast, Chloë started chewing her fingernails and Mummy reached out, quick as a flash, and smacked her hard on the hand. It took me right back to our breakfast table at home in Kent and the stinging slaps administered right, left and centre for any slight infraction of table manners. The look of shock on my daughter's face spurred me to speak.

'Don't hit my children, Mummy. Apologise to Chloë.'

Mummy spluttered like a faulty gas jet. 'I beg your pardon, Isabella? How's she ever going to get a husband with nails like that? You need to paint them with bitter aloes or tie her hands behind her back until she learns. That's what my mother did to me, and look at my nails.'

She stretched out a lavishly be-ringed hand, the nails painted a menacing shade of maroon. I took a deep breath.

'I certainly won't be doing anything of the kind. Please say sorry to your granddaughter.'

'I will not! The very idea. This would never have happened if you'd taken my advice and gone to finishing school. You could have been the wife of a baronet by now, at the very least, and your children would be at a decent boarding school. I blame your father. He was always very lax.'

And with that, she rose from the table and exited stage left. I ask you!

'How are we going to stop her coming out with us tomorrow, Suze?' We'd just finished breakfast and the two of us were cowering in the boot room, watching Mummy stump around the garden like a tweed-clad dragon. The thought of having her along on our day out, lashing out at my unsuspecting friends and their offspring, filled me with dread. Suze grinned.

'Don't worry, Bella. I've got a plan.'

At dinner ('Chicken *again*, Isabella? I hope you'll be varying my diet a *little* more while I'm with you'), Suze beamed guilelessly at Mummy and produced an envelope.

'Happy belated birthday! A little surprise for you.'

Mummy, completely taken off guard, stopped scrutinising my rose-gold salt and pepper cruets (the limited-edition acrylic ones being now just a memory) and put on her glasses.

'How thoughtful. Thank you, Suzanne. Better late than never.'

Suze had managed to wangle a day visit to a local stately home, appropriately moated and turreted, with award-winning gardens. Adding to her enjoyment of the whole experience, the lady of the manor had been at school with Mummy, giving her a chance to criticise the knot garden, the planting and the park. Lunch was included and Suze had booked a cab to take her there straight after breakfast.

'We'll see you at supper, Mummy. We're out for the day too.'

With barely a murmur, Mummy finished her main course and strolled outside to enjoy a cigarette while deadheading my floribunda. Result!

After breakfast on Thursday, Mummy departed and left Suze, the children and me to get ourselves ready for our day out. At Charlene's house, we were greeted by a worried-looking Jake.

'Mum's crying in her bedroom. She's not too good.'

This was terrible news. I'd invested all that precious time in sorting her out and now she'd fallen at the first hurdle. The girls sat down politely in the shabby front room and Jake and Finn loped off to the kitchen. I shared my frustration with Suze, who seemed faintly amused.

'Bella, you can't fix people with anxiety just like that. This is probably a deep-seated issue with lots of complex manifestations. Why don't we go and have a chat to her?'

Charlene was lying on her bed, eyes puffy and face tear-streaked. As soon as she saw me, she burst out crying, gasping that she was sorry, over and over again. Suze took control. Sitting on the edge of her bed, she took her hand and spoke in a calm, gentle voice. I felt redundant. Also, impatient. Why can't people see that determination and self-control are all you need to get over problems like this? I excused myself and went downstairs where the girls were becoming restive. We went out into the garden where they bounced politely on the trampoline for a few minutes before stretching themselves out on the grass and gazing up at the sky.

I'd just resigned myself to having an empty seat in the car when Suze texted.

'We're coming downstairs. Stay calm, get the car ready please xx'

Charlene emerged, a giant pair of headphones clamped to her ears. I restrained my natural curiosity and pulled away from the kerb. I looked in the mirror to see Charlene sitting with her eyes closed, rocking to and fro. Clearly some kind of coping strategy. Suze held her hand and murmured, 'In through the nose, out through the mouth,' over and over again. Far be it from me to question her methods. We'd got the poor woman out of the house and surely that was the main thing.

I pulled into the country park. Claire's battered old car was already parked up and I could see her girls and Lauren's three

236

rushing around the field. I opened the doors and let the children out. Turning round, I could see that Charlene's eyes were still firmly shut and that she had her lips pressed together hard. I raised my eyebrows at Suze, who jerked her head to the right, indicating that I should exit the vehicle.

We'd eaten the picnic and were just about to start making our perambulation of the park when I heard footsteps behind me, and there was Charlene, standing behind me, pale and still, the wind gently lifting her hair.

Jake came dashing over, beaming.

'Mum! You did it. I'm so proud.' He threw his arms around her and, unaccountably, I felt tears in my eyes.

I wonder if Suze would consider relocating from Hong Kong and living with me forever. **#miracleworker #dayatthepark**

Back home, I felt renewed and refreshed. Liane Bloomfield had almost smiled at me twice and expressed sympathy for my situation. I can't report the words she used, but they exactly mirrored my feelings towards my errant husband. Charlene, although a bit jumpy and loath to move from the one spot, had taken a huge step. It had felt good to be out and enjoying my friends' company.

If I had superpowers (and sometimes I think I do), I'd have arrived back at home to find a repentant Mummy eager to make amends and repair our fractured relationship. This was not the case. Over supper, she bombarded us with critical comments about the planting schemes at the Hall. Lunch had been acceptable, but she'd found half a caterpillar in her radicchio and her Earl Grey had tasted soapy. Suze bore all this with good humour but I found myself becoming more and more irritated.

I put the children to bed. When I got downstairs, Mummy was on her fourth gin and tonic and Suze was sipping a glass of rosé. I joined her, but found it terribly acidic. I was a bit surprised. Our wine merchant is normally excellent.

'I saw poor Bertie Pryke-Darby at the club the other day. My goodness, he's aged.'

Mummy had moved on to the social assassination portion of her day. She loves nothing more than to get together with her cronies and pick away at the reputations of their acquaintances. I saw Suze stiffen and glance quickly at me. We both loved Bertie when we were little girls. He was a dear man, so kind and soft-hearted.

'Of course, he was never the same after Arabella ran off with your father. And now he's got Parkinson's. Only five years older than me but you'd put him in his eighties. He's living in some kind of frightful warden-controlled flat, but his brother-in-law (you remember, unfortunate marriage, she had a glass eye) still ferries him around. Well, as I said to Veronica Madingley, if I ever get like that, shoot me! And she said…'

We never found out what Veronica said. Something cracked inside me.

'Can you hear yourself? Why don't you shut up? How dare you say such horrible things about Bertie.'

She stared at me and put down her glass. Slowly. Deliberately. Just like she used to when we were little. It terrified me then and it still scared me.

'I beg your pardon, young lady? What did you say to me?'

Maybe it was the awful, acidic wine. Perhaps it was the memory of Charlene's set, white face as she faced up to her greatest fears. Or (and this was more likely), I'd simply reached the end of my tether with the selfish, rude, snobbish old hag who I had the misfortune to call Mother.

I leaned forward and looked her straight in the eye.

'I said, shut up. Don't you dare come to my house, slapping my children and prancing around like Lady Muck. I didn't even invite you – you asked yourself here so you could gloat over my husband dumping me just like yours dumped you!'

I seemed to have hit a nerve. She leapt to her feet and jabbed her finger in my face.

'He did not *dump* me! What a terribly common phrase. Who are you mixing with to pick up such trashy language? I threw him out because he was sleeping with my best friend! He was weak and pathetic and fell into bed with the first woman who pretended to find him funny. I should never have married him! It was the biggest mistake of my life.'

'I see. And by association that makes Suze and me a couple of mistakes too, does it?' By now I was shouting at the top of my voice. 'You certainly made that pretty clear to us. Have you got any idea how it feels to be sent away from everyone you love at the age of seven? To have your father and the woman who brought you up just disappear? To have to work out how to make it through every day all by yourself? Nanny was far more of a mother to me than you ever were.'

Mummy looked down and swirled the ice around in her glass. I braced myself for a torrent of abuse. I glanced over at Suze, who was gazing at us both with her eyes bulging slightly.

'What a lot of questions, Isabella. Let me try to answer them. Yes. I do know how it feels. I was brought down to see my parents once a day when I was a child. They had no idea what to say to me. They were cold and distant. I lived up in the nursery and when I was six, they sent me away. I was all alone with only my teddy for company, and even he got taken away because Matron said he might spread disease. All they wanted was a boy to carry on the family name and inherit the house. I was a bargaining chip, someone to polish like a diamond and marry off to the first rich young man who came along. Do you know how that feels? You girls had such freedom compared to me. I used to watch you out of the window, swinging in the apple tree, playing hide-and-seek, giving your dolls picnics, and be ragingly jealous of you. I suppose that makes me a bad mother. I had no idea how to be a good one.'

She reached for the gin and refreshed her glass. Then she lit a cigarette. I found I didn't care. Suze was the first to break the silence.

'Mummy, I'm sorry you had such a rough time. You never spoke about it to us. We might have been able to help you.'

She snorted, contemptuously. '*You?* How could *you* help? I turned down two proposals because I wanted something different. I could have had it all – a big house, staff, even a title. But I said no and I held out for love. Then along came your father with his jokes and his easy charm. My parents loathed him so I said yes. All my friends were married already and I didn't want to be left on the shelf. I was the bridesmaid at Arabella and Bertie's wedding and I stood there, looking across at him in his morning suit and thought, "Why not? What if no one better comes along?"'

'The four of us were friends. We all liked the same things and when Arabella and I set up the business, I knew I'd found what I was looking for. It was the only thing I'd ever achieved that I felt truly proud of. Then she went behind my back with your father and broke my heart. I had to hold my head up and ignore all the sniggering and jokes behind my back. It nearly killed me. There wasn't much left over for you.'

Whatever I'd expected, it wasn't this. I tried another mouthful of rosé but it set my teeth on edge. For the first time, I looked at my mother and saw vulnerability.

'At least we're talking, Mummy. Maybe this is the beginning of something. We just wanted to love you, but it was hard with all the rows and shouting. We never really felt you wanted to spend time with us.'

She snorted again. 'I wanted a son, Isabella. I'm not particularly proud of it, but there it is. Girls were worth nothing in my parents' eyes. When we had you two, I was determined to give you the best chance possible to find good husbands and to have a better life than I did. I knew Johnnie Smugge was no good the minute I clapped eyes on him. First, he broke Suzanne's heart and now he's broken yours. I could *kill* him.'

She ground out her cigarette on the edge of my Belfast sink and threw it into the waste disposal unit. I was oddly touched that Mummy wanted to murder my husband. I too was harbouring violent impulses.

'I could kill him too, to be honest. Slowly and painfully. I lie awake at night sometimes thinking about how I'd do it.'

Suze nodded. 'I used to fantasise about pushing him under a train and then telling him that I'd never loved him as he breathed his last.'

Mummy lit another cigarette. 'How about a rare poison? If it was good enough for Agatha Christie, it's good enough for me.'

I wasn't quite sure what was happening, but we seemed to be bonding, if only a tiny little bit and over various ways to dispose of a cheating husband. We sat there breathing in Mummy's second-hand smoke until she announced that it was time she went to bed. Unusually, she kissed us both before she ascended to her chamber. Could it be that she was starting to mellow? **#wonderswillnevercease**

Everyone was terribly polite to everyone else at breakfast. As we finished our tea and granola, Mummy got up to clear away and load the dishwasher. This was quite a departure. Once she'd finished, she announced that she was going to go and have a chat with the gardener.

Suze and I stood at the kitchen window watching her march towards the hapless Ted, fossicking around by the runner beans.

'Maybe we're dreaming, Bella. If we pinch ourselves, we'll wake up and she'll be back to normal.'

Maybe. I was concerned for Ted's safety. He's a nice old boy and probably not used to being confronted with gin-soaked ladies first thing in the morning. Suze put a comforting hand on my arm.

'You're not responsible for her behaviour. You don't have to explain her or make excuses for her. Once you realise that, it's very freeing.'

She was right. Rather than antagonising my gardener, Mummy managed to impress him. She spent much of the rest of her visit out in the garden with Ted, talking about soil types and mulch and goodness knows what. By the time she left, I was almost sorry to see her go. Almost. As she walked out onto the drive, she turned and took my arm.

'You look very tired, darling. You need to take a bit more care of yourself. Maybe pop along and see the doctor? You're probably anaemic.'

She kissed me on the cheek and departed. I was left staring after her, wondering if perhaps she did love me after all, just a little bit. **#amazingrevelations #rarepoison**

September

Exactly a year ago, I started this diary. I look back at that woman, so excited about her new life and all the thrilling opportunities ahead of her and think, 'Isabella, little did you know what was to come.' I could never have predicted that the man I loved so passionately and the woman I trusted and believed to be my friend would betray me so callously. That said, neither could I have foreseen that my dear Suze and I would be friends again. Even Mummy appears to have a chink in her armour. With the children back at school and Ali doing a wonderful job, I'm trying to get used to a new normal.

But I'm running ahead of myself. August was packed with incidents and, if I'm honest, I'm shying away from talking about it. Without Suze, I don't know how I would have coped.

Hard on the heels of Mummy's departure, and with silly season in full swing, Lavinia finally showed her hand.

> *Smugge Is as Smugge Does.* Ubiquitous, self-styled aspirational lifestyle blogger Isabella M Smugge has built her career on family values. Her social media pages are awash with picture-perfect images of her immaculate home, her effortless entertaining, her simpering children and her successful hedge fund manager husband, Johnnie Smugge. What *really* goes on in the house of the woman who constantly refers to herself in the third person? Who *does* she think she is?
>
> Leaving London, the Smugges settled in a sprawling Georgian rectory, worth more than £2 million, and remodelled it in their trademark ostentatious style. Digging up a historic chamomile meadow and pestering

the local council for permission to change the listed building to suit their lifestyle was just the beginning. Friends of the family report that the blogger then used her own children to increase her reach. 'Issy and Johnnie can easily afford to send the kids to private school. But she insisted on getting them in at the village primary, because she thinks it makes her more relatable. She's such a hypocrite.' And that's just the beginning.

Not content with taking three state school places that could be used by local families in real need, Smugge is also calling on none other than the Almighty to make her look sincere. 'Issy had no time for religion back in London,' someone who knows the family told me. 'All of a sudden, she's giving money to the local church, attending some kind of women's support group and making it look like she's exploring faith. She only does it because she thinks it's trendy.'

Does this new-found interest in religion mask a deeper, darker secret? What Isabella M Smugge *doesn't* want you to know is that her husband of nearly twenty years has been doing more than hedging funds and posing for pictures at the Blogger Awards. He's been having an affair with the nanny – such a cliché! She's much younger and prettier than Issy, so it was always going to happen. What goes around comes around. Something you won't know about the family values blogger is that she stole her husband from her younger sister. It's rumoured they haven't spoken since. And yet she pumps out saccharine self-help manuals with titles such as *Issy Smugge Says: It's a Family Affair*. It certainly is!

With a marriage split, family feuds and her fortieth birthday looming, where will Issy Smugge go next? This follower says: stop being two-faced and give us all a rest from your attention-seeking hypocrisy.

I cried all morning. Thank heavens for Suze. Without her, I don't know what I would have done. Mimi counselled ignoring it, but I felt so hurt that my so-called friends were tattling to the papers that I could hardly get through the day. To add to my stress, it being the last week of the summer holidays, the children were being collected by Johnnie and taken away to London for a week.

'They'll be so upset and confused,' I sobbed, gulping down a huge glass of cucumber water. (I'm so thirsty at the moment. It must be all the crying.) 'Seeing Sofija in our flat – my life is falling apart!'

Suze frowned. 'Lavinia Harcourt is an empty vessel, Bella. We both know that. People read those words and forget them almost instantly. Maybe it's time to give Lavinia a taste of her own medicine.'

I liked the sound of that. It was a risk, going up against a woman who had the ear of half of the UK's population, had her editor over a barrel and had won Journalist of the Year five times in a row, but maybe it was worth considering.

That evening, Suze and I lay on the sofas in the family room plotting revenge on Lavinia. According to Claire, I should be forgiving the miserable old bag, not trying to get my own back. As if!

'Listen, Bella, I feel a bit responsible for all this.' Suze was looking serious. 'You were doing what you always did, protecting your little sister. Who knew that mean old Lavvie Harcourt was going to end up sleeping her way to the top? That must be how she got that job, right?'

I entreated Suze not to give it another thought. In my line of work, you have to get used to a few ups and downs. Johnnie's had a few fallouts with friends and clients along the way too. Several years after we got married, we were super-close to a couple who we thought would be friends for life. He worked with Johnnie at the bank; she was a music PR. We were always together and we had the most fun. Johnnie had to make a difficult decision at work and the guy took it badly. He blamed him for taking over a client and not being transparent about it. With the benefit of hindsight, I can see that Johnnie was wrong. But back then, it was dog eat dog.

I dreaded saying goodbye to Suze. Lavinia's comments about hypocrisy had stung. Was that how people saw me? Maybe I should forget the whole church thing and content myself with buying new play equipment.

My reverie was interrupted by Suze pouring herself another glass of red and asking me a question.

'Here's a thought, Bella. If you could go back and say one thing to your younger self, what would it be?'

I was intrigued. What *would* I say to little Bella Neville? 'Ring Childline? Beg Daddy not to go on holiday to Italy? Run away to the circus? Stand up to Mummy?' I genuinely didn't know.

Suze was smiling. 'How about, "I love you"? If you really meant it, there would be no room for judgement, fear or anger. Imagine a life lived like that.'

I couldn't. Fear and anger had stalked me throughout my childhood and now everyone was judging me. A wave of sadness washed over me and I found myself bursting into tears yet again. What would I do when she went home? I didn't think I could carry on like this. **#alone #miserable #hypocrite**

I insisted on driving Suze to the airport and stood watching her walk into the departure lounge. Then I drove to meet Johnnie and the children at a coffee shop down the M11. I won't talk about that, if you don't mind. It was horrendous.

I felt desperate, alone, wretched. I was counting the hours until school began again.

Maybe Lavinia was right. Maybe I was a hypocrite.

The first day back at school was bliss. I had the whole day to myself, free to write, post and take photos. I got home, sat down for a minute and the next thing I knew it was lunchtime! I gazed at my pallid visage in the mirror and asked myself, 'What's happening to me?' Maybe Mummy was right. I could be anaemic. All the carbs I'd been eating had made me feel really bloated too. I booked an appointment at the doctors for a check-up.

The doctor obviously doesn't know what he's talking about. To be on the safe side, though, I'll pop into the pharmacy and pick up a test. Just to rule it out.

How can two little blue lines make your heart sink into your boots? What on earth am I going to do? I can barely cope with the three children I've got, let alone a vulnerable newborn.

The only tiny piece of silver lining in this cloud is that I won't have to buy a new coffee machine. There's nothing wrong with it. My taste buds always went crazy with every new pregnancy and this one's no exception.

Today, Lavinia led her column with a nasty little attack on a member of the Royal Family. So what if the poor girl's gone for a fringe and worn the same dress three times this year? She turned her attention to me a little further on.

> *Anyone for Affirmations?* Self-satisfied aspirational lifestyle blogger Isabella M Smugge likes nothing better than giving the rest of us advice. How ironic, then, that she finds herself a single mother, minus her Eastern European nanny, alone in her pretentious Suffolk mansion, worth around £3 million. Only last month, Ms Smugge was telling us that 'Your Only Limit is You'. She also shared that 'People Only Throw Shade Upon What

Shines'. Today, her marriage in ruins and her future uncertain, Issy Smugge doesn't look nearly so shiny.

The attention-seeking blogger is quick to jump on any bandwagon she thinks will benefit her. Only a few months ago she was imploring us to 'Be Kind', but she herself is rather short on that quality. A fellow pupil at the £8,000 per term exclusive girls' boarding school St Dymphna's has seen the other side of Isabella M Smugge.

'Isabella always wanted to be the queen bee. She was jealous of some of the younger girls because they were so much prettier and more popular than her. One night, she sneaked into their room and assaulted one of them. She cut off her hair while she slept! Then she lied about it and she was never brought to justice. All of us have kept our silence for all these years, but we can't remain quiet any longer.'

As if this shocking act of barbarity wasn't enough, former schoolmates confirm that Isabella Neville (as she then was) was pretty handy with her fists too. 'I remember seeing her attack a much younger girl and punch her to the ground. She always had a violent streak.'

Ms Smugge tells us that 'The Only Difference Between a Good Day and a Bad Day is Your Attitude'. It looks as if it could be a little more complex than that!

Staring at the screen in my writing studio, I took stock. I'm separated from my husband who's been sleeping with my au pair and everyone knows about it. I miss them both. No one knows that. I'm unexpectedly and disastrously up the duff. I feel sick every morning. I have put on half a stone. I think I saw cellulite on my thighs last night. One of Britain's most powerful journalists has a vendetta against me and she's got people tattling away to her, over which I have no control. I've got a spot coming on my chin.

My life is over!

I've always been very careful to keep my bedroom a peaceful, calm, tech-free zone, but needs must when the devil drives. Lying in bed, on my phone, scrolling back through my content, I realised that some of it wasn't particularly honest. No wonder I was such an easy target for Lavinia. I never showed the mess, the fails, the mistakes. Maybe it was time for a new direction. I've always prided myself on moving with the times. Everyone's banging on about being kind and authentic. It's time I did too.

I was just nodding off to sleep when it came to me in a flash. Of course! 'Open Brackets'. It could be my Next Big Thing. No more, 'From Tramp to Vamp'; less of the picture-perfect posed shots.

Next day I messaged Mimi with my brilliant idea, and got writing. I took a moodily lit shot of my rose-gold salt and pepper mills and, instead of telling my readers where to buy them, I wrote a witty little paragraph about the fate of the acrylic originals.

I invited the children to make cakes when they got home from school and took shots of the inevitable mess. Flour all over the worktops, a broken egg on the floor, wonky cupcakes and watery butter icing. Instead of throwing a rosy glow over it all, I posted the photos with no filters and a self-deprecating little paragraph. I think I may have hit on something here. Mimi is very pleased.

The next day, Lavinia's deadly rival ran a little something in her 'Net Results' column.

> Recent victim of the Bitterest Woman in Fleet Street, award-winning lifestyle blogger Isabella M Smugge has risen above the insults and come out fighting. Open Brackets? Bravo, Issy Smugge! We love you.

In your face, Lavinia Harcourt! At this rate, I'll have hit three million followers by Christmas. As I said in my inaugural 'Open

Brackets' blog, 'Everyone's got at least one set of brackets, but lots of people make it their life's work to hide them. It's so easy to pretend, or to make things sound better than they really are. Honesty, letting your slip show and revealing the awful truth about what really happens when you let your children loose in the kitchen is encouraging and, I hope, says to readers, "It's not just you. We're all in this together."'

I feel proud. I feel – almost – happy. Now all I have to do is get Johnnie back and my life will be on track again. #newbeginnings

Claire wasn't on the playground this morning. I must pop over for coffee soon. Charlene occasionally drops Jake off at school now. It feels pretty good to know I had something to do with that.

There was a hint of autumn in the air tonight. I cleaned up after tea and gazed out of the window at the trees waving in the wind and a thin spiral of woodsmoke curling out of the chimney of the thatched cottage next door. I put the children to bed and made a point of spending time listening to them talk to me. I was always in such a rush before. Open Brackets. I have to remember that.

The sound of my phone beeping woke me up from a deep sleep. My texts had gone crazy! There was one from Lauren which made no sense.

Babes, have you read Tom's message? Poor Claire – gotta pray she'll be OK xx'

I scrolled back down. Everyone seemed to be offering to pray or look after the children or both. What on earth was going on? I finally located the origin of all the activity, a group message from Tom.

'Claire collapsed tonight and has been rushed to hospital. She's lost a lot of blood. Please pray if you're praying people. She's unconscious and her vital signs aren't good. Thank you. Tom x'

My own problems paled into insignificance beside this terrible situation. What would I do without Claire in my life? How could she die? Being married to an actual vicar and going to church every Sunday of her own free will had to count for something. But what did I know? I was just a hypocritical, attention-seeking, publicity-hungry woman who had spent her entire life thinking about herself.

I walked downstairs and sat in the kitchen in my big, beautiful house, the only sound the ticking of the clock. With each minute, Claire's life was ebbing away. I felt desperate, anguished, hopeless, all emotions I've become all too familiar with of late. I read and reread Tom's message. Was I a praying person? Did I even believe that God was up there? As I looked back over the last twelve months, it seemed that something or someone had been at work in my life. As I sat in my kitchen, an abandoned wife, a pregnant mother, a restored sister, what could I do?

I bowed my head. I felt like an idiot but there was no one there to see me.

'Dear God. This is Issy Smugge. I expect You know my name. Please don't let Claire die. I would be so enormously grateful. I'll do anything. The church roof was just the start. New loos, new kitchen – anything, please just don't let her die. Many thanks. Amen.'

As prayers go, it wasn't going to win any awards, but all I could do was hope that someone with clout was listening. Outside, I could hear the wind sighing in the trees and the soft autumn rain falling on the terrace. Ten miles away in hospital, Claire was fighting for her life. Tears dropped slowly on to my hands as I faced the possibility of life without her.

I got up, turned off the light and walked slowly upstairs. 'Dear God, please save Claire,' I whispered, as I walked into my bedroom. Lying in the dark room, sleepless and tearful, I entreated someone who may not even be there, 'Please. Please. Please.'

I've got no time for superstition, but as I spoke the words, I felt the tiniest lifting of the weight on my shoulders. Was it my imagination, or did I feel a gentle touch on my arm? If only God *was* like Daddy, kind, loving and compassionate, someone who understood my pain. I remembered what Sue had said at Friday group. My eyes swimming with tears, I visualised my father standing in front of me, his cheeks ruddy, his hair windblown and his face alight with love, just like that day in Whitstable. I squeezed my eyes shut, put my hands together like a child and asked again.

'I promise to be good and not say horrible things any more or look down my nose at people. Please, can You make Claire better? Thank You. Amen.'

The wind rustled in the trees outside my bedroom window and I heard an owl hoot. Was it a sign? Probably not, but all I could do was hope.